# STORIES FROM
# THE TREE HOUSE

To Charlotte—
go out
And get some
world records
too...

WRITTEN BY
## JUSTIN MATOTT

D1443039

## ACKNOWLEDGMENTS

To the original buddies - E. **Gabriel** Mando Matott and J. **Peter** Mando Matott!
May the wisdom of Father Mando always guide you both
and may Charmando find his rightful place in history…

### IZ ODO ODOL

Also to Alyssa and Andrew DeMey. Thanks for reading this manuscript before it was really readable!
J.M.
To Hannah Bragg and Gail Schiedt for their help with Design, Layout and Pre press.
D.S.

### WARNING

Mr. Matott does not advocate the use of any illegal firecrackers.
The stories in this book that speak to the fun of using fireworks are for reading entertainment only;
please understand that fireworks can be very dangerous. After all, if something is designed to explode,
it generally will, and does not take into account upon what or whom. Please use common sense
when thinking about using fireworks, and always have an adult present. If considering undertaking
some of the dare-offs and other pranks performed in Mr. Matott's imagination, remember much of it
is imagination and not reality. A special note: this book is indeed primarily fiction, though it must be
admitted that Mr. Matott had a full, rich and adventurous childhood from which to draw.
He also has numerous scars to prove it. BE CAREFUL OUT THERE!

### THE GABRIEL WORLD BOOK OF RECORDS

Text copyright © 2010 by JUSTIN MATOTT

Design and Layout Buster York Creative. www.busteryorkcreative.com
Interior illustrations copyright © 2010, David Schiedt.
Jacket illustrations copyright © 2010, David Schiedt
All rights reserved under International and Pan-American Copyright Conventions. No part of
this publication may be reproduced or transmitted in any form or by any means, electronic or
mechanical, including photocopy, recording, or any information storage and retrieval system,
without permission in writing from the publisher.
Requests for permission to make copies of any part of the work should be mailed to:
Permissions Department, SKOOB BOOKS,
P. O. Box 631183
Littleton, CO 80163.
Library of Congress Cataloging-in-Publication Data
**THE GABRIEL WORLD BOOK OF RECORDS** written by JUSTIN MATOTT.;
Illustrations by David Schiedt - 1st ed. p. cm.
Summary: ISBN 978-1-889191-27-0 {1. chapter book series. I. David Schiedt - ill. II. Title First edition
A B C D E
To contact JUSTIN MATOTT regarding his work, please see his website at www.justinmatott.com.

Printed in China
Manufactured in China. Production Location: Guangdong, China. Production Date: 6/30/10. Cohort: Batch 1

# CONTENTS

# PROLOGUE

My finger traced along the pages of the stiff new book, flipping forward, then backward hungrily. I wanted to bend the corners to mark my favorite feats in my Guinness Book of World Records book, but the truth is I would be bending almost all the pages because each page seemed to hold a mystery, magic, or inspiration.

"PAGING GABRIEL PETERS! PAGING GABRIEL PETERS! ITS TIME FOR DINNER! THIS IS YOUR THIRD AND FINAL CALL!"

Dad's shout sounded like the people who page you when you are at the airport, but a little bit angrier, more like my brother's as it boomed up the stairs, down the hall and flooded under the door to my bedroom. His yell was even louder than the music coming from my 8-track stereo.

My dog Frisky's ears went up, and he turned his head curiously to watch the door.

"O-KAY, Dad, I'm coming!" I yelled from my bedroom.

"ONE MORE MINUTE AND I'LL FEED YOUR FAVORITE PEPPERONI PIZZA TO THE DOGS!"

Dad yelled up the stair to me in the angriest voice he could muster, which really wasn't too angry. I could tell he was trying to sound mad and wasn't... yet, but I really didn't want to test that. I was huddled under my covers in the upper bunk of my bunk beds, staring at a picture I just couldn't believe was even real in my new book. My finger was tracing the text, and my other hand was scribbling fast in my notebook.

I knew Dad wouldn't really feed my pizza to Frisky and Friskier because they always get sick when they eat greasy food and puke on the carpet. Besides, Dad's favorite breakfast of all time is cold pepperoni pizza, and further besides, both of the dogs were huddled inside my bedroom at my door moaning and growling to get out because they could smell the pizza downstairs.

Frisky's whole body and especially his fuzzy ears were actually shaking since he wanted the pizza so bad. He started to woof-growl, and to prance with his front paws the way a horse does.

"One bad apple don't spoil the whole bunch girl..."

The Jackson 5 blared from my phonograph's 8-track as I sang along at the top of my voice, still wondering what all the fuss about girls was. I mean, I kind of had a crush on a girl named Amy last year, but that was mostly because she smelled nice and was kinda pretty. Actually, she was really pretty.

I wasn't even sure why I liked her with my friends telling me she and her friends had cooties and all, but still I did. When she gave me a special Valentine on Valentine's Day, different than the one she gave the other boys in my class, my stomach felt all funny and Dad said she was the first in a long line of girls who would upset my stomach. Mom smacked Dad on the shoulder and then laughed so hard at that one that I thought she was going to spray milk out of her nose the way my brother Carl does when I tell funny stories at dinner.

I shook my head to clear my thoughts and realized how far away I am sometimes in my imagination.

Dad's favorite family night is pizza night and he doesn't like it unless everyone is gathered around the table for it. I was trying to think if I even heard the doorbell ring when the delivery guy dropped off the pizza. NOPE, I HADN'T! Even though pizza is my favorite food of all time, I had so many other things on my mind that I had put my stomach on hold for probably the first time in my whole life.

Carl's voice, which now was almost as low as Dad's, bellowed up the stairs, "Yeah, Chicken-Little, I'm eatin' all of your pizzaz right now!"

Why was it the whole time they were yelling for me my favorite album was playing? I nudged the play button on the stereo on top of my dresser with my big toe without even leaving the upper bunk. "Never can say goodbye, no nononono... every time I think I've had enough... Don't want to let you go..."

"Come on, not more corny girl stuff," I said to myself, looking at the album cover of The Jackson 5. I told my dogs, "Michael Jackson's afro is so cool. I wonder if my hair would ever do that?" but the dogs were far more interested in the smells coming up the stairs from the kitchen.

I could hear Mom's growl coming up the stairs too now, "Carl, once and for all STOP CALLING YOUR LITTLE BROTHER NAMES!"

"NOW! GABRIEL!" Dad yelled.

"Sor-ry Dad, I'm coming!"

Wow, he was really being impatient. I mean it couldn't have been more than a couple minutes since he called up last. I jumped down off of my bunk and switched off my stereo, thinking of how dumb it is that Carl always calls pizza "pizzaz" and thinks that is really cool for some reason. I also knew Carl's threat as usual is an idle one since I know my mom would never let him eat my dinner. Usually I wouldn't be late for pizza, but I just got the new Guinness Book of World Records, brand-new edition, and as hard as I tried to put it down, I kept saying, "Just one more..." The Guinness Book of World Records is clearly the best book ever!

Every year I get the new edition and read it cover to cover in bunk and in my tree house, comparing last year's records to the new ones. Some seem to never change, and some just get bigger, heavier, stranger and cooler. I plan to spend the whole day tomorrow up in my tree house reading it.

My favorite part of the book is the stuff people do to get into the book without really trying (I guess). Like the guy with the extra long, totally gross curly fingernails, the tallest and the shortest people in the world, the lady with the really, really tiny waist, and the man with the beard of bees. Man, one time I caught a huge bumblebee in my cupped hands and got stung. I have never felt such an electrical kind of shock go through my body, and then the pain from the stinger — OUCH! I can't imagine what would happen if hundreds of bees decided all at once to sting my face!

The phone rang. I grabbed it off my dresser before my brother could get the phone downstairs.        "Hello? Hey Andy... Nothing, just reading the new Guinness Book... You got it too? I know, that's what I was thinking... We could...."

"Gabriel, NOW!"

Dad was standing on the other side of my bedroom door, and I could tell he was really steamed, not just pretending to be mad anymore. Dad is pretty relaxed usually, but not when it comes to pizza night.

Frisky and Friskier started to wag their tails furiously as they realized Dad was on the other side of the door, and that meant the door was going to be opening, and soon.

"Hey Andy, I really gotta go. Yeah... write down ten records you think we could break... 'kay, see ya, buddy.' I hung up the phone. "Coming, Dad! Sorry!"

I opened my door, and both Frisky and Friskier almost took Dad out at the knees as they raced to the kitchen where the delicious pizza was waiting.

"Dad, I have to go to the bathroom, is that okay?" I asked.

"Make it really quick, Buster!"

I knew Dad wasn't really mad anymore when he called me Buster.

As I passed by him, Dad rubbed the top of my head.

"Son, you really need to come when you are called. We all are waiting for you."

"Sorry, Dad."

I walked into the bathroom and closed the door. In a little while, I ran down the stairs and pulled up to the table where everyone was waiting for me. I folded a slice like Dad does and stuffed the pizza into my mouth as fast as I could, ignoring Mom's scowl.

"Gabe, slow down and eat your salad, too..." Mom said as she watched me folding another entire triangle of pepperoni pizza into my mouth.

"Yeah, you big Chicken-Piggy," Carl snarled.

"Mmmfffsfrrrry m..." I tried to spit out at my big brother.

Mom barked, "Gabriel, don't eat with your mouth full!"

"Bfut mo-omhowf can I eat unlef my mouf is ull?" I asked, moving the huge lump of chewy, cheesy pepperoni pizza to one side of my mouth.

"I meant, don't talk with your mouth full!" Mom growled.

Dad and I burst out laughing, and I accidentally sprayed pepperoni pizza on Carl across the table.

'GROSS, YOU LITTLE CHICKEN-CRETIN!'

Carl was bright red as he wiped my pizza spit off of his face with a paper napkin.

'Chicken Cretin?' Dad and I asked at the same time.

'It means stupid,' Carl said under his breath.

'Carl, STOP calling Gabriel names all the time. How many times do I have to tell you that? One more insult and you are in your room for the night and no more pizza and no chocolate Sundae!' Mom barked.

I folded a third slice of the gooey pizza and stuffed the cone into my mouth, 'Or if ithpithaz?' I smirked under my breath.

Mom threw an evil glance across the table, so I swallowed before I spoke again.

'Don't worry about it, Mom. I could really care less what Carl thinks of me! Sticks and stones may break my bones… but…'

'I'll break your bones,' Carl mouthed at me, but Mom caught him and gave him 'THE LOOK'.

Carl just glared across the table at me, like I was the one who started it.

"How come he never gets in trouble? He just launched
a pepperoni spit bomb at my face and you don't even say
anything!" Carl scowled.

Mom started, "Well, I don't think he meant to..."

"Yeah, if I did that, I would have to go live in my room for a
century or longer!" Carl's eyes filled with tears.

I felt bad for him. My brother did do a lot of boneheaded
things, but there was no reason to always yell at him. After all,
his dumb insults didn't even bother me. I just thought it was
totally lame that he had to add "chicken" to every insult. I guess
it was just a habit now.

"It's okay, Carl, don't cry. I'm sorry," I pleaded.

"I'm not crying, you big chicken-idiot!" Carl snarled.

"CARL!" Mom growled and slammed her fist on the table,
which sent Friskier scurrying to the other side of the room.

"You see, Gabe makes fun of me for just being a human and
you don't even get mad at him," Carl whined.

I stomped my foot, "I wasn't making fun of...."

When I stomped my foot, Frisky joined Friskier.

"Gabe, maybe it's best that no one says anything more to
make it worse," Dad murmured.

"But, I..."

"GABE!" yelled my folks. Both of them stared me down.

Carl looked at me with total satisfaction. But I really hadn't
been making fun of him... this time, anyway.

The rest of dinner everyone was pretty quiet. Frisky and
Friskier made their way back under the table, hoping for falling
pizzaz.

I felt bad for Dad, since pizza night is always his favorite.
First I made everyone tense by being late, and then Carl
had to go and be so rude.  Dad sighed really loud and then
carried his plate away from the table and into the living room,
preferring to dial out in front of the television.  He switched
on this corny television show called Hee Haw, and just as soon
as I was excused and did the dishes I rushed back up to my
bedroom, skipping the chocolate Sundae too, to take more notes
about the Guinness records and plan what me and my buddies
would do to get into the book next year.

℗

(Dad was showing me in this book on his desk how the
author gets to protect what they write with this symbol ℗, so I
decided to put it on every page of my new journal so my dumb
brother can't take my brilliant ideas and copy them down for
his homework assignments, especially the ones about Glenn the
Sea Monkey℗ hehheh.  Oh, you just wait to see what I have
planned with a monster sea monkey!)

# TIME TO MAKE IT INTO THE RECORD BOOKS

I am going to see if the guys from The Secret Brotherhood of Boys want to try to set some world records so we can get into the book! I have some ideas about what we can do. Like, I got this idea that we could create the world's largest spit pool ever with gallons and gallons of gooey, slimy saliva. I looked up "spit" in Guinness, and the only thing they have in the record book is about distance.

I started singing while I was scratching notes about the records we could set. I started to sing, "You don't spit into the wind..." I drew a little picture, "and you don't pull the mask off the old Lone Ranger." I jotted down a note about spitting, "... and you don't mess around with Jim...." Man, o man, I love that song. Anyway, the only spitting records are distance of spit, and distance of spitting watermelon seeds.

There is nothing in the book about making the world's largest spit pool, which is the record I think we could set. I figure if we got Tony's little sister Bianca's wading pool and put it right under the tree house, we could fill that thing in no time flat. We could all spit all day long and then sleep in the tree house at night, tied to a branch and lying on our stomachs. We'd be hanging over the edge a little so we would drool all night into the pool.

I'll bet my dad would take some pictures and help me get someone from the Guinness Book Of World Records over here from Ireland to verify our spit record. We could get a ton of lemonheads and atomic fireballs and bubble gumballs up at the Bait Shop, because those always make your mouth fill up with syrupy drool.

A couple of weeks ago we had a secret meeting and decided it was time to have a President of The Secret Brotherhood of Boys. I wanted Andy to win, but it was a top-secret ballet where everyone wrote down just one name and put it in my baseball cap. I got all but one vote, and that one was mine, which was for Andy.

So now as the President I have to call the meetings and I have to run them too. I called a secret meeting of The Secret Brotherhood of Boys for the next day using our secret code words and telephone tag order that Tony wrote out for each of us, so we would remember to use code names. To start, I call Andy (Secret code name STUTTER), he calls Butch (Secret code name B-DOG—dumb, huh? But he made that one up. Isn't there a rule somewhere that you can't give yourself a nickname?), Butch calls Tony (Secret code name TOENAIL), Tony calls Craig (Secret code name GREG, which is SO dumb on account of the fact that it sounds the same and also is the name of my one my dumb brother's best friends, and is practically the same name anyhow), Craig calls Murph (Secret code name WARBOY, though Murph argued hard for WARRIOR but lost) and Murph calls me (Secret code name PETERS, which is so dumb since it is my last name and not so secret), and Murph calls me to make sure the whole thing works and comes back around.

When we all got to the tree house, I told everyone my first order of business is going to be to change these dumb names to something cooler like: SPIKE, FONZIE, ELVIS, RODNEY AND RED. We also were supposed to each have ten ideas written down for records we might set, but of course no one did. Andy was the only one with more than three ideas, so it would be up to me to decide.

First we all talked about the whole nickname thing, and how it wasn't really working.

Eddie said, "My dad says nicknames just happen."

"How?" I asked.

"I guess he got his nickname one time when he was riding a mini-bike and flew over the handlebars into a big patch of cactus!"

"What's his n-n-nickname?" Andy asked.

"HOLY FLIPPER!"

That one cracked us all up, because we could see Eddie's dad pitching over the handlebars of a mini-bike.

"Why 'holy'?" Eddie asked.

"DUH!" we all snarled. "Cactus?"

We talked about it for awhile, but in the end we decided nicknames were dumb and just stuck with what came natural; dummy, hey you and yo bro!

Tony yelped, "Wouldn't that be so cool if we all had mini-bikes?"

"I'll never get one. Mom said no mini-bikes, no motorcycles," I murmured.

Eddie said excitedly, "Hey, did you know the Lawn and Leisure place is going to start selling Indian Motorcycles?"

"Yeah, they hired m-m-my b-brothers to help b-build a dirt bike track b-b-behind the store," Andy said. "B-But it w-won't b-be ready until n-next summer."

"The man that owns Lawn and Leisure is super cool," Craig added.

"Yeah!" everyone agreed.

Sometimes when we were going fishing, we would stop in the store and just stand in the air conditioning and buy a pop from the soda machine. The machine was always stocked with Dr. Pepper, Red Cream Soda, Root Beer and Seven Up. The man would let us drive the riding mowers around in the parking lot, and sometimes he even gave us candy bars when we came in to get a pop.

"Jimmy t-told me that h-he is g-going to l-let kids ride the motorcycles if they b-bring a note in from their parents," Andy added.

"COOL!"

"AWESOME!"

"I CAN'T WAIT!"

"UGH!" I said, feeling horrible. I knew Mom would never give me a note, and all of my friends were going to get to ride the motorcycles without me.

"What's the matter, Gabe?" Craig asked.

"I'll never get to ride. Mom is totally against motorcycles on account of my Uncle Howie getting really hurt on one when he was a teenager," I growled.

"M-Man, that st-stinks," Andy scowled.

"Yeah, but while you guys are riding motorcycles, I'll be zooming around in my jetpack!" I teased.

"Yeah, right —hic, what jetpack — hic?" Butch's usual grumpy voice came from below us, because he was late getting to the meeting.

"Oh, I'm going to win one by selling stuff from one of those contests!" I declared.

I leaned out and pretended I was going to spit on Butch. He ducked around the tree and then shinnied over to the steps.

"For real?" Craig asked.

"There's no such —hic thing as a real jetpack —hic. That's just in the —hic comics and on TV —hic!" Butch snarled, now below us on the steps and coming up.

"Well, I guess we'll see about that, huh?" I snarled. "Not just that, but I am getting a real metal detector too! I am going to find so much treasure!"

"—hic —hic —hic..."

I looked around the tree house at my friends, who looked at me admiringly and a little jealously. "Okay, back to the business of world record setting!" I demanded.

Butch was coming through the cutout in the tree house where the rest of us in The Secret Brotherhood of Boys were, and Murph was coming across the gravel road fast, heading toward us.

"—hic —hic —hic..."

Butch had the hiccoughs for two days straight. I flipped through my Guinness book from the index to the page I was looking for. "Hey, there's a record right here for hiccoughs. This guy has been hiccoughing for thirty years. Maybe Butch can beat that record!" I laughed.

"Is it true that the only way to get someone to stop hiccoughing is to scare them?" Tony asked.

"—hic —hic —hic..."

"Nah, that's an old wives tale," Eddie jumped in.

Andy had a funny look on his face, "Huh? Old w-w-wives t-tale?"

"What, you've never heard that before?" Eddie asked.

"—hic —hic —hic..."

Butch kept hiccoughing. He tried to hold his breath. He asked us to try to scare him, but that's like trying to tickle yourself. If you know it's coming, you don't get scared.

Okay, check it out, guys. I was lying on my stomach in the tree house and the guys were in the tree house with me, but Butch was now lying against a huge tree branch, trying to get rid of his hiccoughs.

"Did you guys know that a guy has been hiccoughing since 1922? Listen to this: He contracted it when slaughtering a hog. His first wife left him and he is unable to keep in his false teeth," I read directly from the book.

"Oh, it's th—the c—c—curse of the evil h—hog!" Andy laughed.

"—hic —hic —hi...c"

"Oh my gosh, listen to this, there's this other guy in England back in 1769 who hiccoughed so loud that you could hear it a mile away!" I read proudly.

"SHEESH! That is loud!" Craig whistled.

"Shh... check this out too. This seventeen—year—old guy sneezed for 155 days, and this fifteen— year—old girl yawned continuously for five weeks." I opened my mouth and made myself yawn, which turned out kind of funny, because right after I did, Tony yawned and then Butch, which was hilarious because he hiccoughed and yawned at the same time, and before I knew it everyone was yawning including me.

"Ahh —hic Ahh —hic Ahh —hic..."

Murph turned out to be so excited about his ideas to set a record that he didn't even climb up into the tree house. He jumped on to the rope swing hanging right below us and began to read his list off to us.

"1. Everyone—wears—combat—clothes—and—has—to—dogcrawl—ten—miles."

"WHAT?" several of us shouted, because Murph always is so excited and talks so fast that it is hard to understand him.

The last time Murph was at my house, I told him the other guys would like him more if he slowed down a little and didn't

talk about
war all the time. I
noticed he has been trying.
"2. Everyone-has-to-wear-
combat-fatigues-and-climb-up-and-
down-the-rope-to-the-tree-house-
one-thousand-times-without-using-
his-feet."

Butch growled, "-hic I'm fatigued
just listening -hic to this dumb list -hic!"

"Yeah, c-c-come on, M-Murph, we can
read." Andy joined in, hanging his head down
from the tree house right above Murph. "Just
give us your list."

"COME TO ORDER! Murph, if you are
going to join this meeting, you have to be in the tree house," I
demanded as the newly elected President.

When I began to explain my own record-setting idea to the
guys, they were all really excited about it.

"Okay now, check this out, guys. We have to decide if we could
do something like this."

I began to read from my Guinness book, "The greatest
distance achieved at the annual tobacco-spitting classic at
Raleigh, Mississippi is 31 feet one inch..."

"-hic Thirty-one feet? That's like -hic one third of a football
field-hic! That is a long way -hic to spit!" Butch calculated.

"Wow, Butchie, Er, B-Dog, is a brainiac! He figured that out
so fast," Tony laughed.

Butch punched him hard on the shoulder and snarled, "Shut
up, Toenail -hic. What kind of a --hic nickname is Toenail?"

"Hey, cut it out, Butch-Dog! You're going to knock me out of
the tree!" Tony screamed.

"With -hic any luck I will..." Butch sneered. "And you're late
-hic!" he snarled at Murph, who had just popped his face up
through the hole we crawl through. "You know if you are late you

have
to buy everyone
gumballs at the Bait Shop next time!'

"When-did-we-make-up-that-rule?"
Murph asked.

"We? -hic You ain't even part -hic of we yet!"
Butch barked back.

"Come on guys, cut it out! Butch, stop being
so mean to Murph all the time!" I commanded
as his President. "Now everyone shut up and
listen!"

I couldn't believe I was talking to my
friends like that, but they all did just what I asked.

"Ahem, now where was I?" I continued, "In the 3rd
International Spittin', Belchin' and Cussin' Triathlon, Harold
Fielden reached 34 feet 1/4 inch at Central City, Colorado.
Distance is dependent on the quality of salivation, absence of
cross wind, two-finger pucker and the coordination of the back
arch and neck snap. Sprays or wads smaller than a dime are
not measured."

"-hic -hic -hic"

Tony said, "Spittin', belchin' and cussin'... sounds like a good
idea to me, 'cept if I cuss my mom will wash my mouth out with
soap."

Butch chimed in, "-hic Yeah, me too. -hic Let's just spit and
-hic belch and..."

"Oh-come-on-ladies,-in-WW2-there-were-tougher-contests-
every-day-in-the-foxholes-just-to..." Murph interrupted.

"Enough with the -hic war talk, Murph-hic, sheesh," Butch
scowled.

"...Keep-the-men's-minds-off-of-the-horrible..."

Andy chimed in to break the constant tension between
Murph and Butch, "Hey M-Murph's g-g-got a ton of g-gas, how
b-bout we get a hundred c-c-cans of beans and..."

"-hic -hic -hic"

'Oh, come on, no one is going to fly from Ireland to hear Murph cut one a million times!' I said, snorting through my nose on account of laughing too suddenly. 'Oh man, that would be so cool, like mustard gas... Okay, how bout this...'

The guys threw record-setting ideas around for a long time.

I finally interrupted and went back to my spitting idea. I explained the whole thing to them, and everyone seemed to like it. We were all sitting around in a circle when Andy snorted so loud I thought his nose would blow off, and then he was laughing really hard.

'What's up, Andy? What's so funny?' I asked.

'—hic —hic —hic'

'Wh-What if...' Andy was laughing so hard and snorting so loud in between breaths that he couldn't get it out. 'Wh-Wh-What if M-M-Mr. Stolz...' he couldn't finish without laughing. Finally he blurted out, 'Wh-What if Mr. and M-Mrs. Stolz w-were in our sp-spitting contest?'

'—hic THEY COULD FILL A BABY POOL —hic IN TEN MINUTES —hic!' Butch screamed.

'Yeah, say it, don't spray it, Stoltzie baby,' Tony said.

Eddie was laughing so hard, he almost tumbled out of the tree house.

Andy was still laughing as he chortled, 'Every t-t-time I am at p-piano l-l-lessons I get a sh-shower...'

Butch was laughing too, '—hic Remember the time —hic Mr. Stolz was so mad at us —hic that he...'

'You mean when he was Santa Clod the Spitter?' Eddie spurted.

It went on like that for a long time, and when we finally got back to my idea for record-setting madness my stomach hurt so bad from laughing that I could hardly talk.

'—hic —hic —hic'

θ

Well, that's how we started a year of trying to set records.

It sure looked like this year was going to be a bonanza for me. Finally I was going to be on the big yellow school bus with my buddies, going to the same elementary school they all did. And finally, finally, finally I was going to get to be a fifth grader.

Plus, since I was changing schools, no one except my friends would know that I had to repeat last year, so this would be a much better school year for me. Besides, new schools meant no more uniforms and even better, no more Sister Mary Claire!

But school was still a couple months away, and we had tons of work to do before we went back to school if we were going to see our names in the Guinness Book of World Records! We were going to be famous, really famous!

CHAPTER TWO

# BIG DEAL BICENTENNIAL

There are only three more days to go until one of the biggest deals in a long, long time. It is July 1st of 1976, and that means the U. S. is about to have a big deal birthday. I thought my Grandma was old, but the country is going to be 200 years old in just a few days.

My Uncle Stewie and Uncle Howie, mom's brothers, are coming to celebrate here in Colorado with us. I am excited to see them, but mostly I am excited because they are bringing Gran with them and she is going to stay with us for a couple weeks while my uncles go to Yellowstone and fish all over Wyoming and Montana. They'll then come back and pick her up to go back to Kansas, where they all live.

Gran is a lot of fun, but I have never seen her when she wasn't at her farm in Kansas, so I wonder what she will do with all her time. There are always so many chores to do on the farm, and Gran is the one that seems to do most of them. My grandpa is usually taking care of his livestock and the grain fields, leaving Gran to take care of the chores in the house, barn, and around the farm where they live.

My Auntie Leslie is coming too at some point. Auntie Leslie is my dad's sister, and she weighs like ten thousand pounds. "More to love of me, eh?" is what Auntie Leslie says to me, and I think she is funny. She has stayed with us a ton (no ton pun intended) of times, especially because her husband (my uncle Chester) died a long time ago, so she travels a lot. My uncle was really, really fat too, and Dad told me it caused his body a lot of trouble, so he died. I should be sad, but I only met him once when I was a baby, so I don't even remember him.

My uncles are planning a two-week fishing and camping trip, so they are dropping Gran off for a nice, long visit. They are going to bring tons of firecrackers for the big Bicentennial celebration. They promised to keep the sky lit up in our neighborhood all night long.

I can hardly wait.

☺

I awakened early on the Fourth of July to the sound of my uncles joking with Dad downstairs in the kitchen.

"We just drove straight through, stopped for gas a few times, but we made great time!" Uncle Stewie said, recounting the all-night trip.

"Yeah, that new pickup is great. The cassette deck lets you listen to all kinds of good music when you are between cities and the radio doesn't come in too well. Beter'n my old 8-track!" Uncle Howie chimed in.

I walked across the hall into the bathroom and looked out the back window as I peed. Gran had gone straight to the vegetable garden and was throwing weeds onto the lawn. I could see her from the bathroom window.

I ran back over to my room to get dressed, threw on a pair of shorts and a t-shirt and peeked out my window, which faced the front of the house. There was the truck they were talking about. A really cool shiny blue pick-up with a white and blue camper top was sitting in front of our house. I hoped my uncle would let me sleep in it overnight. It would be the coolest clubhouse for The Secret Brotherhood of Boys meetings!

I ran down the stairs and was picked up by Uncle Howie.

"WOW, who is this? I haven't seen my nephew Gabriel yet, but this kid is a head taller than he is, and doesn't have an eye patch. Who is this intruder?"

"Uncle Howie, cut it out, you know it's me!" I giggled.

Uncle Howie started to tickle me, which made me almost pee my pants, even though I had just been in the bathroom.

"Wait 'til you see Carl. He looks like the missing link. Like someone hit him with the ugly stick!" I laughed.

"Gabe, that is not nice!" Mom said.

"Sorry Mom, I didn't see you there."

Mom was standing behind my Uncle Stewie getting things ready for an old-fashioned farm breakfast.

"That doesn't matter. You shouldn't say things like that at all," Mom scowled at me.

"Sorry."

I hung my head and acted like
I was sorry, but I wasn't. Carl said
all kinds of mean things to me,
so to me getting him back a little
seemed right.

"Say things like what?" Carl
came bounding down the stairs,
obviously delighted to catch me
in the middle of a good chewing
out. "How can anyone sleep with
Grandma making so much noise in
the backyard?"

"Oh my gosh! Look at you, Carl."
Uncle Howie stood next to him.
"Geez kid, you are as tall as me."
It was almost true. "You been eatin'
your groceries, boy!"

Uncle Stewie gave Carl a bear
hug and said, "You got a little ways to go before you catch
me." Carl tried to pull away, but that just made Uncle Stewie
squeeze harder.

Uncle Howie saw the look on my face. "Don't worry about it,
Gabe. I was always the runt, too. Look at me; I still am!"

"That supposed to make me feel better?" I scowled at him.
"Who you calling a runt?" I asked under my breath.

My uncles went on and on, making a big deal about how big
my brother was. They were challenging him to arm wrestle and
ignoring me, so I slid the back screen open and walked out onto
the patio. My gran, who was still pulling weeds like it was her
own garden turned when she heard the back door open. A huge
smile crept across her face. I ran into her arms and gave her
a tight squeeze.

"How is my handsome young man?" she asked.

"Good, Gran, how are you?" I squealed.

"Well, I'm better now that I finally got to see my favorite
little boy."

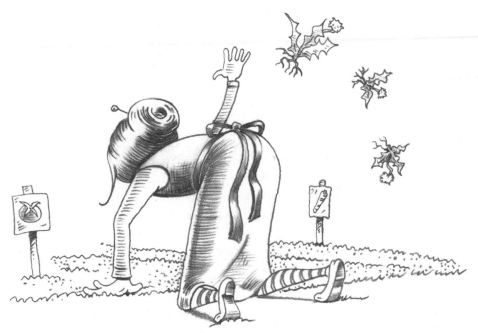

Gran squeezed me really, really tight.

There was that description of me as puny again. How come Carl got to be big and I didn't?

"I'm not little, Gran," I shot back, looking down at my feet.

"Oh pooh, I don't care if you grow to be ten feet tall! You will always be my special little boy. S'got nothing to do with size."

When I raised my eyes up from the ground, Gran thumped the end of my nose with her index finger.

"Okay," I shrugged.

Grandma held my shoulders and looked into my eyes.

"Now, I got a surprise for you," she said.

"What is it?"

"It's in the truck," Grandma said and started walking in that direction.

"Is it a dead, headless chicken?" I smirked.

"Don't you sass me, boy," Gran laughed

I started thinking about the last time we saw each other – how she had freaked me out so bad by twirling the chickens in the air like lassos so we would have some supper.

"Now, you come on," she told me.

We walked through the garden to the front yard and out to the curb. Gran reached into the truck and pulled out a bag, handing it to me.

"Open it," she said.

"What is it?" I asked, excited.

"One way to find out," Gran smiled.

I tore into the sack and found a big bag of salt water taffy.

"Yum, I love your taffy, Gran!"

She nodded as I looked next at a package wrapped in a brown bag. I pulled the tape off, and started to open the bag.

"A book?" I asked dismally.

"Oh, not just any book, Gabe, THE BOOK! This book is one of the best books ever written about a boy, for a boy."

Grandma looked excited about it.

I shrugged, raising my eyebrows I read the cover out loud. "Where The Red Fern Grows?"

"The candy's from me, the book's from your gramps. You n' me are gonna read that book together if we can find the time."

That certainly made the book more interesting. "Great!" I said, and looked closely at a picture of a boy with a flashlight and his dogs on the cover. It made me think of how many times I had gone on journeys in the fields with my two dogs, Frisky and Friskier.

"We'll start tomorrow night after all this doggone Bicentennial's hoopla has died down," Gran said.

"Do you want to sleep out in the back yard in my tent?" I asked.

"You got an extra cot in that tent?" Gran said, rubbing the lower part of her back. "Can't sleep on the ground anymore with this old back."

"Yup!"

"Then your tent it is!" Gran looked across the gravel road toward the pond and nodded upward. "That there your tree house, Gabriel?"

"Yup!"

"Then we'll read up there some too."

"You can still climb trees, Gran?"

"WHAT? You never seen me up in that hayloft of mine?" she sneered.

"Yup!"

I started laughing, thinking about the last time I was diving off the hayloft into the huge pile of hay below, and Gran threatening to do so too, but never actually doing it.

"Can we read some in my Guinness World Book, too?" I wondered.

"Sure, I love all that weirdo stuff!" Gran cackled.

"I'm gonna get into that book this year, Gran," I insisted.

She rubbed my head as she said, "Well, I'll just bet you will... Hmmm... World's Weirdest Grandma?"

Just then Carl and my uncles came out the front door.

"Hey, Grandma," Carl said.

"Hay's for horses, mules and goats, I'm your Grandma and I eat oats!" Gran cracked herself up.

Carl rolled his eyes. "Like I haven't heard that one a million times before!"

I shot him a dirty eyeball and mouthed, "BE NICE YOU BIG IDIOT!"

Carl half-heartedly hugged Gran, but when she squeezed him, it was something fierce.

"Now, don't you think just cause you're a head taller than I am that you can go being like that," she told him.

"I didn't do anything," Carl complained.

It was the strangest thing; Carl and Gran were like oil and water. I couldn't understand how anyone wouldn't think my gran was the greatest, but somehow Carl just saw the weird in her. I saw it too, but I liked it.

"I got something for you," Gran told Carl.

She reached into the truck again, and pulled out a bag that looked similar to mine.

Carl muttered, "What is it?"

"Open it up," Gran said eagerly.

Carl tore the bag open unceremoniously. "Salt water taffy? I can't eat this; it sticks to my braces." Carl growled rudely.

I shot Carl the dirty eyeball again and mouthed the word "JERK."

"Then give it to Gabe; he loves it! Open the other one. It won't stick to your braces..., hopefully."

That's the great thing about Gran; it's really hard to rattle her cage.

Carl pulled the small bag out and ripped it open.

"Holy Guacamole, that is the coolest pocketknife I ever saw!" my big brother hooted.

Carl pulled the bottle opener open, then the sharp blade and started working on trying to pull out another one of the blades.

Gran smiled, "Well, that's from your Gramps. I protested, but he insisted."

"You would," Carl muttered under his breath, but we all heard him. Uncle Howie, who had just been watching and listening and fooling with his new truck cuffed the back of Carl's head, maybe a bit harder than he had meant to for talking to Gran that way.

"Ow! What the heck?" Carl snarled.

"Well, aren't we grumpy?" Uncle Stewie asked.

"Grumpy? How 'bout just the biggest jerk in the world?" I chimed in.

"Whatever!" Carl stomped off, flicking the blades of his new pocketknife.

We all watched Carl heading down the hill in a big huff.

"Oh, first year teenagers are the worst! The whole bunch of them should be put on ice for a decade till they turn back into human beings if you ask me." Gran laughed and pulled me to her and ruffled my hair. "But my Gabe isn't going to be like that when he's a teenager, are you young man?"

"Uh, no!" I couldn't imagine ever being as rude as my brother.

"Now, let's go have some breakfast!" Gran said, and the four of us headed into the house as Carl sulked on his own.

☻

That night when it got dark, my uncles and Dad were out in front of our house lining up a huge arsenal of firecrackers, fountains, rockets and other gear. I was watching from my window, but wanted a closer look so I shuffled out of my bedroom window, across the roof and then up onto the highest point of our roof. My uncles unloaded box after box from the back of the camper.

From my high spot I could see the fireworks beginning downtown in the city park. All over our neighborhood little kids were running around with sparklers, and groups were gathered in all the backyards. Smoke was curling from just about every backyard from the barbecues everyone was having. The smell of roasting meat was heavy in the air, and some gunpowder smells reached my nostrils too. Our neighborhood had been one big party all day. It seemed everyone thought it was a big deal to celebrate the Bicentennial Fourth of July.

I looked up at the weird old lady's house that everyone talks about. There are so many stories about her around here and nobody really even seems to know her. I felt kind of sad thinking that she is probably a lot like my grandma, kooky, but totally cool too. It was dark, except for the one light you could see burning in there night and day. I wondered if she was lonely living on her own like that.

Suddenly, a huge, bright explosion went off in the street right in front of my house, and then  a huge rocket whooshed upward right past me, barely missing my head. I ducked down as close to the shingle as I could get. Another rocket exploded way above me, then another and another.

"HOLY SMOKES, STEWART, YOU RIGHT NEAR TOOK MY EAR OFF WITH THAT LAST ROCKET!" Uncle Howie screamed, bending down over a huge fountain while he lit a punk with some matches, which is a stick that looks like my older brother's incense, but doesn't put off the same kind of stink when you light it.

"Uh, sorry, Howard, but move back or you'll take one of 'em in the face," Uncle Stewie yelled over the high-pitched screaming one of the spinning fountains was giving off in the middle of the street.

As more and more of the firecrackers lit up the sky above our house with their color and explosions, I could see Butch, Tony and Andy running up the hill toward my house. Then Carl's friends were gathered in our side yard, and after fifteen minutes of my uncles firing off rockets and fountains, our yard was flooded with people. I didn't even notice that Murph had climbed up onto the roof and was sitting just a few feet from me, making comments about how the night sky looked like it did when we did aerial assaults on the Nazis.

From where I was perched I watched Carl and Greg belly crawl to the back of the camper. They both grabbed what looked like thick packs of firecrackers and stuffed them down the front of their pants, covering them over with their t-shirts. I watched them belly crawl back to the side garden, and then they snuck over to my dad's little bench, which is up against the fence.

They both pulled the packages out of their pants and stuffed them down under the bench. Then they returned to their group.

Pretty soon Carl and his buddies headed down the gravel road. I watched them and saw that they were meeting up with a group of girls down by the street light where everyone goes to play hide-n-seek. Carl and his friends are all about girls nowadays and Carl is ALL ABOUT Denise! As they walked down the road toward the lake, I could see Carl was holding hands with Denise.

By now my friends were all either up on our roof or over in the tree house watching the spectacle. They didn't even seem to notice when I shinnied down off the roof and snuck down to Dad's garden bench. I reached under the bench and found two huge bricks of Black Cat firecrackers and a small brick of M-80s, which were supposed to be like an eighth of a stick of dynamite. I stuffed them under my shirt, and while everyone was out in the front watching the spectacle I rushed into the back door and ran down to the crawlspace. I unloaded the bricks of firecrackers under a box of Christmas lights that no one would be needing to go near for a long time.

Uncle Howie and Stewie were true to their word. They put on a show like none I had ever seen before. Everyone in our neighborhood talked about it all summer.

☉

The next morning from my bedroom I could hear my uncles talking in low voices in the front yard as they gathered all of the burnt firecrackers off the lawn and the gravel road, stuffing the trash in a bag. I hurried out the front door in my pajamas, feeling guilty that I had in a way stolen from them by hiding the firecrackers when I should have just given them back.

Uncle Howie was going between the garage and the camper bringing food they had put in our freezer for their fishing trip, so I climbed into the pickup with Uncle Stewie.

"Hey, little buddy, you trying to be a stowaway?" he asked me.

"What's that?" I asked, playing with the knobs on the little stove in the camper.

"It means you are trying to sneak into our truck to go along on our journey," my uncle laughed.

"No, I want to tell you something," I said sheepishly.

I told Uncle Stewie the whole thing about being up on the roof watching Carl and his goony friend stealing. And then I told him the rest. He thought it was really funny that I had double-crossed Carl's double-cross, and then told me he had seen Carl and his friend doing it, but it didn't really matter to him because they had so many firecrackers and "boys will be boys." He and Uncle Howie still had another box left that they never used, so it was no big deal that the other firecrackers had gotten taken..

"So you don't want them back?" I asked.

"Gabe, you're a big boy now. You know how to handle those things, right? As long as you are really careful, I am going to trust you to keep them," Uncle Stewie said, and patted the top of my head. Then he got out of the camper and told me to wait right there, and then he went into the cab of the pickup and came out with two huge bricks of pop-bottle rockets. He stuffed them into the brown paper sack and told me to use them wisely, but that if I got the chance I should use them in a prank against Carl and his buddies the way Uncle Stewie used to get back at his big brother, who now was his best friend—my Uncle Howie.

"If anyone gets hurt, your momma will skin me for giving these to you, so mum's the word! AND LIKE I SAID, BE REALLY, REALLY CAREFUL!" Uncle Stewie stressed.

"I promise!" I said excitedly. Then I snuck the bag into the crawlspace, thinking about how cool my uncle was. I snuck back up into my bedroom and peeked out the front window and watched them climb into the pickup and drive away. They would be back for Grandma in a few weeks.

I got my journal down from the shelf and started making notes about the kinds of prank possibilities there were with firecrackers.

# SOMETHING'S IN THE AIR

Andy and I were lying on our backs on the hill next to my yard after he flew over the handlebars of his bike. I was laughing at him so hard I almost peed my pants. His arms and legs are so long that he looked like a giant **daddy-longlegs** spider that got caught in the wind and went spinning through the air.

"Wh-What were you l-laughing at, P-P-Peters?"

I could tell Andy was kind of mad at me for laughing because he hardly ever calls me Peters. After a little while he started to laugh too, realizing how funny it must have looked.

"Uh, nothing..." I muttered and scanned the sky. I was squinting really hard and tracing the sky with my finger. "CHECK IT OUT DUDE, ITS A TYRANNOSAURUS REX EATING YOUR LAME DOG, TEX!"

Every time we lie on our backs, we look for wild stuff in the clouds and sometimes even make up funny stories. I was talking about Tex here. He's Andy's dog, and supposedly a white poodle, but I had never seen him white. Usually he is dirt yellow with big orange-eye-crust boogers running out of his eyes, and his paws and belly are so dark from dirt that he leaves paw prints on your pants when he jumps up on you, which he constantly does. Tex barks all the time in a high, yippy voice, and if you ever pet him he just pees. No one really likes him very much, but he is my best friend's dog, so in a way I kind of have to like him.

"HEY! D-Don't b-be mean to my d-dog!" Andy barked.

Andy is always kind to his pooch, 'cause only a jerk would be mean to an ugly dog like Tex.

"I'm not being mean to him. It isn't like he understands English!" I defended, glancing over at his dog, which had once again escaped the yard.

"P-P-Poodles are the sm-smartest dogs of all d-dogs! You're always t-t-talking to your d-dogs like they understand. Why do you th-think your d-dogs could understand you, but not m-m-mine?" Andy insisted." Uh, because he isn't a real dog," I snorted.

"Take it b-back, P-Peters!"

"Huh uh..."

"I m-mean it!" Andy thumped me hard on the shoulder, but I guess I had it coming for making fun of him flying over his handlebars and for making fun of his dog.

"Sheesh, I'm just kidding around," I thumped him back.

"I kn-know... Hey, I-look at that huge c-corvette d-d-driving right into a f-fat lady!"

Andy pointed toward the mountains at a big, dark cloud coming over the foothills.

"All I see is your big girlfriend's..." I started, but he cut me off.

"Huh? M-My g-girlfr... I d-don't h-have a g-girlfr... T-T-TEX, GET B-BACK HERE YOU L-LAMEBRAIN!" Andy sprang to his feet and headed toward where Tex was escaping. "C-Come on, G-Gabe!"

It was too late though. His dumb dog was running down the ditch barking at something, and he was heading toward Killer's house. If that dog Killer got hold of Tex he would be a grease spot on the gravel. I couldn't see what Tex was barking at. It was probably just a stick, but right then I half wished it was an alligator.

Luckily, Tex doubled back away from Killer's house and bounded toward my house again. Andy kept running around trying to get a hold of him. I just stayed right where I was, and Andy came back within a minute exasperated with his idiot dog.

This whole thing was nothing new. Andy's dog Tex was always escaping his yard, and today he had been following me and Andy around and barking nonstop ever since Andy flew off of his bike. It was driving me and Andy totally nuts.

Then again, my dogs go everywhere with me, but Tex never really gets to leave his yard on account of being so annoying and not knowing how to stay out of the street. Somehow though he always finds a way to get to freedom. You have to hand it to him for that.

Andy plopped down on the ground and rolled onto his back right next to me and sighed really loud.

I squealed, "Look at that dragon! See that long jagged pink tail that is coming up from the ground! That's his tail!"

"Hmmm, n-n-nope, I d-don't see it, but I see the biggest p-p-poodle g-getting close to that d-d-dragon and it is g-going to eat it!"

"Yeah right, lamebrain, like a dog could eat a dragon!" I laughed.

"Yeah, if th-there was a d-dragon! That looks m-more like a prairie d-d-dog."

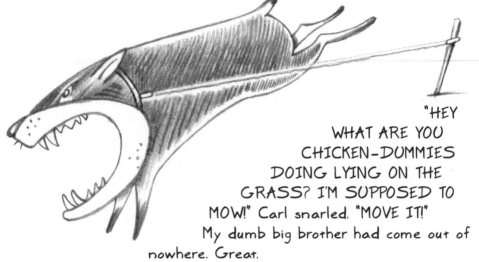

"HEY WHAT ARE YOU CHICKEN-DUMMIES DOING LYING ON THE GRASS? I'M SUPPOSED TO MOW!" Carl snarled. "MOVE IT!"

My dumb big brother had come out of nowhere. Great.

"Sh-shut up Carl," Andy said under his breath.

"Wh-what d-d-did you s-s-s-say, Andy?" Carl glared angrily.

I jumped up and yelled, "Carl, you are such a jerk! Don't make fun of Andy or..."

"Or what, chicken-dunce? I'll give you two a haircut with the mower if you want."

My brother laughed a bit too loud at his own dumb joke.

"Oh, yeah, that's so funny I forgot to laugh, lamebrain. Get lost, loser, or I'll tell Mom that you are bugging me again!" I threatened.

"Loser?" Carl snarled at me. "Who you callin' a loser, chicken-jerk?"

I responded in kind, "You are the world's biggest jerk. Just leave us alone."

Carl pushed me back down and kneeled on my chest and gave me a nipple twist or a "p-p-purple n-n-n-nurple." as Andy called it. "How d'ya like these apples, chicken-loser?"

Gran popped her head through the kitchen window, where she had obviously been listening, "Carl, why don't you pick on someone your own size? Leave those boys alone."

"Oh Grandma, we're just kidding around, aren't we boys?" Carl pushed his knees down on me for emphasis.

"Why don't you boys push back? Andy, he isn't much bigger

than you really," Gran snarled.

"OW, GET OFFA ME YOU BIG, STUPID JERK!" My chest was burning and all I wanted to do was something to hurt Carl. All of a sudden Andy, who now stood about an inch shorter than Carl but weighed half what Carl did, jumped up and knocked Carl off of me.

Carl looked completely shocked, but he regained his tough guy act and jumped on Andy, pinning his arms down. Then he straddled his chest and cut a huge one on him.

I started laughing so hard that Andy snarled at me, "Nice, P-Peters, I d-d-defend you and you j-just l-laugh when your big j-jerk-o brother cheeses on m-me?"

"Cheeses?" I acted dumb.

"Yeah, he cut the cheese!" Andy growled.

He had a good point about having defended me, but I was laughing too hard to do anything about it. So was Gran.

Andy was screaming now, "Oh my g-gosh! Carl, you sm-smell like you d-died, get offa m-me, NOW!"

Just then one of Andy's brothers, Johnny-or-Jimmy, showed up. Johnny-and-Jimmy were identical twins and they were Andy's big brothers. I think Andy was the only one of us that could tell them apart, but they both hung out in the Goon Squad; that much we did know!

"Carl, what are you doing on my brother?" he asked.

Gran was still laughing hard when she closed the window, as if things were going the way they should.

"Tormenting. What's it to you?" Carl barked back.

"What?" Johnny-or-Jimmy snarled.

"HE JUMPED ME! SO I AM JUST GIVING HIM SOME OF HIS OWN MEDICINE," Carl yelled.

"Yeah, that's cuz you were making fun of the way he talks,"

I whined, rubbing my chest, which was still smarting.

Johnny-or-Jimmy's face went totally red. "WHAT? PETERS, I TOLD YOU LAST TIME YOU DID THAT, THAT IF YOU EVER MADE FUN OF ANDY'S STUTTER AGAIN I WAS GOING TO BEAT THE CRUD OUT OF YOU."

Carl jumped up. "Yeah...? Give it your best, Epstein!"

Carl stood as tall as he could and lunged at Johnny-or-Jimmy.

Johnny-or-Jimmy curled up his fist and shoved it so hard into Carl's face that I thought his nose was going to shatter. Blood spewed from Carl's face and his face went white. If there were two guys in the neighborhood Carl usually backed down to, it was Johnny and Jimmy. Carl wiped his nose across his sleeve and started laughing like a crazed maniac, lunging again at Johnny-or-Jimmy. Johnny-or-Jimmy and Carl were

rolling around on the grass, punching and cussing each other
out. Gran was just watching from the window. I knew if it were
my mom she would be trying to break the fight up, but Gran
seemed to be kind of enjoying it. Probably because she was tired
of Carl's dumb attitude.

Andy and I watched with total fascination as two of the
toughest guys in the neighborhood, my brother and Johnny-or-
Jimmy, beat the crud out of each other. During it they kept
talking in language that could get them both in trouble.

The whole time, Tex was barking and nipping at Carl. So
Carl threw an elbow, catching the poodle right across the chops.
Tex whimpered and ran to the other side of my yard where
he surprised Flop, my funny narcoleptic cat who looks like a
giant walking meatloaf with hair, while he was stalking some
grasshoppers in the garden. Flop came running out from behind
some big cabbages, his tail twirling in a circle behind him, and
chased Tex out of our yard.

Just then my mom stepped out onto the back patio. "What's
all the yelling about?"

"Oh man, they're dead," I whispered loud to Andy.

"D-Dang... this is going t-to be great!" Andy smiled.

"Hey, you think there is a world record for getting your big
brother grounded the longest?"

We both cracked up at that.

Gran leaned out the back door as though nothing was going
on, "Boys, do you want a grilled cheese sandwich?"

I nodded my head. "Do we have tomato soup?"

"Well, what's a grilled cheese without tomato soup, hon? Andy,
would you like one, too?" my mom asked.

Andy looked at me with a total confused look on his face.
Why was my mom ignoring the sounds coming from the backyard?

"S-Sure, th-thank you, Mrs. P-Peters."

"Tell Carl that when he and Jimmy are done playing around
I will have sandwiches on the picnic table." Mom turned and
went back into the house.

As she left, I noticed the wire coming from Mom's ear. She

was listening to her favorite radio show on my transistor and most likely hadn't heard a thing.

"WOW, my mom is totally oblivious," I laughed.

"Wh-what does that m-mean?" Andy sputtered.

I spun around and looked at Andy. "What does what mean?"

"Wh-What does that w-w-ord oblivious m-mean?"

"Oh, it means not aware of things right under your nose..."

Andy just shrugged and turned back to the action.

"I turned back to see Carl and Johnny-or-Jimmy lying on their backs panting and sweating.

"Wow, Carl, your left hook has improved," Johnny-or-Jimmy puffed.

"Yeah, thanks Jimmy. Hey, check that out." Carl was pointing at a huge cloud that was passing over the house. "It's a bear eating a STUPID poodle."

I couldn't believe my ears. Since clouds are white and puffy, I guess everyone sees something eating a poodle.

As usual, when guys fight, it is settled and over. A few minutes later we were all sitting at the picnic table eating grilled cheese sandwiches, tomato soup, and icy cold lemonade.

"Hey Andy, I know another world record we could make!" I spurted in between gulps.

"WH-WHAT?" Andy looked excited.

"World's biggest jerk for a brother!" I snarled at the two dirty guys on the opposite side of the table.

"Wh-which one w-would win?" Andy smirked.

"Watch it Epstein, or I will cut one on you again!" Carl glared at us.

"I think they'd tie!" I laughed.

"Try it Carl and I'll whip you again!" Johnny-or-Jimmy said, but he was laughing.

"Whip me? Oh, not sure that's how it went," Carl said, thumping Johnny-or-Jimmy on the arm.

"Yeah, who's bleeding?" Johnny-or-Jimmy thumped Carl back harder, and pointed at the tip of Carl's nose and his sleeve, which had a long streak of blood on it. Just then

Jimmy-or-Johnny came running into the backyard.

Pretty soon Carl and Johnny-or-Jimmy were rolling around on the grass again, huffing and puffing and growling at each other. Then Jimmy-or-Johnny joined in.

I whispered, "Pssst, Andy, how can you tell if that is Johnny-or-Jimmy or Jimmy-or-Johnny?"

"H-How c-can I t-tell?" Andy looked at me like I had two heads.

"That's what I said, cheese-cup-Charlie!" I smirked.

"C-Cuz one's a j-jerk and the other's a b-b-bigger jerk!" Andy laughed. "And, wh-who you calling ch-cheese-cup-Ch-Charlie?" He punched my arm.

I punched Andy back, and then ran up and gave Carl a cheese cup while Johnny-or-Jimmy had him pinned down and Jimmy-or-Johnny was pulling on Johnny-or-Jimmy's shoulders.

"GABE, YOU ARE A SUCH A DEAD MAN!" Carl screamed in agony.

Johnny-or-Jimmy was laughing so hard he fell off of Carl and rolled onto the ground. "Ha ha, your little brother got you with the deadly cheese-cup surprise!" Johnny-or-Jimmy dog piled onto Jimmy-or-Johnny and started wrestling him.

Carl ran after me. I ran into the house with Andy and hid behind Mom and Gran.

"Let me at that little chicken-creep!" Carl snarled.

"Carl, stop it right now. What are you doing?" Mom asked.

"That little creep cheese-cupped me! I'm going to murder him," he growled.

Gran snorted, she laughed so hard. "Cheese cup? As in, who cut the cheese?"

I just nodded, always shocked that my Grandma was so frank and so not like other grandmas at all.

"Is that the same as a Dutch oven?" Gran smirked.

"Mom! Don't teach them that!" Mom scolded Gran.

Gran just smiled.

"You're the one that cut one on Andy first!" I yelled.

"What's a cheese cup?" Mom asked.

"You d-d-don't w-want to know, Mrs. P-Peters." Andy looked mortified.

Jimmy-or-Johnny came in the back door covered with grass stains. "This is a cheese cup!" He cut one really loud into his cupped palm and then held his hand over Carl's face. A second later he ran out the back door laughing so hard he tripped and was sprawled out on the back lawn when Carl jumped on his back again.

Gran exploded in laughter.

"MOM! DON'T ENCOURAGE THEM!" Mom shouted at Gran.

"Boys don't need encouragement, if you haven't noticed! Do you remember all the evil things Howie and Stewie used to do to you?"

"I've tried very hard to forget, Mother!"

Gran just kept chuckling.

"Oh, why didn't I have girls?" Mom whined.

"Oh, please!" Gran sneered.

"YOU ARE SO GOING TO GET IT, EPSTEIN!" Carl's voice echoed throughout the back yard, and then he and Andy's brothers were once again rolling around laughing and beating on each other.

Andy looked at me and said, "I th-think they would t-tie for w-world's b-biggest loser brother."

"Two cheese cups in such a short time! Maybe there's a record to make here," I laughed.

Mom just smiled, giving me that I have no idea what makes a boy tick look and nodded her head. Gran was still just laughing really hard.

"So, answer my question, Andy. How do you tell Johnny-or-Jimmy apart?" I pressed. I wanted to know.

"J-Johnny smells like p-peanut b-b-butter and k-kitty litter and..."

"WHAT?" I yelled.

"J-Just k-kidding. Johnny has a h-hairy m-m-mole on the side of his n-n-neck," he answered.

"GROSS!" I yelled.

We both turned onto our backs to watch the clouds drifting by.

# OUR OWN SPEEDY GONZALES

The time with Gran had gone so fast. It was hard to believe my uncles would be back in only a day to pick her up.

At breakfast Gran looked across at me and said, "Gabe, we didn't really get a chance to read the book together like I planned, but I have enjoyed spending my evenings with your folks. I hope you will read it very soon; it is a great book! I want you to tell me all about what you think of it when you read it, okay?"

I shrugged, "Sure, Gran, that's okay," but I felt disappointed. I thought my Auntie Leslie would be here by now, and she wasn't, and here Gran was already leaving and we hadn't spent my bedtime together reading.

Mom and Dad were going to take Gran to see a tourist place called Estes Park, where my uncles would meet them. Even though I didn't mind long drives and I loved spending time with my gran, Mom said I couldn't go; that I had too much to do. So Mom and Dad left Carl in charge of me, which made me mad. I decided I would disappear while they were gone and Carl would never know where I was until Mom and Dad came back.

I hugged Gran hard and told her I loved her. Maybe we'd get to go back to her farm for Thanksgiving this year.

☺

I heard Carl up in his room talking low into the phone, so I picked up the downstairs phone really quietly and cupped my hand over the mouthpiece and listened in. Carl was talking to Denise, and I could hear some other girls giggling in the background. They were making some plans, and it sounded too mushy for me to listen to.

Not five minutes after Mom, Gran, and Dad drove off, Carl snarled at me, "Get lost, chicken-dork. I'm hanging out here with my friends, and we don't want any of you little germs around, get it?"

"Ohhh, is Denisie-poo coming over?" I jeered.

Carl jumped out of his chair, pinned one of my arms behind me and started giving my other arm an Indian rug burn.

"Say how bout' you make like a tree and leaf!"

"DORK! Who says that kind of junk?" I shot back. I wasn't giving up, not yet.

"Say it!" Carl growled, pushing his nasty breathing mouth up to my ear.

"IT!" I screamed and started laughing.

"What?" he growled.

"You said to say 'it!" I laughed like a madman, but my arm was starting to really hurt, bent up like that.

"What're you talking about, chicken-pukeasaurus?" Carl snarled

"You are weird, you know that?" I asked.

"SAY IT OR LOSE YOUR ARM!" he barked.

"Say what?" I screamed.

"Say, 'I'll make like a tree and leaf!" he insisted.

"I'm not going to say that. That is so stupid!"

He hiked my arm up behind my back a little more.

"OW, CUT IT OUT STUPID!" I yelled. "I'm going to tell Dad when he gets home, and he is going to skin you!"

"I'm terrified, chicken-dummy!" With that he let go of my arm and pulled me down the stairs to the basement. He opened the crawlspace door and pushed me in. Then he closed the door and pushed something heavy in front of the door.

It didn't matter to me. I heard his heavy footsteps upstairs as he clomped over to the kitchen. He must have dialed the phone because I could hear him through the floor, "Coast is clear, come on up to my place!"

I belly-crawled to the other side of the crawlspace and pushed my body through a small opening by the window-well. Now I was outside, and Carl thought I was inside. I waited for a little while and then watched through the kitchen window as Carl opened the front door and greeted Denise and two girls. A few minutes later his dumb friends Greg and Jimmy came through the door, too. They all flopped down in front of the television.

The girls were on one side of the living room, and the boys were on the other. I just can't understand what is fun about that! They were too boring to spy on, so I left.

☺

I went down to Eddie's house, and from there we called a meeting in the tree house. The plan for us to make it into the Guinness book for the world's largest spit pool was on.

Butch and Andy came running up the street holding a wading pool over their heads and jostling each other as they ran. From the tree house they looked like some weird outer space creature with a huge blue disk for a head and four legs. They threw the pool down right below the tree house and clambered up the steps.

Craig, Tony, and I were spread out in the tree house trying to figure what was going to work. In a sketchbook we had written—WORLD RECORD ATTEMPTS BY THE SECRET BROTHERHOOD OF BOYS (no lame-o big brothers allowed!)

Butch's face appeared through the hole you have to climb through to get onto the tree house platform.

"I liked Gabe's idea, but how about the world's deepest spit pool? No one has ever done that!" Butch was huffing and puffing as he clambered in.

"That is totally the grossest thing I have ever heard, Butch. Let's do it!" Tony yelled.

"I know; cool huh?" Butch was smiling ear to ear as he and Andy both lay on their stomachs and aimed long strings of spit into the wading pool. "BOMB'S AWAY!"

"More like loogies away!" Tony laughed.

"Hey, do loogs count?" Butch asked.

"There aren't any rules, lame-o, we are inventing a whole new record!" I snapped, kind of mad at Butch.

Butch started shinnying up the tree above us. "Hey Andy, can you get your mom's little movie camera? You know the one she is always using at your birthday parties?"

"I c-c-could ask h-her; wh-why?"

"So we can film the whole thing. You know, we gotta show an empty pool. And then if we film it getting filled, those guys from the Guinness book will know it ain't water or anything!"

"I'm n-n-not sure my m-mom will like that idea," Andy frowned.

"Don't tell her then," Butch snapped.

"Yeah right, Butch, we're gonna use all of Andy's mom's film to record drool? We can use my camera," I interrupted what was sure to become an argument.

"Oh yeah, okay," Butch shrugged.

It was weird. Butch was acting like the idea to make the spit pool was his by changing it from biggest to deepest. Guess that's okay, though, since Butch doesn't get much recognition for his ideas, because usually they are so dumb no one wants to go along with them. It was his idea that time to sneak down to Mean Mrs. Rickles when we both almost got murdered. Still, it kind of made me mad, but I decided to just keep it to myself. The real trick was to get all of us to work together to get into the book together.

While Tony, Craig, and I went back to sketching out the way it would work and Tony, who is really good at math, started to calculate how long it would take and how many of us we would need, the rest of us talked about other records we could set or break.

We were interrupted when Eddie came running up. "What's up, guys?" he asked.

We explained the idea to him.

"Cool. We need something that won't hurt to tie to our legs at night so we can keep from falling out of the tree, but still can drool into the pool," he suggested.

"Like what?" I asked.

"How 'bout that rope Craig's dad uses to pull us on sleds from the back of the dune buggy?" Butch asked.

"No way! That stuff is so scratchy!" Eddie said.

"Wuss!" Butch snarled.

"You are!" Eddie shot back, looking like he was going to fight.

"Sh-Shut up g-guys," Andy barked.

Suddenly Eddie yelled, "Hey, my dad has a bunch of neckties. How 'bout I bring some of those up, and we use them to tie to our legs at night?"

"You sure your dad won't get sore about that?" Butch asked.

"What he doesn't know won't kill him!" Eddie ran off in the direction of his house.

"I still think Craig's dad's rope is a better idea," Butch sulked.

I pulled my binoculars out of my hiding place and watched Eddie running pell-mell down the hill. Then my eye caught Mr. Patchett. "What the heck is he doing?"

"Wh-Who, Eddie?" Andy asked.

"No, Mr. Patchett..." I focused the knob.

Andy grabbed for the binoculars, "Let m-m s-see!"

"Hang on...."

Mr. Patchett was walking around the lake with a wrist rocket on his arm, aiming and sending rocks into the water.

"I'll bet he's trying to get the monster carp with his wrist rocket!" Some have said the monster carp is the size of a shark. The lake is pretty small to have a carp that big. Carp eat everything so if I were a fish, I think I would plan on moving out of this lake.

Andy grabbed the binoculars out of my hand.

"Hey!" I yelled.

"H-He is so w-w-weird!" Andy snarled.

"Look who's talking, weirdo!" I growled at him, not too happy about him grabbing my binoculars.

"H-H-Here c-comes Eddie!" Andy moved his arms, mimicking Eddie's motion. "Here."

Andy tried to give me back the binoculars. I just ignored him and went back to the sketch with Tony.

Andy looked over my shoulder, gave me a side hug, and said, "D-Don't be s-sore at m-me, G-Gabe... I j-just w-wanted to s-see what you w-were looking at!"

I pushed him away and punched his shoulder, which was as good as saying I forgave him.

Andy pushed his face down near the sketchpad, thinking out loud. "Wh-what ab-bout building a f-f-fifty-foot bike j-jump and jumping over s-s-seventy-three c-cars like Evil Knievel on my brother's stingray?"

"Yeah, right! He uses a motorcycle not a bicycle dummy!" Tony laughed.

"Th-that's why it's b-b-better you m-moron, and would be a n-new r-record!" Andy snapped.

Butch was lying on his stomach again, trying to spit in the center of the wading pool when he growled, "Oh look everyone, it's Murph the Smurf! Who invited you anyway, WARBOY?!"

"SHUT UP BUTCH, WE CAN USE HIS SPIT!" Tony barked. "The more the merrier!"

"Too bad we're not trying to fill it with hot air. Murph could do that single-handedly," Butch growled.

"What do you have so against him?" I asked.

"What don't I?" Butch responded.

Eddie scrambled past Murph and up the tree house steps, throwing ties at us. "Man, I never ran that fast in my life!"

Murph came running up, to lie panting down under the tree. Whenever we were up in the tree house, it was amazing to realize how much our voices carried over the pond and down the ditch. Everyone in the neighborhood seemed to be able to hear the conversations.

Murph ignored Butch's next comment,"What-about-catching-
one-hundred-bull-snakes-and-taking-a-bath-with-them, like-
a-foxhole-in-the-Vietnam-war?"

I gave Murph the signal to slow it down. He was talking so
fast no one could really understand him.

"Yeah, right!" I mocked. "Whose mom is gonna let snakes into
the house? Not mine, that's for sure! Remember when I had that
bull snake in my closet and it got loose and my babysitter told
my mom? NO CHANCE!" I scowled, and noticed Mr. Morris on his
back porch. He seemed to be listening to us.

"With-like-a-thousand-Estes-rockets-strapped-to-your-
back,-I-bet-you-could-jump-the-train-from-the-sandstone-
canyons!" Murph suggested.

"There's n-no w-w-way!" Andy laughed, just imagining one
of us trying it.

We all started to chuckle and I think Mr. Morris did, too.

Murph said, "I-think-once-you-got-to-the-top-of-the-canyon..."

Butch yelled, "Hey, let's strap them on, Murph, maybe you'll
fly to Vietnam!"

"LEAVE MURPH ALONE, BUTCH!" Tony yelled.

"Yeah, lay off, man!" Eddie chimed in.

Murph had climbed fast up the steps, and now the tree house
was getting a bit too crowded.

"M-M-Murph's one of us n-n-now!" Andy added.

Murph thumped Andy on the arm, his way of saying thanks.

"W-Watch it, M-Murph, you'll knock m-m-me out of the
tr-tree, and I don't have any rockets to blast me off before
I splat on the ground!" Andy snorted, and they both started
laughing.

Murph sneered at Butch, and uncharacteristically kept his
mouth shut.

I reached into the pocket of my jeans, and pulled out three
grape gumballs that I stuffed into my mouth. The lint on them
kind of grossed me out, but I left it on. I figured it would add
a little volume to the spit I was going to deposit in the pool.

My spit kept drooling down in this long purple mass, and
then the breeze seemed to carry it all the way over to the
ditch, totally missing the wading pool.

"Tony, add the wind to your calculation," I called out.

"Man, Gabe, you are a moron. How can you miss the pool?
You're right over it!" Butch laughed.

"Moron? Me?" I made a small spitball, rolled over and
launched it at Butch. A grape glob landed on his chest and
drooled down in a straight line.

He acted like he got hit with a bullet and started rolling
around, yelling, "I'm hit, by the purple moron monster!"

Butch was chewing on a red pixie stick, and let go a huge,
stringy spit which hit me square on the back.

"Oh no, not my church clothes!" I hollered. "You spit on my
church shirt!"

"Peters, I bet you made that whole thing up. There was no
kid that cried about that; it was YOU!" Tony smirked.

The church clothes thing went back to an old joke about this
kid at St. Joe's who would always challenge people to a water
fight at lunch and then start crying because he got wet. He
would howl through his tears, "NOT MY CHURCH SHIRT! MY MOM
IS GOING TO KILL ME!" It was ridiculous for him to want to
start a water fight and not get wet. The problem with a water
fight in the lunchroom was it got you in a ton of trouble with
the batwomen, and people usually used their milk instead of
water, so at the end of the day you would stink like bad cheese
from the crusty milk on your shirt.

"Yeah right, puke breath. Like I care about my clothes!" And
with that I let a long purple drool go from my lower lip down my
own shirt to my belly button.

I started laughing so hard it hurt. "I'm trying to hit the pool,
Butchie!" I turned back to my stomach and let out a long purple
drool, this time actually hitting the pool.

Mr. Morris was listening to us, because I saw him laughing
at what we were talking about. Then he went back inside.

Butch and Craig were hacking loogies down into the pool, and all the guys now were lying on their stomachs joining in.

The bottom of the pool started to look totally cool and disgusting, with tiny pools of yellow from the lemonheads, purple from the bubble gum, and red from Butch who was still sucking on pixie stix and swishing saliva around in his mouth until the drool poured out over his lips and down into the wading pool.

"Okay-so-if-we-acted-like-we-were-POWs,-we-could- get-some-rope-and-tie-a-noose-around-our-ankles-and- then-tie-it-to-the-tree-branch-and-sleep-up-here-on-our- stomachs..."

"MURPH!" I gave him the warning look. Everyone paid more attention to him when he was calmer.

"...hanging-out-just-a-little,-and-then-all-night-long-we- would-drool-and-fill-the-pool-while-we-were-sleeping!" Murph continued.

"Already thought that one out!" Eddie said happily, showing Murph his dad's neckties.

"Yeah, but I ain't actin' like a P.O.W. This isn't about some dumb war, this is about setting a world's record, MURPHO WARMONGER!" Butch growled.

"Whatever...." Murph resigned, sighing.

"But, that's a good idea, Murph! We could tie our legs to the tree," I added, thinking how weird it was that all of my friends were suggesting things I had already suggested in our Brotherhood meeting when I introduced the idea of getting into the Guinness book in the first place.

"You kn-know, w-w-we are just p-p-practicing right n-now, because we d-d-didn't t-take any 'before' p-pictures with Gabe's c-c-camera!" Andy said.

Tony mumbled, "Well, once we get started, we have to keep going—evaporation, wind, dry mouth..."

"Dry mouth?" Butch and I said at the same time.

"Duh, you can only make so much spit at a time, guys," Tony filled us in.

So we were all lying on our stomach spitting down into the pool when this kid I have seen before at school and sometimes riding in the back of the bus came running up the gravel road as fast as I have ever seen anyone run. He looked like that Speedy Gonzalez cartoon because he was fast and he was wearing a funny round cowboy hat tied to his chin.

"Hey kid, where're you going?" Butch called out from our perch on the tree house.

The kid looked like he did everything in fast motion. He stopped running and stood there squinting up into the tree to see who was talking to him, and then looked surprised to see all of our faces hanging off the side of the tree house. We must have looked like a plywood monster with multiple heads.

"Over here," Butch motioned with both arms. "Aren't you that kid that gets off the bus down at the highway?"

"Yeah!" The speedy kid stared straight up into the tree
at us like we'd known each other forever.

"What are you doing around here?" Tony asked.

"It's a free country isn't it?" he responded between breaths.

"I wasn't saying you shouldn't be here, I just haven't seen
you up here before, that's all," Tony answered. "So, what are
you doing?"

"Running." He looked at Tony like he was a total moron.

"Yeah, we can see that. What're you running from?"
Tony said a little more forcefully in response.

The kid shrugged his shoulders and looked into the pool
that was now multi-colored globs and blobs. "Nothing."

"What's your name, kid?" Tony asked, like he was The Secret
Brotherhood of Boys' official spokesman.

"How come you ask so many questions?" The kid lifted his
hat off and wiped the sweat on his forehead with his sleeve.

"I like questions. What's your name?" Tony responded.

"T-Bone!" the kid said, jumping from one foot to the other
like a frog dancing.

"T-T-T-B-Bone? What k-kind of a n-name is that?"
Andy asked. "That's your r-r-real n-name?"

"Why do you talk like that?" T-Bone asked innocently.

"T-T-Talk l-like what?" Andy said, smiling really widely.

"Never mind." T-Bone suddenly looked kind of embarrassed.

"So, is that your real name?" I asked to break the tension.

"Nah! My name is Ray T. Garza; the T is for T-Bone, which
is what my gramps calls me. I live with my grandparents in
the little green house behind the U-Pump-It gas station. My
Gramps owns the gas station. What the heck are you guys
doing with this wading pool?"

"NONE OF YOUR BEESWAX!" Butch scowled.

"B-B-Be nice, you m-moron!" Andy barked at Butch.

"We can't chance a stranger finding out what we are doing.
He could spoil it," Butch whispered, but a bit too loudly.

We all gave Butch a dirty look. "Maybe we'll invite him to
help!" I snarled.

Andy, Butch and I climbed down the tree to get a better look at this kid named after a steak. Andy threw the football that was lying next to the pool at Butch, thumping him right between the shoulder blades.

"Ow, you big dummy!" Butch scowled playfully at Andy.

A big grin spread across Andy's face, "W-We're even n-now...."

Butch had smacked Andy in the face with the football earlier, and Andy had told him he was going to get him back.

"Can I play with you guys? I've got a wicked arm for quarterbacking. My gramps says I will go pro with my golden arm."

I shuddered at the thought of the golden arm. I remembered the story about the man with the golden arm we had heard at camp in which this guy who has lost his arm has one made of gold and then loses it. At night the arm crawls across the ground looking for the man who says in a really spooky voice, "I'M THE MAN WITH THE GOLDEN AAAARRRRMMMM." You say that real spooky like when you are telling the story and when the listeners least expect it you yell and jump at them, which makes everyone jump.

While T-Bone, Andy, Butch and I threw the ball around, Murph, Eddie and Tony took the wading pool into the pond and washed it out so we could start officially with witnesses (my mom and Dad) and my camera. Murph was saying something about synchronizing our watches and beginning at 0-five-hundred-hours or something military like that of course, and the rest of us just figured we would start at five o'clock.

"I gotta run, guys!" T-Bone said suddenly and turned, starting down the gravel road. Then he turned back around and laughed, "Get it? 'Gotta run,' and I am running!"

We just nodded as T-Bone went running down the gravel road back toward his house.

"Do you think Speedy Gonzalez could beat Spiderman in a footrace?" I asked no one in particular.

"Duh!" Butch sneered.

"Not a duh! Spiderman is faster in the air on his webs, but Speedy Gonzalez is both feet on the ground fast!" I smirked.

"You are SO dumb. It is a mouse against a superhero guy!" Butch scowled.

"Uh,-well-it-is-really-a-spider-against-a-mouse-if-you-want-to-be-technical," Murph added, glancing my way 'cause both of us knew he had caught himself and slowed down.

"SHUT UP MURPH!" Butch growled.

"Spiderman isn't a spider. He has spider powers, but he is a man," Tony added.

"Technically he is a man, but his whole deal is spider power!" Eddie chimed in.

We argued like that for about half an hour, and then no one said anything for a while. I started thinking that The Secret Brotherhood of Boys could use a fast kid to run our missions, and to be our spy when we were planning secret attacks on our brothers.

"Hey guys, what would you think of asking T-Bone to join the brotherhood?" I said out loud.

"Totally! But the hat's gotta go!" Butch exclaimed

"Cool kid! I like the hat!" Tony snarled at Butch. "Maybe we should all wear hats. Sherlock Holmes did, and we are supposed to be detectives, right?

"No doubt!" I added. "So, do we let the speed-demon in the club?"

"Roger-that!-Now-I-won't-be-the-only-newbie-and-Butch-will-have-someone-else-to-abuse!" Murph exclaimed.

"I w-w-wonder if he sp-spits as g-good as h-h r-runs?" Andy shrugged.

"What the heck should he do for initiation?" Butch asked.

"I don't know, but I need to go to the Bait Shop and get some film for my camera and some of those sour bubblegum balls to make me pucker all night and spit and drool like a fool!" I said, totally excited about setting a new record.

I headed down the gravel road and all the guys followed me. We went past the U-Pump-It on the way. T-Bone was looking out the window where you paid his Grandpa for gas. I ran over there and asked him if he wanted to meet us back at the tree house at five o'clock. I told him I would tell him then about our record and our clubhouse.

T-Bone's grandpa rubbed T-Bone's head and said something in Spanish to him, then smiled at me with all five of his teeth showing. He had the same kind of hat on that T-Bone was wearing.

"My Grandpa likes your glasses," T-Bone said shyly.

"Tell him I like his hat." Then I ran toward the gravel frontage road to meet up with the other guys on our way to see Joe at the Bait Shop. As I did, I hollered back, "Five o'clock, T, bring a sleeping bag, it could be a loooooong niiiiight!"

T-Bone leaned out the U-Pump-it window and yelled, "Hey kid, it looks like someone shot you in the back!"

"Red pixie spit!" I yelled back, and could hear T-Bone explaining it to his Grandpa in Spanish and the two of them howling with laughter.

# CHAPTER FIVE

# WEIGHING IN ON MY AUNTIE

My favorite picture in the Guinness Book of World Records is of Earl Hughes. You can ask me anything about him because I have his page memorized. He was so fat that after he died, he had to be lifted with a crane and buried in a piano case. I was thinking that it might be fun to have him in The Secret Brotherhood of Boys but we couldn't meet in the tree house on account of the fact that he would break the tree. Besides, according to the Guinness book, he died.

There's a picture on that page too of twins that ride motorcycles; they also are SO huge.

As I looked at the awesome page, I decide I definitely would get into this book next year.

Right now I am gonna call another special meeting of The Secret Brotherhood of Boys to go over the details of how we can get into the book. I'm thinking that my Auntie, the one we call "the sofa," might be able to win the heaviest lady category. She is huge, like more than three or four times the size of my mom. I heard my mom earlier telling my dad that my Auntie Leslie said she weighed a ton. I looked that up in my mathematics book, and that means she weighs two thousand pounds. Earl Hughes only weighed 1,069 at his top weight, so that tells me that if I can get my Auntie onto a scale and have the people from the Guinness company verify it, she will be the new world record holder by far!

The heaviest woman in the book is Mrs. Percy Pearl Washington, who they think weighed in at 880 pounds, even though their scales only went up to 800. That means my Auntie could totally take this category by more than double! There are other people mentioned in the book that were close, but one of them is totally crazy. You see, they say Mrs. Flora

May Jackson weighed 267 pounds when she was only eleven years old, and 840 pounds when she died. She was in show business, and they called her "baby Flo". Me and Butch were figuring that this Baby Flo lady weighed as much as him, me, Andy, Craig and my dogs Frisky and Friskier when she was our age, and THAT IS TOTALLY CRAZY!

Auntie Leslie is staying on our foldout couch right now because Dad says it is too hard for her to climb our stairs. To figure out how we could see if my Auntie would qualify, I thought maybe our veterinarian's office could work to weigh her. After all, the vet's scale had to weigh horses.

"Dad, not to be rude or anything, but how much does Auntie Leslie weigh?" I asked when I went downstairs.

Dad looked at me like I had lost my marbles. "Shhh, Gabe, keep your voice down. You don't want to embarrass her.

"Oh yeah, right, sorry. Does she really weigh two thousand pounds?" I whispered.

Dad wrinkled up his face. "Where did you hear a crazy thing like that?"

"Mom said Auntie said that," I whispered.

"What? Why would she say that?" Dad questioned.

"I dunno. Mom just said she said she weighed a ton."

"Oh Gabe, that was just a figure of speech. A big figure... hehheh, er... excuse me, that wasn't nice," he admitted.

"What does 'figure of speech' mean?" I asked.

"I meant she was exaggerating, of course. No one could weigh two thousand pounds. My car weighs close to that!" Dad insisted.

"There's this guy in my book that weighed over a thousand pounds."

"Isn't that stretching it a bit?" Dad asked.

"No really, you wanna see?"

"Perhaps later," Dad said, looking around to make sure my auntie wasn't listening in.

Auntie Leslie was outside under the tree with Mom, talking.

"So how much does she weigh?" I asked, still whispering.

"Probably somewhere close to 250. But you keep that to yourself."

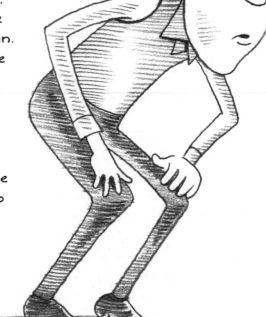

"Holy guacamole, Mrs. Flora May Jackson weighed 267 pounds when she was only eleven-years old, so she must have been huge as a little kid too!" I spurted out. "She also weighed 840 pounds when she died as a grownup," I added, in case my dad hadn't read the page.

"That's over three times as big as Auntie Leslie. Why are you asking? And how do you know all this stuff?" Dad asked.

"I memorize pages out of the Guinness book," I said proudly.

"Strange picks to memorize, son." Dad rolled his eyes at me. "So, why are you asking about Auntie? I know you guys are trying to get into the Guinness book, but you aren't thinking of..."

"Never mind," I said, suddenly embarrassed. "I mean, I was just curious, that's all."

"This wouldn't have anything to do with your Guinness quest, would it, young man?" my dad scolded. "Because even the mention of that to your lovely Aunt would hurt her feelings."

I instantly felt very ashamed of myself. I loved my Auntie, and I would even if she weighed 840 pounds. I decided right then and there that the only way to get into the book was to do it myself and not use someone else.

"I'm sorry, Dad."

"Don't be sorry to me. I'm actually surprised at you, Gabriel."

My dad's face said it all. He was disappointed in me, and that was the worst feeling of all.

# RABBIT ~~DIARY~~ JOURNAL BLUES

I was telling mom about my journal and how I was writing a lot of things about school last year and the mean old Batwoman. Mom suggested that I also write about my life outside of school, which for the most part is fun, but of course I have been writing about that anyway.

Mom said it is important to learn not to dwell on the negative when there are so many positive things to think about. She told me that is why Uncle Morris always seems negative and cusses so much, because he keeps thinking about his wife being so mean to him and all.

My other uncle is my favorite uncle. Uncle Dwayne is a librarian at a college, and he was my dad's college roommate. So he's not really a brother like a real uncle is. But we're pretty close, and he bought me another journal for my birthday.

I think the adults in my life are trying to tell me something.

The only journal I never wrote in was the one my brother gave me as a joke, to make fun of my habit of putting my nose in the journal and writing every day, which is by far the last thing he would ever do. The journal was covered in blue rabbit fur, with a chain that held a blue rabbit foot attached to it.

I thought about the poor rabbit that gave his very foot and his life for the stupid cover on the journal, and just couldn't get over it. Somehow it was different than the jack rabbits that I was making into a coat for my Grandma. It seemed humiliating for a rabbit to be dyed blue and used for a kid's journal.

I kept the rabbit fur journal for a little while, and then I couldn't take it being in my room anymore. Andy and I buried it in my backyard. It may well be the only blue rabbit that had a full funeral with a song and everything written for it.

I thought it was a good idea to write the rabbit song on one of the pages from the pitiful journal. Andy and I sang the song to the rabbit after we buried it and the journal with a big carrot, and with a big bunch of flowers from our garden. We sung the words to the tune of Happy Birthday.

I can't exactly tell you the exact words because we nailed the paper to a cross and planted it at the burial site, and when the sprinklers came on it ended up looking like one big watercolor smudge. But anyway it went something like this when we sang it together:

*'Little rabbit, poor you*               *'Little r–r–rabbit, p–poor you*
*Little rabbit, poor you*                 *L–Little r–rabbit, poor you*
*You were a nice bunny*                   *You w–were a nice b–b–bunny*
*But they dyed you all blue...'*          *B–But they d–dyed you all b–b–blue...'*

I saw Andy wipe his eyes. Andy's always like that, a real nice kid, and he would cry at the drop of a hat. Andy said some big words at the rabbit journal's gravesite due to something he had seen in a movie one time. His words were really different than the prayers we say, because Andy is Jewish.

One thing Jewish means is his family doesn't celebrate Christmas and Easter and some of the other things my family always celebrates. But the truth is Andy likes Santa Claus; he just doesn't tell his family. Andy even asked me to teach him the prayers of our Catholic faith. Now, whenever we have a snack, if I start to eat without blessing my food, Andy starts to cluck his tongue the same way my granny does when she thinks someone shouldn't be doing what he is doing. Then he bows his head, folds his hands and says a Catholic prayer he has heard a million times on account of the fact that he eats dinner at our house a lot. But he can never recite it quite right: B-B-Bless us our L-Lord, for b-birthday g-g-gifts, that we receive f-from the c-county through Christ, oh L-Lord, amen. (Just so you know how it actually goes, we say: Bless us oh Lord, for these Thy gifts, which we are about to receive from Thy bounty through Christ our Lord, amen.) Andy slaughters it every time, and it just cracks me up.

My mom always laughs into her napkin when Andy volunteers to say our prayer before dinner. My mom thinks it is totally cute and tells me that Andy is a really good influence on me. Dad thinks it is super funny, since Andy isn't even a Catholic or anything. Carl thinks Andy's stutter is funny, but he doesn't really make fun of him anymore since Andy's brother punched him for doing that. He can be really mean to me most of the time, but he is almost always nice to Andy now.

Mom really likes Andy, and feels sorry for him because his dad drank and then he used to act mean. At least now Andy's dad is getting better and is much nicer to everyone.

The first time my mom told me that Andy's dad drank a lot, I thought that was a good thing. She is always telling me to drink more water. But then she told me he drank booze and that it wasn't a good thing in his case. It's kind of like the time the priest at our church had to drink up the entire communion wine that was left over and then couldn't stop. He had to leave our church to go to some farm where I guess they don't have communion wine. Weird that a priest would want to be a farmer, but he might be back cuz maybe he will be allergic to cows or something.

Tonight Andy sat down across from me at the dinner table and said, "Mrs. Peters, I have been practicing the other prayer that you all say. Can I say it now?"

Mom smiled and nodded.

"This ought to be good," I said under my breath, and Carl snorted and tried to cover up his laughing by clearing his throat a bunch of times.

Andy thumped my arm and started to pray, "Our F-Father who d-does art in heaven, H-Halloween is the day, thy k-kingdom came, it's all the s-same, as earth is a p-part of heaven." (Just so you know how it actually goes, we say: Our Father, who art in heaven, hallowed be Thy name. Thy kingdom come, Thy will be done, on earth as it is in heaven....) I always forget to ask Mom why God is a 'Thy,' and other people are a 'they'.

Mom stood up and hugged Andy. "That was just perfect Andy."

We all just sat there wondering what was going on; he had been so off it was ridiculous. But Andy just hugged my mom back really hard.

Andy cracks me up, cause he really thinks that is how the prayer goes and I never like correcting him, because he gets enough of that from all of his four older brothers. Now that Mom told him it was "perfect," he will never try to really learn it for real, and we will always have something to laugh about.

Andy is the best friend a kid could ever have. He never makes me feel stupid when I tell him things that really bug me. Sometimes when we sleep out in the tent and it is just Andy, me, and my dogs and a million crickets singing, we talk and talk and talk. We tell each other what we want to be when we grow up, and where we want to live.

We both want to live right here. We think our neighborhood is just about as good as it gets. But we also think it would be cool to have Brandon Anderman's house here in our neighborhood, and be rich and fly planes and both have a cool big motorcycle and jetpacks and all kinds of fancy cars and trucks. We go on and on like that for hours, and it never gets old talking to him.

Andy thinks I'm the greatest guy in the world, too, and that is a good thing when most people think you are a dork. He is and always will be the best guy in my book.

*e*

Well, the day Andy and I buried my rabbit fur journal was
the last day of June. Summer was going way too fast, and I
was kind of excited to go back to school, since I would be going
with Andy and the guys.

One of the hardest things about going to a different school
is that I would watch the bus pick up the other kids at the bus
stop and wish I were with them. It was hard to be the only
one who didn't go to the neighborhood school. Life's not
supposed to be this hard for a kid, is it?

Life would be perfect if I never had to leave my tree house
or the pond. I wish I could just live up there with Andy and the
other guys in The Secret Brotherhood of Boys and never come
down. That would be so cool. We could have this system with a
bucket where my brother and the other big brothers would have
to be the slaves and put food in the bucket and then take care
of the bathroom bucket. We would live up there and grow beards
when we got older and never have to go to school again and
never, ever have to deal with mean people! Oh, yeah. And of
course, Frisky and Friskier would live up there with us, and Flop.

Well, come to think of it, it might be better if we all lived in
a house and just hung out in the tree house during the day.

# OPERATION "GET THE GOONS"

I called Andy and told him to start The Secret Brotherhood of Boys' phone chain. We needed to meet, but this was going to be a totally different kind of meeting from most of ours. School was right around the corner, and I had a big idea.

"Andy, I want everyone to meet at my house, in the garage, in half an hour."

Andy asked, "Why n-not the tr-tree h-house?"

"Cuz I have something to show you guys, and you aren't going to believe it!" I exclaimed.

"O-kay, n-no hints even?" Andy asked.

"NOPE! You'll know soon enough."

I hung up quickly.

Murph called a little while later, verifying that the phone chain plan worked and everyone had been called. Eddie was downtown with his mom and so he wouldn't be there at first, but we could catch him up on things later.

One by one, the brotherhood assembled outside my garage door.

I pulled the curtain in my bedroom back and peeked out. I could hear Butch and Murph bickering as usual, so I pushed the window open.

"SHHHH.... this meeting is top secret! I'll be right down."

I slipped through the halls into the basement, then eased out the door into the garage, leaving the door propped on account of its squeak and all. Then I lifted the garage door as quietly as I could and motioned the guys into the garage. When they were all in, I shut the garage door back down.

"Did anyone follow any of you?" I asked.

"Uh, do you see anyone that's not in the club?" Butch asked sarcastically.

"Come on then," I whispered, holding my finger in front of my lips and indicating that they should come in the house, but very quietly. They followed me to the crawlspace.

I let the door down, and everyone climbed in. I pulled the string to make the bare light bulb pop on, and it lit up a corner of the crawlspace. Then I pulled the strap on the backside of the crawlspace door, pulling it shut behind us and latching the inside latch.

"My mom is in the living room right above us, so keep it down!" I whispered.

"What's the big secret, Gabe?" Tony asked.

"Yeah, what g-g-gives?" Andy whispered.

"Everyone sit in a circle," I commanded. There was a painting tarp lying on the dirt, which we all gathered onto. I pulled the box labeled CHRISTMAS WREATH/OUTDOOR LIGHTS out of the way, and shoved the big grocery bag into the middle of the circle. "Okay guys, prepare to be amazed!"

The looks on all of their faces were funny as they waited to see what was so top-secret. I dumped the bag out onto the tarp, and the bricks of Black Cats, pop-bottle rockets, and M80s spilled into a big pile.

"CHECK IT OUT GUYS!" I whispered.

Everyone had something to say.

"HOLY GUACAMOLE!" Butch spurted.

Andy's eyes were as big as saucers. "D-D-DANG!" he shouted.

Craig whisper-yelled, "SWEEEEET! LETS BLOW SOMETHING UP!"

"OH-MY-GOSH!-THOSE-ARE-M80S!-THOSE-BLOW-UP-UNDER-WATER!" Murph said, already thinking tactically about what could be done with them. He was always going on about underwater warfare and the Navy Seals.

"SHHHH!" I gave them all the evil eye.

"WHERE D-D-DID YOU G-G-GET THOSE?" Andy said, way too loud still.

"SHHHH! SERIOUSLY, KEEP IT DOWN!" I reminded the guys again.

"ARE YOU KIDDING ME? THIS IS AWESOME!" Butch squealed.

'SHHHHH! I MEAN IT! WE CAN'T GET CAUGHT, YOU GUYS! IF WE DO, WE'LL NEVER GET TO USE THESE!' I growled in a low shouting whisper.

That finally got through to them. The thought of having such an incredible thing as these and not being able to use them was more than any of them could stand. But it shut them up. Then everyone started bouncing the big bricks of firecrackers in their hands and playing hot potato with them, feeling the sheer weight of the incredible, explosive powers spread out in front of us.

Murph scowled, "These-M80s-when-all-lit-together-could-blow-up-the-bridge-down-at-the-lake!"

"Who'd want to do that, lamebrain?" Butch gruffed. "That's a great place to fish from."

"I-didn't-say-I'd-want-to,-idiot.-But-in-wartime,-they-use-sticks-of-dynamite-to-blow-up-roads-and-bridges,-I-was-merely-saying..." Murph snapped back.

"Give us a break already with your dumb war talk!" Butch growled.

I interrupted, "Come on you guys, knock it off. We have business to discuss. By the way, we are called a brotherhood for a reason. You two need to stop fighting all the time!"

"Oh yeah, brothers never fight!" Butch growled back.

"Wh-Where did you find th-these?" Andy stammered, his eyes still wide like saucers.

I told them the whole story; how Carl had taken them from my uncles, and then I had taken them for them and hidden them. Carl had never said a word about the fact the firecrackers had gone missing, because he couldn't. How would that look to know he stole from his own uncles?

"So, we're going to use them to prank the goons!" I exclaimed.

"Hey-Gabe-how-come-you-always-call-them-goons?" Murph asked.

"Yeah, what's a goon?" Craig asked.

"A bully, a thug, a dumb big brother; that's a goon!" I exclaimed.

The doorbell rang upstairs, and we all just froze. We could hear Mom getting up from the couch and walking over to the door.

"Why, hello, Eddie."

We could hear Mom through the floor just perfectly, so that meant she might be able to hear what we were talking about down in the crawlspace.

"OH-MAN-EDDIE'S-GOING-TO-GIVE-US-UP-DOWN-HERE!" Murph panicked.

"SHUT UP, MURPH!" Butch yelled. "Do you want Gabe's mom to hear you?"

"You shut up too, Butch! Jeez, you guys, you are going to get me in a ton of trouble!" I put my finger up to my lips, telling them all to be totally quiet. "We are going to have to start using our walkie-talkies more when we have secret meetings," I whispered.

"Yeah, if we can figure out how our stupid brothers won't listen in," Butch growled.

I could hear Eddie's voice both inside the house and outside from where I was sitting up against the front wall. "Hello, Mrs. Peters. Is Gabe here?"

"SOUNDS GREAT MOM!" I kissed her on the cheek again, half because she is the greatest mom in the world and half because I was so relieved that she hadn't heard my knucklehead friends talking too loud and I wasn't going to get skinned for having so many firecrackers in the crawlspace.

"Okay, well you boys come out to the picnic table in the backyard in half an hour, okay?"

I looked at my Mickey Mouse watch and said, "Thanks Mom, you're the best!"

I went back down to the crawlspace and told the guys what happened and about lunch. You would have thought my mom's menu was from the Ritz-Carlton's best restaurant the way they all started smacking their lips and talking about how great my mom was.

I started in again, "I have a couple ideas of how to get the goons. Either when they are all down in their high-and-mighty dirt fort that they don't ever let us go in, we could throw the firecrackers in there..."

"No, that won't work. There's nowhere to hide up there, and they would pound us into the ground," Craig said.

"Okay, even better, when they are down by the lake with all of the girls we can launch the pop-bottle rockets at them and they'll never know what hit them!" I yelled.

"AWESOME!" Eddie yelped.

"But, won't they know it's us?" Craig asked.

"Carl would never suspect it was us if we did it right, because he doesn't know I have them. So the first time we use them, we will only use the pop-bottle rockets. But we will have to rely on hand signals and good escape routes, so when it all goes down we can get out of town!"

"We're going to town?" Eddie looked totally confused.

"Forget it, Eddie, it's just a figure of speech," I explained.

"A figure of what?" Eddie looked like his brain was going to explode.

"Yes, he and the other boys are all down in the crawlspace. Go on downstairs," Mom said in a sing-songy voice.

My blood went cold. "How did she know we were down here?" I wondered aloud.

"Okay, thanks." Eddie said.

I heard him step into the house, and start walking over to the stairs leading down.

"Oh, Eddie, you'll probably have to use a secret knock or something," Mom laughed.

"Uh, okay. Thanks Mrs. Peters..."

Eddie sounded like a bull elephant coming down the stairs, and then he knocked on the crawlspace door.

Murph had already slid over to the door and muttered, "PASSWORD?"

"Uh, I don't know it," Eddie said

"Request-denied-Private-Edward," Murph growled through the door.

"COME ON MURPH LET HIM IN ALREADY!" Butch yelled.

"Okay,-jeez-keep-your-shorts-on." Murph unlatched the door and Eddie scooted in with all of us.

"HOLY COW! WHERE DID YOU GET ALL OF THOSE?" Eddie yelled when he spied the fireworks.

"Seriously guys, my mom is right above us and she obviously knows we are down here, so keep it down!" That time I must have sounded really angry because everyone just sat there looking at me like I was a madman. "As a matter of fact, I'm going upstairs to see if Mom says anything so I can find out how much she knows. If I stomp three times in a row, you guys need to move out and leave through the garage door and meet me up in the tree house in half an hour... that is if I don't get grounded for the rest of the summer because of your big mouths!" I scooted to the door and left, leaving it open just in case they needed to escape quickly.

I walked up the stairs and closed the door leading down, so if they escaped Mom wouldn't see them leaving. I plopped down on the couch next to Mom and kissed her on the cheek. "Hey, Mom, what's up?"

"Oh, nothing, just catching up on some of my reading that I never get to when classes are in session."

"Do you like being a teacher?"

"Yes, I do!" she smiled, not looking away from the book.

"Hmmmm, so...?" I said casually.

"So what, dear?" Mom sighed. I could tell she wanted to get back to her reading.

"So, what're doing now?" I asked.

"Honey, I just told you. What are you doing?" Mom looked at me suspiciously.

"Nothing," I said a bit too suddenly.

"Sounds like you are having one of your secret meetings in the crawlspace. Don't you usually do that in the tree house?" Mom asked.

I noticed mom's headphones were sitting next to her. "Yeah, but this is a top secret meeting, and Carl and his goons bug us a lot when they see us up there."

"What's the meeting about?" Mom asked.

"It's a secret, Mom. Come on, you were listening in on it, weren't youuuuu?" I chided her.

"No, actually I was listening to some Beethoven when I heard the doorbell ring," Mom said matter-of-factly.

"Huh, how did you hear the doorbell then?" I said suspiciously.

"Well, I didn't have it up too loud, but don't worry; I wasn't listening in on your secret meeting.""

"So, how did you know we were in the crawlspace then?" I pursued it.

"Well honey, when a group of boys go tromping through the house, no matter how quiet they are trying to be, you just know," Mom smiled.

"Oh, sorry." I said sheepishly.

"Nothing to be sorry about, Gabe. Would your friends like to stay for lunch? I have some Ball Park Franks, Velveeta cheese sandwiches and lime Kool-Aid, and Mrs. Morris brought over a couple of her famous peach pies. I can top those off with some cinnamon ice cream."

"Forget-about-that,-let's-get-back-to-Operation-Get-The-Goons!" Murph said excitedly.

"SWEET! THIS IS GOING TO BE RADICAL!" Craig chimed in.

"Gabriel, time for lunch, sweetie," Mom called from the backyard patio.

"Yeah, sweetums, we better wrap it up," Butch said snottily.

"Yeah,-baby-cakes,-we-better-move-our-sweetheart-booties!" Murph added laughing, and Butch thumped him on the arm playfully.

I scooted to the door, opened it and then shut it back down really quickly and latched the door, "No one gets out alive, boooohaaaaahaaaahaaaa!"

But I slid the latch open again, and Craig and Eddie came tumbling out from putting their shoulders to the door to try to push it open. Soon the herd of elephants was coming up the stairs and out on to the back patio.

We set out a detailed plan, and then quickly I went back down to the crawlspace and buried the firecrackers back in their hiding spot. I then returned back to the patio where Mom was setting out a feast in the backyard.

CHAPTER EIGHT

# THE BIG BLOW-UP
# BACKFIRE BUNGLE

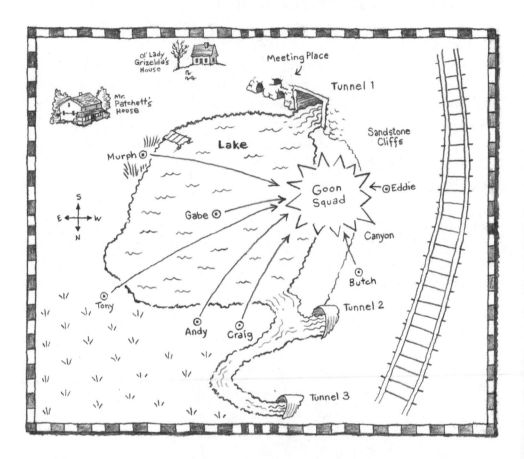

We only had two more weeks of summer and then we were back in school, which means tests, studying, classes, and shoes instead of bare feet. So we wanted the summer to go out with a bang, literally. The Secret Brotherhood of Boys met down by the lake and finished our plan we now called 'Operation Get The Goons'. Murph drew what he called his 'tactical military map' on this tiny notebook he keeps in his flak jacket, which actually really helped when he showed us the positions everyone would have to be when our big brothers were in place. Murph came dressed in military fatigues and had painted something on his face, which made it all green and black.

Andy had overheard his brothers talking to Carl and the others in the Goon Squad about meeting the girls down by the lake right after dark and so it was decided that that is where THE BIG BLOW was going to take place.

We all sat by the river that flowed into the lake, just below the caves in the sandstone cliff, and discussed how it would work. It was decided that only two people would use the walkie-talkies on account of how loud they would be and how sound carries across the water.

Murph said, "First-objective-is-to-get-in-and-out-without-being-found-out.-If-the-mission-goes-as-planned-we-will-all-live-through-the-night,-but-I-pity-anyone-who-gets-captured-during-this-mission!"

"Aren't you being a bit dramatic?" Eddie asked.

"Drama-is-the-business-of-danger,-and-boys-tonight-we-are-the-brokers-of-danger-and-drama!"

We all just looked at Murph and marveled at how serious he was taking this.

"We-will-have-to-go-inaudible! If-they-hear-us-talking-on-the-walkies-we're-good-as-dead-or-at-least-P.O.W.s!"

"Almost afraid to ask... what's a P.O.W?" Tony sneered.

"PRISONER-OF-WAR!-SUBJECT-TO-TORTURE-OR-WORSE!" Murph barked.

"Shhh, guys, be quiet in case they start to show up," I said, and just then we spotted three girls with Denise walking along the railroad tracks and disappearing behind the sandstone canyon where the train rumbled through at night and shook the ground all around. They were surely going to the other side of the canyon and would follow the trail down into the little valley where we always spied on them. They had no idea what they were in for on this night.

We all hunkered down lower into the tall weeds and watched.

Murph pulled a pair of binoculars from his belt. "Ahhhh,-here-comes-Andy's-brothers.-Soon-the-fireworks-will-begin...-literally!"

We all laughed at how official Murph acted, and how in his element he was.

Eddie asked, "Murph, are you going to be in the Army when you grow up?"

Murph snapped as though he were insulted, "Navy-Seals-Private!-The-Murphys-are-Seals!-My-Dad-was-a-Seal!-I'll-be-a-Seal!-my-brother-Boney-will-be-a-seal!"

"More like a Navy Juvie-Seal!" Butch snarled.

"Oh-yeah,-why-don't-you-say-that-to-his-face-tough-guy?" Murph snapped at Butch.

Butch just studied his feet, the look on his face was pure terror at the thought of confronting Boney Murphy.

Tony, who was on lookout across the field, would be able to see our victims gathered in their spot and he would signal Butch with the walkie-talkie when everyone was in position. From where I would be, I would clearly see Butch's flashlight signal to begin the BIG BLOW. We were so excited we could hardly stand it. It was starting to get dark and soon they would all be coming. It was time to get them back for all of the mean things they had done to us.

We were in a spot that no one could see us, but we knew we would see them. There were only three ways to get to their "secret" place, and from where we were we could see all three.

The plan had come together; we were ready. Each one of us, seven in all, were going to be in different places around the lake. Butch would be on the sandstone cliffs, in the highest cave. Murph would be near Mr. Patchett's house down in the weeds (truly dangerous because of Mr. Patchett, who always seemed to be right there when something was going on, but Murph had the least seniority in the club, so he got the short straw). Eddie would be up on the sandstone canyon wall where the train goes through, the highest and most visible place because it was right above our big brothers' hiding place. If he accidently kicked a rock and it tumbled down, it would give us up and we would all be tortured. Eddie was the best person to be up there because he could climb like a monkey, very carefully. Andy and Craig would be up on the path leading around the lake, which was dangerous because it was the most likely way the goons would go to try to escape our air raid, so Craig and Andy would have to hurry and hide. That would mean they would be scooting down the embankment into bull snake alley, which we knew at times contained hundreds of snakes, although usually they were only out when it was really hot. Still, that many snakes anywhere could make anyone's skin crawl.

As I mentioned before, Tony would be stationed as our lookout in the field where we built the monster jump last winter on which Sawyer broke both of his arms. Being in the field could be really dangerous because you are totally out in the open, and it is the field that a lot of times the older brothers cut through to get to the lake. So they might try to escape across the field, and if they did, there would be nowhere to hide at all.

Finally, I would be out on the raft in the middle of the lake, which was by far the most dangerous position on account of the fact that you have to row in and tie the boat to the dock and you are literally in the middle of the lake, but I figured when it was dark I could lay flat and they wouldn't even know I was there if everything went well. If it didn't and I could swim fast, I might be able to get to the opposite edge of the lake from where all the action would be going down.

I needed to be on the raft because it was the only place at the lake that all of the other positions could see me waving my punk, which I was going to use to light the pop-bottle rockets. When I waved the punk, everyone was to count down from ten to one and then ignite their pop-bottle bunch and aim it right over where our brothers and the girls would be.

Each of us would have twelve pop-bottle rockets apiece and our walkie-talkies. We knew that the big brothers wouldn't be on any of their walkies as long as they were with the girls. The plan was that at exactly nine o'clock we would signal each other with the walkies and each one of us would light our twelve pop-bottle rockets with a twisted fuse set in an actual soda pop-bottle (which required us to visit the Lawn and Leisure to get a pop and to check on the Indian motorcycle track progress).

On my go, the seven of us would aim all twelve pop-bottle rockets right above where our dumb brothers were hanging out with their girlfriends. That was going to be eighty-four explosions right above their heads all at once, which was sure to scare the girls so bad that they would come out of their hidey-hole screaming at the tops of their lungs! As soon as they were panicking and coming out of the little valley they hang out in, we would fire off the second round of eighty-four. It would be like they were coming from everywhere and nowhere all at the same time.

The goons wouldn't know which way to run, or what to do.

☺

We all went to our positions. As I rowed the boat slowly out to the dock, the oars made small splashing sounds as they broke the water. I could see in the last of the night's light a dark yellow and pink band across the top of the mountains. The stars were twinkling like someone was turning on switches. The sky went from dark blue to black, and thousands of stars hung over my head. The moon was about half-full and was already overhead, so the reflection on the water looked really cool. Every time one of the oars dipped in, the moon rippled and wiggled and then back to the rounded moon I was used to. And then it all became squiggles in the water again.

Eddie was wearing a funny miner's cap his Grandpa had given him that had a dim light on it. I saw him coming over the crest of the sandstone canyon right as the last light of the day disappeared. I could see the light on his miner's cap and knew he was standing right above the spot where the teens were now gathered.

Because I was in the middle of the lake, I could hear everything. I could hear Craig and Andy talking in low murmurs. Even though I couldn't actually hear what they were talking about, I wanted to tell them to stop talking in case the Goon Squad could hear them, too. Then I heard the crackling of Tony's walkie-talkie as he whispered to Butch that all were in position. Butch signaled to me from his cave by flashing twice quickly with his flashlight. From the path Craig and Andy flashed twice, too. Tony answered with a double flash, and Eddie waved his hand in front of the miner's light twice.

We heard the low voices of my brother and the other goons and then sudden explosions of silly giggling coming from the four girls creeping out of the canyon and right across the water. They sounded like they were standing right there on the raft with me. The girls seemed to giggle at just about everything my dumb brother said, especially Denise. I couldn't really understand that since I just didn't find Carl too amusing at all.

Murph had a flashlight with him as he crouched down in the weeds. He had covered the top of the flashlight with some kind of a red plastic, which muted the color, but I could hear him talking to himself just across the lake in a military way: "...-positions-Private-Murphy-prepare-to-take-the-hill..."

"Psst, Murph, shut up already!" I growled, sure that my voice would carry right to him as he was on the edge of the lake.

"Sorry,-General-Peters."

I could hear him splashing in the shallow waters surrounding the lake.

Suddenly the raft moved as though a big wave had lifted it. The dread I felt thinking about the legend of the Indian in the lake seized me. Mr. Patchett had put in all of our heads years ago the legend of the Indian who comes out at night and haunts the lake area. It still made my skin crawl to think about him lurking in the weeds with a tomahawk ready to attack us at any moment.

I knew I had to push the thought out of my mind, or I wouldn't be able to control the mission. But I couldn't help but think about the prospect of this whole thing backfiring, and me—instead of rowing to the shore—having to dive into

the lake water
where the dead dog, the
Indian, the possible ghost of the
girl who drowned and maybe even
the monster carp hung out. Any one of
those things could drag me to the bottom of
the lake. Which was worse, that or one of the
Goon Squad capturing me? I made myself push
the thought out of my mind. I looked around one
more time, licked my lips, took a deep breath and
lit my punk.  I started waving it slowly in the air, making sure
it was as high as I could lift it, so everyone could see it from
his positions. I heard the crackle of the walkie-talkie and the
command to count down was given.

I counted down inside my head: ten, Mississippi ... nine,
Mississippi ... eight, Mississippi ... seven, Mississippi ... six, Mississippi
... five, Mississippi ... four, Mississippi ... three, Mississippi ... When I
got to two, there was a series of whooshing noises going right by
my face and sparks trailing as they climbed into the air and
exploded, just as I was readying to light. Someone needed to
teach Murph how to countdown. But then I thought of how fast
Murph talks, and his timing made more sense. I realized then
that I was right in Murph's line of fire for the target. I hit the
deck and lost count, but I set the punk to the twisted bunch of
fuses and put my arm up in the general direction holding the
pop bottle over my head. WOOSH, the sparks from the dozen
pop-bottle rockets singed the hair on my arm as they headed
off to blow up over the Goon Squad meeting. The pop-bottle
rockets were zooming in from every direction; it looked like a

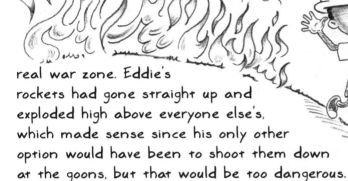

real war zone. Eddie's
rockets had gone straight up and
exploded high above everyone else's,
which made sense since his only other
option would have been to shoot them down
at the goons, but that would be too dangerous.

Everyone seemed to have hit his target, because
the whole sandstone canyon above the Goon Squad
meeting was alight and an instant commotion began.
It was totally cool. The plan had worked really well—
or so I thought.

A blood-curdling scream, which sounded too high to be one
of the Goons and too low to be one of the girls, punctured the
air, as did the report of dozens of pop-bottle rockets exploding
like a Fourth of July display right on target. It brought a huge
smile to my face and whooping from every direction as The
Secret Brotherhood of Boys felt true victory. More screams
were pouring out of the canyon.

All of a sudden the weeds on the hill started to glow red in
about ten places. Before I could even launch the second round,
the Goon Squad was piling out of the canyon and onto the
path right toward where Craig and Andy were. The girls were
shrieking and the Goons were helping them out of the canyon
and down the path. I saw Andy and Craig scramble down the
embankment right into bull snake alley.

Eddie was running right down on top of the Goon Squad
instead of hunkering against the sandstone cliff as we planned,
so he could fire his second round off right over their heads as
they went down the path either way. But Eddie was screaming

at the top of his lungs, "I'M HIT! OW! STOP! DON'T FIRE ROUND TWO! STOP! COME ON GUYS, I MEAN IT!"

What nobody thought through or calculated on Murph's brilliant map was that when you aimed right over where the Goon Squad was, you were aiming directly at Eddie. We had planned it out and had said under no circumstances was anyone to yell commands or anything that would let on who had done this prank, but against my better judgment because I realized Eddie was seriously in trouble, and since the other guys had already whooped and hollered, I started to yell, "CEASE FIRE! STOP THE SECOND ROUND!"

The moon and the second round of pop-bottles from Murph, Tony and Butch who had already lit and aimed was just bright enough to illuminate Eddie tumbling down the  embankment, screaming and rolling like a cowboy who has just been shot off of a cliff. WOOSH, WOOSH, WOOSH, WOOSH went Murph's rockets right past my face again and then they arced up, hitting the hill

and exploding. I hit the deck, but I tumbled sideways and my foot went off the raft. Suddenly I was in the inky black water, and the thought of the Indian in the lake hiding terrified me. I began to swim toward the shore.

Eddie must have rolled right past where the Goons and girls had been standing down into the stream that runs out of the lake on that side, because I could hear the splash from where I was. He was writhing like a snake and screaming that his skin was on fire. He had been hit by at least five of the pop bottle rockets.

But what was really on fire was the entire sandstone hill. The old, dead brush had gone up instantly, and the fire was spreading sideways across the hill like lava coming down the side of a volcano.

Mr. Patchett flew out his back door screaming, "WHAT IN TARNATION IS GOING ON OUT HERE?"

The goons and girls ran right past him. The girls were still screaming but I could hear the goons laughing and yelling at us that we were all dead.

As soon as the coast seemed clear, all the guys started running from their positions to where Eddie was still screaming at the top of his lungs. I made it to the other side of the lake without getting pulled under by the Indian, and when I got there everyone was stomping out the fire that was still spreading across the hill. Mr. Patchett was yelling something about calling the fire department, and that just made everyone stomp that much harder.

Instead of calling the fire department, Mr. Patchett and now a few other neighbors, including of all people our scout leader Deak were running up the sandstone canyon with shovels and hoes. Everyone went to work on the fires, and by the time we were done stomping and shoveling and hoeing, we were all wet with sweat and huffing and puffing. Eddie was sitting on a rock next to the lake crying.

Mr. Patchett gave us all a good chewing-out, and told us how irresponsible we were. We all just nodded and acted like we felt worse about it than we did, but the truth of the matter is we got our brothers really, really good!

Deak walked over to where Andy, Tony and I were talking and said, "So, you boys responsible for this mess?"

I looked at Deak, and my pride for the prank started to vanish. "We didn't mean for the hill to catch fire, we were just trying to get our brothers back for..."

Deak interrupted me; "We'll talk about it at our next scout meeting. We'll also talk about maybe figuring a way that you boys can replant some stuff on the hill so it won't be so unsightly."

When Deak walked away we all just looked at each other helplessly. Somehow we knew that we were going to be paying for this prank for a long time to come.

When Mr. Patchett and the other men walked back to their houses assuring each of us that our parents would be called, we all walked over and circled around Eddie. Murph and Butch flashed their flashlights on him, and it looked like he had measles the size of quarters on his neck and chest. There was one on his face, too. The pop-bottle rocket that hit his face missed his eye by about half an inch, and had burned his whole eyebrow off. The burns were already blistering up, and Eddie was in a lot of pain. I started to shiver from the lake water, the sweat and the fear of what was to come. Eddie was moaning, "I could smell my flesh burning! A couple of them blew up when they hit me!"

Andy helped Eddie to his feet. "Oh m-m-man, sorry, that st-stinks man!"

"Yeah, really, sorry bud," everyone in the brotherhood said. We all felt terrible.

"Well, I think I'll go home," Tony said.

"Me, too," Butch whispered.

"Anyone want to sleep in my tent?" I asked.

Eddie said, "Better not. I kinda want to be home when Mr. Patchett calls my Mom and Dad."

"Jeez, I don't. I kind of think I want to run away before that happens," Tony said meekly.

"H-Hey, wh-who w-wants to jump a t-train for California with m-m-me?" Andy asked.

"Oh-come-on-you-guys-what's-the-worst-thing-that-can-happen-to-us?-Stop-acting-like-a-bunch-of-sissies!-At-least-none-of-the-Goon-Squad-got-ahold-of-us."

"Look!" Craig screamed, pointing toward Mr. Patchett's house.

Coming around the lake was Carl and the other goons; they looked like they were coming for revenge now. Andy and I grabbed Eddie's arms and pulled him up the small hill. Then we all started running across the field toward the crazy lady's house, because at this point, what other choice did we have?

CHAPTER NINE

# MUDBUGS

The big blowup down at the lake meant I was grounded the week my birthday fell in. Even worse, it was the last week of summer, and the only time I could leave my yard was to go to my scout meeting where I was going to get a lecture.

Part of my punishment was no birthday party, which was fine because everyone in The Secret Brotherhood of Boys Club was grounded too, so nobody would have come anyway. It's funny, Mom and Dad were mad at me about what we did, but even madder at the fact that I wouldn't tell them where I got the firecrackers. Butch had been a snitch and given me up as the supplier of the firecrackers as soon as Mr. Patchett caught us. I'm no snitch like Butch, so there was no way I was ever going to tell on my uncles, and that is what got me extra grounded, which is Mom's way of saying not only don't you leave the yard, but no dessert and no treats for the whole time you are in grounding prison.

Deak called a special meeting for the scout troop, and we got an hour lecture about fire danger from a fireman. I guess that was as close as our troop was going to get to the firehouse until we proved ourselves again.

After we all got ungrounded, Deak made us dig plants out of the field near the lake and replant them along the hill where we had burned all of the old plants. It was hard work, but when we were done we felt better about ourselves.

Eddie had to stay in the house for two weeks with salve and other stuff on his burns. It turned out he had six really bad burns that were going to leave scars, and the one over his eyebrow would always be visible and about half of his eyebrow would never grow back. We thought he looked really tough that way, and wished we had cool scars. But to hear Eddie tell it the pain was not at all worth it.

☺

So because my birthday was not a big deal this year, Dad's birthday was going to be the last big celebration of the summer before everyone went back to school. For Dad's special day, my parents usually have an adult party for their friends to celebrate, and our family always has a "just us" party for each person's birthday.

Dad's birthday meal was going to be surf and turf, because this year was a big one — turning thirty-five, which I guess is a lot.

Mom got some of Dad's favorite thick steaks from the butcher in the next town over whom we go to for real German sausage in October, since Mom is from a big German family and she likes to celebrate like they do in the "old country" (that is what she calls Europe). Dad grew up in upstate New York, near Maine, where lobster is "a dime a dozen." When he was raised there, his family feasted on lobster and steak all the time, since his dad raised cattle. "It reminds Dad of the birthday celebrations he had when he was a boy!" Mom said, almost as excited about Dad's birthday as he was.

I walked into the kitchen, and there was this giant pot that Ol' Man Waldtrout lent my mom with these four crazy-eyed creatures with giant pincers. They were a hundred times bigger than the crawdads we'd catch in the ditch, and which Mom boiled up one time and we ate their tails with hot sauce and ranch dressing.

My dad thought we were crazy to do this. "Why are you eating mudbugs?" he asked us.

For some reason, my dad's people always called crayfish or crawdads "mudbugs."

"They're just mini-lobsters, Dad," Carl said in between bites.

"Not the lobsters I knew when I was your age!" Dad made a face. "Ugh, mudbugs... Do you know what those things eat?"

"DA-AD, don't gross us out! They're good! Come on, give them a try," I begged. But Dad just nodded his head and walked out of the kitchen.

I looked at the lobsters in the pot now and felt sorry for them. They all kept moving around in small circles and were climbing all over each other trying to get out. How could you boil something alive like that? The doorbell rang, and I was surprised to see T-Bone standing on my porch with Andy.

"Come on in, guys," I invited.

When Mom went into town I grabbed the pot off of the counter. It was really heavy to carry it full of water and lobsters across the street, but Andy grabbed the other handle and T-Bone held the bottom of the pot. We had to do something to help the poor things.

I started to slip the four lobsters down into the pond, one by one.

Andy had a worried look on his face. "Gabe, seriously, if I d-d-did this my dad would k-kill m-me!"

"Yeah man, lobster's expensive," T-Bone added.

"Well, Mom isn't going to be too happy, but how can she just boil them alive like that?" I moved the giant pot closer to the water.

"You are g-going to g-g-get k-k-killed!"

"Andy, stop saying that. No one is going to get killed. I might get grounded again and all, but when I tell them why I did it, they'll understand... don't you think?" I asked, getting a little nervous.

"Mmm, n-no, Andy said.

"No way, Jose!" T-Bone looked at me as if I were totally crazy.

Carl came out the front door and started running across the road right at us.

"Duck!" I yell-whispered.

"Holy c-crapola, he l-l-looks like he's going to k-k-k-kill us."

"Holy crapola? What the heck is 'holy crapola'?" T-Bone asked, lying in the weeds next to the ditch.

Carl ran right on by the pond and out into the field like his tail was on fire.

"He doesn't even know we are here, you big dorkorama, and you sure like using the KILL word, don't cha?" I thumped Andy's arm.

He looked at me, scowled and then gave me a huge frog bubble. A frog bubble is when someone uses his knuckle to punch usually your bicep, making a knot in the muscle jump up like a frog.

"You ask me about crapola, and you call me a dorkorama?" I shot back.

We both started laughing pretty hard. I rubbed my arm and planned to get him back with his own frog bubble when he least expected it.

T-Bone just looked at us like we were both crazy and started making big circles around his ear, "Loco!"

*

Right before I dropped the lobsters into the water they looked up at me with their stickball eyes, which seemed to rotate around like a slinky, and then as I set one on the bank it turned and skittered down into the muddy water backwards. I thought they would probably first introduce themselves to the crawdads, which were like their second cousins or something. I figured their claws would ward off any snakes or other creatures that wanted to eat them, or so I thought.

After we dropped the lobsters into the pond, both Andy and T-Bone thought it was time to get going.

Andy told me, "You are g-g-going to g-get m-murdered when your m-m-mom finds out what you d-d-did, and I don't w-want to be around to w-watch!"

"Me neither, see ya!" And with that, T-Bone was running fast toward the highway.

All of a sudden I had a real sinking feeling. I looked into the muddy water to see if I could catch them again, but they were nowhere to be seen. I was so nervous about mom coming home that I just sat up in the tree house watching the gravel road for her car. When her car came rumbling up the hill, I slowly crawled down the tree and crossed into my yard.

When Mom got home and found out what happened, she was steaming mad. "Gabe, how could you do such a thing? You have ruined your dad's party!"

I felt so bad; Mom was actually crying. "Mom, I, I was trying to..." I couldn't even think of a way to explain myself. I just knew somehow I had to get those lobsters back.

I went across the gravel road to the pond and tried to find the lobsters. But there was no sign of them anywhere. I looked and looked for a long time, but realized I would never find them. I'd hide at the bottom if someone wanted to boil me alive and eat me, too.

Mom never mentioned it to Dad because I guess she didn't have the heart to ground me again, since summer was the best time of the year. We had steak and some other good food, but none of it tasted good to me after what I did. I was trying to be nice to the living creatures, but it backfired really big.

When I told Mom I would pay for the lobsters, she started crying again. How can trying to do the right thing make you feel so bad, I wondered?

A few days later near the grate where the water pours out of the pump into the irrigation ditch I found two of the lobsters. They were all white and dead. Something had been chewing on them a lot. I found out that lobsters can only live in saltwater, so we might as well have eaten them, because in a way they drowned.

Carl knows a lot about animals, and when I told him what I had done and why he said, "What a chicken-dunce you are, Gabe! Which would you rather do, drown or boil? Boiling takes no time at all, but drowning for a lobster takes all night in sheer agony. Their lungs fill with muddy fresh water, and they suffocate slowly. It is a painful death."

I felt horrible. I wasn't sure Carl knew anything about it, but he sure was making me feel lousy.

Then he added insult to injury, "By the way, we aren't finished with you little pukes for what you did down at the lake. You can't run forever, you know."

A shiver ran up my spine just by the way he said that. Holy crapola, I felt like a real dorkorama!

θ

Then I got this idea: what if I took pictures of one of the lobsters crawling along the mud bank of the pond next to a regular crawdad? THE WORLD'S LARGEST CRAWDAD, now that could make it into the Guinness Book of World Records, couldn't it? We had been so busy doing other things that we hadn't finished our plan for the spit pool. We would have to get back to it.

# CHAPTER TEN

# FLUSH

We are at that point when the summer is starting to feel more like autumn. Even though they mean the same thing, I like the sound of autumn better than fall since I sometimes fall off my bike but I never autumn off my bike or anything else for that matter.

The mornings are cool enough that I have to wear a sweatshirt, and then by afternoon I back in my t-shirt. Soon all of the lal rivers under the tunnels, the ditch and ponds will be icing over, and the critters underwater will be sleeping for the rest of the fall, winter and some of the spring. So, if I was going to make a fortune selling fish to the man at the Pet Shop, I was going to have to get a move on it really soon.

Today I finally figured out why my dad always kids around with me about naming all my fish 'Flush'. I keep three fish bowls in my bedroom, and asked for a huge aquarium for my birthday, which I didn't get. Sometimes I keep little frogs from the pond in one of the fish bowls, but that backfired on me the time Carl thought it was funny to put four little frogs in the toilet. Mom went into the bathroom and you could hear her scream a mile away. Of course, I was the one who got in trouble because I had brought the frogs into the house and Carl said I did it. I had been doing so many boneheaded things this summer that Mom just believed him when he told her that, even though I tried to explain that this time I had nothing to do with it. Mom made me take them over to the pond and let them go. So much for my frog farm, but I will try again. Maybe I could set the world's record for the largest frog farm? And then for the largest frog!

Mostly I keep goldfish in the bowls ever since I won two goldfish at the school carnival. The prize came for guessing how many jellybeans were in this giant plastic Coke bottle that was almost half as tall as me. I got to keep the jellybeans too, which made me sick after a few days of munching on them constantly. I put the rest of the jellybeans in a giant bag and hauled them up into the tree house for our Secret Brotherhood meetings. They were a big hit. Not only did they taste good, but they were really good ammunition in our slingshots. I had about a million welts on my arms and legs from our jellybean wars. It was a good thing I was wearing my glasses too, because one of the jellybeans hit my left lens so hard I thought it was going to shatter. And if you sucked on about five of the jellybeans at a time, you could make the grossest spit drool hang for a while until it plopped down into the wading pool below.

Once Frisky and Friskier were lying in the shade below the tree house when the rain of jellybeans started. Frisky started walking around eating them. Friskier took one taste and spit it out and went back to the shade. I think she ate a black licorice bean because she was making the same face my grandma makes when she is cleaning the poop out of the chicken shack or when she is mucking out the stalls.

Frisky kept walking around with his nose right on the ground though, sniffing and chewing, sniffing and chewing. I cracked up as I watched him spit out the black licorice and chocolate ones. He looked so funny with his tongue sticking way out of his mouth while he was trying to eject them without letting his teeth touch them. He kind of looked like a wolf with his teeth pulled back like that. He probably ate a million jellybeans before he went back to the shade. This was going to backfire on him, because he threw up jellybean goo all over the place later and I had to clean it up. But it was kind of worth it because he threw it up all over Carl's bed.

☺

One time I put a handful of guppies that I had caught down at the lake into one of the bowls. I thought maybe I could figure out how to make them have a million baby guppies that I could sell to Joe up at the Bait Shop for the catfish catchers. But the next morning all of the guppies were floating on their backs. I was so disappointed I put the bowl on my windowsill and forgot about it. A few days later, after the sun had been warming the bowl during the day, the worst smell came from my room. It was like rotten guppy stew, and no one could go upstairs for the rest of the day without gagging. When I went in to get the book, I noticed some of the guppies were falling apart like they had actually been cooked by the sunshine. That was when Mom

made the rule of keeping my goldfish bowls on the bottom level of
our house. The only thing down there is her sewing room, a bathroom
and the crawlspace. Dad and I built these cool shelves down there
where I could put cages and the fish bowls for my fish, salamander,
toads, and frogs. Plus I have a tarantula terrarium there with two
tarantulas I named Creepy and Creepier even though they are really
nice and like to crawl all over you, which I don't mind but which really
gives my mom the willies.

Butch tried to give me his bearded lizard, but Mom was still shaky
about any reptiles coming into the house. I bought a tall cage at
a garage sale for the occasional wounded or abandoned bird, and
on the bottom shelf there was enough room for the huge wire cage
Squeaky and Squeakier, my guinea pigs, lived in. Moving them down
here made Mom particularly happy, since she was always saying they
stunk up my room. Dad even hand painted this funny sign and hung
it over the door at the bottom of the stairs; it said — 'GABE'S ZOO,
PEE-YOU'. Of course, at some point Carl decided to be funny and
wrote over it, 'GABE'S CHICKEN COOP,

ALL HIS ANIMALS SMELL LIKE POOP!' He drew a picture of a chicken pooping on it too, and that is what got him in a ton of trouble with Mom. She made him go to his room and rewrite Dad's sign, which just cracked me up because Dad thought Carl's addition to the sign was funny, and actually I did, too. Mom didn't.

When Dad and I were setting up the shelves and trying to make sure we wouldn't be in Mom's way, I told him, 'Dad, if I had a fifty-gallon aquarium, I could turn two fish into two hundred. I can get about fifty cents apiece for one, so I could make a hundred dollars. If I made a hundred dollars, I could buy a bearded lizard to go with the one Butch wanted to give me to keep it company and... wait, no, I could buy a mom — or dad — bearded lizard to marry Butch's one, but first I would have to figure out which is which.'

Dad was looking at me with a huge smile on his face. I wasn't sure if that was a my son is so weird smile or if it was a hey that's a good idea smile, which got me all excited, 'Dad-do-you-have-any-idea-how-much-a-bearded-lizard-baby-would-make-me?-And-what-if-they-have-litters-like-kittens?-I-need-to-find-out-if-they-have-litters-or-not!-I-could-be-a-millionaire-and...'

Dad shook his head and smiled really big, 'Shoot,-why-wouldn't-you-just-buy-a-mom-and-dad-alligator?-Do-you-have-any-idea-how-much-an-alligator-baby-goes-for?-You-could-just-let-them-take-over-this-floor-and-keep-the-door-locked-and-the-other-cages-out-of-reach!'

'Are you making fun of me, Dad?' I sniffed.

Dad rubbed my head, 'No buddy, I love your enthusiasm, and I have no doubt that someday you are going to be a millionaire. I've never seen someone have so many ideas to sell stuff!'

'DID YOU SAY ALLIGATORS!? GREAT IDEA, DAD! Can you loan me the money to buy some alligators now?'

'Calm down, buddy, I'm just kidding. I can just see your mom if we came home with alligators. We'd be living out back in the doghouse!' Dad rubbed my head again.

'I know, I know.' I was disappointed, and then suddenly less-dangerous ideas hit me. 'But Dad, what if I got...'

I went on and on with combinations of two reptiles, male and female, that would have so many it would have filled Noah's boat, until I could tell Dad wasn't really listening anymore.

We finished the shelves, and then had some of Dad's favorite Neapolitan ice cream on the porch. "You know, Gabriel, I really do think you are going to be a very rich man when you grow up."

"WHY?"

"Because you are always looking for the next way to make a buck. If you aren't selling something door to door, you are selling stuff from your bedroom door. You are the only kid I know who can buy a box of bubblegum for two dollars and make ten dollars selling it to other kids."

I started laughing. "Well, I do like the cold hard cash-e-o, Dad-e-o!"

"Yes you do, my man, yes you do! Cash- e-o?" Dad chuckled.

"Dad-e-o?" Carl interrupted from the doorway leading out onto the back patio.

"Mind your own beeswax, jerk-e-o!" I barked.

"What a chicken-dork-e-o!" Carl muttered coming out the back door.

"Jealous-e-o?" I sneered.

"Of what?"

"Chicken-butt!" I rhymed, just to get a rise out of Carl.

"Why would I be jealous of you?" he scoffed.

"Chicken-pooh!" I rhymed again.

"Dad, make him stop!" Carl complained.

"Chicken-plop!" I continued.

Dad was grinning now.

"Seriously Gabe, I'm gonna..."

"Chicken-bunna!" I moved around behind Dad's lawn chair just to be safe.

"DA-AD, are you going to make him stop or not?"

"Chicken-snot in a pot, smells a lot, like Carl who's got..."

Dad intervened, "Well, Carl, as I remember you kind of started..."

"Chicken-farted, it's retarded, don't get me started... sorry, Dad, I just had to."

"GABE SHUT UP!" Carl snarled.

"Chicken-butt-up! Chicken-cut-up!" I just kept going, to egg him on.

Dad stated matter - of - factly, "Carl, you are the one that hyphenates the word 'chicken' all the time."

"Chicken-rhyme! All the time!" I went on.

"I can't stand it!"

"Chicken-bandit..."

"Gabe, ENOUGH!" Dad wheeled around at me, though I wasn't sure why. He had just seemed to be defending my right to fire back.

"Chicken-tough! Chicken-fluff!" Then I clapped my hand over my mouth indicating that I was done, and thinking maybe doing it to Carl was one thing, but my dad... well that was another.

"I'm so outta here!" Carl gave me a look that said, "Wait until later when Dad's not around."

"Chicken-dear!" I called as a parting shot.

Carl mouthed the words, "I'm going to kill you!" when Dad wasn't looking at him.

"Not scared poop-e-o!" I sneered back in air talk.

Carl let out a giant, frustrated scream and ran across the gravel road toward the field where he and some of his goony friends were digging their multi-room fort.

The goon had been complaining at dinner last night about constant cave-ins and asking Dad for advice. What he didn't know is that some of us little brothers were sabotaging them, by pushing dirt back in after they had gone. We would sit up on top of the dirt hill over the part of the field where they were digging their "secret fort" and spy on them with binoculars. When they left, we would sabotage all of their work. It just doesn't pay to be mean to your little brother sometimes.

"So about those alligators, Dad..."

"Son, I think you have enough animals to keep you busy for a little while. Perhaps some other time we will discuss it."

"Really?"

"Really! But I'll have to work on your mother for a while before it happens," my dad smiled.

# CHAPTER ELEVEN

# PET SHOP BLUES

I ride my bike to the Bait Shop all the time, and the Pet Shop is a few miles away so Mom lets me ride there, too. The man who owns the Pet Shop is a nice guy who always chews on a cigar and is about the shortest man I have ever seen. He has a dark five-o'clock shadow all the time, and wears tank tops that are supposed to be white but are actually gray, like the ones my big brother wears to his gym class.

The guy lets me pet the puppies and help him feed the other animals. I always ask him about the animals, and tell him that I want to have a zoo or a Pet Shop when I am a grown-up. One time, when he asked about why I had a whole box of grape bubble gum under my arm while riding on my bike, I told him about my bubble gum and candy store. I told him about how I made a bunch of money by marking it all up individually and selling it to the other kids in my neighborhood, mostly those kids whose moms won't let them cross the highway on their bikes to go to the bait shop themselves. He seemed really impressed with my ideas about selling and business, and now always wants to talk to me about that stuff when I just go in there to see the puppies.

"Kid, dese goldfish will have little goldfish, and by the end of da year you would have hundreds of goldfish if you kept dem all. I'll make you a deal; all dis stuff costs about nine bucks. You pay me half now and the rest I'll credit at twenty-five cents a fish until you have paid it off, kay? I always need da udder kind of critters, too. So if you see any lizards or greenback frogs, you bring dem in to me for some cold hard cash."

A great thing about this was that when one of our neighbors, Mr. Povich, moved he had a huge garage sale, and he gave us about a hundred fish bowls that his kids had used. Dad thought they could come in handy someday for some kind of a project or another, but they ended up just collecting dust in the crawlspace like so many of Dad's collections. I knew Dad would let me line them up in my downstairs zoo to start my fish empire now. I was going to be rich!

My first successful sale at the pet shop—actually it was a trade I made—was for a yellow-and-black spotted salamander that was crawling in our window-well that I named 'Sticky'. I took him to the pet shop, and the owner traded me two goldfish and some fish food for him. It was hard riding my bike all the way home with a big baggie full of water and two sloshing fish. I figured they were going to be pretty dizzy by the time I got them home.

When I was almost home, I saw a huge bull snake stretched out across the shoulder of the road that I almost rode over. I had to get off of my bike and find a place to set my goldfish down so I could move the snake off of the road and into the field where a car or a bike wouldn't run over him. I started thinking about slinging him over my shoulder and taking him home or, better yet, back to the pet store. I could probably trade this big guy for just about anything. But I couldn't stand the thought of a big old snake that was free to roam the fields one

day and then in some glass box the next. I wondered then if now, with my downstairs zoo, Mom just might say yes to a snake. I could keep him in the big open air cage my guinea pigs are in and put them in a pen.

Who was I trying to kid? There was no way Mom would let that happen. I eased the big guy into the tall grass and he hissed. "Oh yeah, I am so scared snaky-dude."

I picked up the fish bag and started to pedal along, I realized that when I set the fish bag down, there must have been a small stick or something on the ground, because a small hole sprung out some water in my fish bag. By the time I got home I had lost more than half the water in the bag, and now it was really squirting all over. I had to pinch the hole shut as I jogged upstairs to my room and poured the whole thing, fish and all, into the empty bowl.

I decided with all of the trauma the fish had taken just getting to my house, that I would keep them on my dresser for a few days before I moved them to my downstairs zoo. I had totally forgotten Mom's rule about fish in my room due to my guppy soup incident.

Dad came into my room and looked at the goldfish bowl. "You better move those downstairs before Mom sees them in your room."

"Oh, yeah! Oh man, don't tell her, Dad!" I felt a little panicked and grabbed the bowl. On my way out of my room, my foot caught and the whole bowl went flying into the hall. Gross, greenish water splashed all up and down the hall wall, and the two fish flipped around on the carpet, their mouths moving like they were talking, trying to breathe. Dad grabbed the bowl and filled it with water from the bathtub and we put the fish back into the bowl. I carefully hurried downstairs to my basement zoo, de-chlorinated the water, and set them with the others.

Dad came down and looked at all of my animals.

"I named them Ricky and Lucy, just like the funny people on that television show."

My dad just laughed and said, "Gabe, you should just name them both Flush."

I thought it was a weird thing to say, until the next morning when I went down there to see how they had done, and they were both floating upside down and all the gold in them was gone. They looked like two weird ghost fish. I looked at the water, thinking that it should all be gold since the color had drained from the fish somewhere. I felt a bit discouraged, but I think riding them home on my bike and then hurling them into the hall is what killed them. Maybe Dad would take me up to the pet store this time to get Ricky Junior and Lucy the Second.

The idea of having a fish empire came to me the day Andy and I decided to start a frog farm, which gave me the idea to sell guppies and goldfish, too. Every kid wants a pet, and not all kids' moms will let them. But almost everyone can have a fish because they don't make a mess or anything. So, I decided to get some goldfish and let them make more goldfish, which I could sell to the man who owns the pet store for about twenty-five cents each.

After the first Lucy and Ricky croaked, the man at the pet store sold me gravel, food, and two fish, which he said were definitely a good mom and a dad. He didn't even charge me for them because the first Ricky and Lucy died so fast. I felt a little guilty about leaving out the hall part of my story to the pet

store man, but I did tell him all about the ride home the fish
had.

Well, Ricky Junior and Lucy the Second only lasted three
days before they croaked, which is funny because if a frog dies,
do you say it croaked? No, because someone would think you
were just saying that they were talking. The point is, the fish
kept dying, and that is why Dad said to call them all 'Flush'—
I guess because we sent them to the ocean through what Dad
called "The Toilet Portal".

Anyway my first mom and dad fish died, and then my
second mom and dad fish died for no reason. Dad even drove
me and them home from the store, so there was no trauma. But
that didn't stop me from going back to get more, because the
pet store man told me the second time that he had a five-day
policy for me and me alone: "If your fish don't croak 'for five
days, they's yours fo good, but if they do, youse come on back
and I'll replace 'em everytime. But do me a favor—don't bring
dem stinky dead fish in ta me to show me. I trust youse. If
youse says they croaked, they croaked!"

The dude is a really nice man, but his stubby cigar stinks
and always is hanging out of his mouth because he already
smoked most of it, and the rest he chews, which is ultra gross!
"Now you wanna watch one of dose boa snakes eat some
meece?"

"YEAH!" This would be the third time I saw the boa eat. It
was amazing to watch.

That gave me an idea. "What if I caught a bunch of mice in
the field by my house? Would you pay me for them?"

"No way Jose, dose meece got diseases. I wouldn't never feed
my snakes no wild meece. 'Sides, mice are a dime ah dozen.
Stick with da fish, kid, dat's where the real money is."

I couldn't really figure out why he was calling me "Jose" or
why he always called mice 'meece', but it was really cool to
watch what happened when he dropped those mice down into
the huge terrarium that was in the center of the store. All of
a sudden every boy that was within a mile from there was

running into the store to watch the snake strike and then
swallow the mouse whole.

"Some kids," said the shopkeeper, "seem to know 'xactly when
I'm gonna feed me snakes. Dere's always a crowd."

What happened is the snake raised his head and stared
the little mouse down. The mouse was skittering around trying
to find a safe place, but everywhere he went there was more
snake. Then as fast as a lightning bolt hits the ground the
snake's head snapped forward and his huge jaws clamped down
on the mouse. A turd dropped out of the mouse, and then
slowly the little furry body disappeared. It was totally cool and
disgusting all at once. "One time I had me a two-headed snake!
You shoulda seen that weird thing."

"What did you do with it?" I said excitedly, hoping maybe I
could trade him some fish or something for a two-headed snake.
I was just sure it could be some kind of Guinness record.

"Oh dat poor ting didn't make it through the first week. It
was a freak youse know. Nature took care of it!"

"SHOOT!" I said too loud out loud and then covered my
mouth.

He dropped another mouse into the glass cage. In a blur, the
same thing happened with a quick strike, coil and the mouse
was about to go in the business end of the snake. Then we
moved on to the next cage. This time the shopkeeper pulled out a
small rat.

"Check out me Anaconda; now dis one ere's an eatin'
machine!"

"Have you ever heard of an African Rock Python?" I asked
excited to tell him what I knew.

"Well, I 'ave now. What about em?" He muttered through his
cigar.

"They say it's so evil it comes out of the egg striking at
anything that moves." I watched him dropping rodents into cages
and felt half sorry for the furry critters, but even more sorry
that I didn't get feed the snakes myself.

"Well dat ders a purdy mean baby." He sneered.

# CHAPTER TWELVE

# NO MORE MEAN MRS. RICKLES

A FOR SALE sign went up in the Rickles' yard. I never thought in a million years I would say this, but I am kind of sorry to see her go. Ever since Mr. Rickles died, we have left her alone and she us. It just didn't seem right to prank someone who had such a sad thing happen, even if she was really mean.

She doesn't yell at us anymore when we walk down the ditch behind her house, and for the first time since I can remember no one smashed down her corn crop right before she could harvest.

I never thought it was fun at the time to have her yelling at us, but there was something exciting about it. We would always be trying to figure out if today was the day she would scream at us from her back porch.

Her son Ryan never came outside much anymore. He never hung around with us before, maybe because we are a few years older, but we would see him with some of the younger boys riding bikes and even sometimes playing games of catch in the road. On rare occasions he and his friends would come to the streetlight to join in on a game of hide-n-seek, but they were always the first to get called in before the games really even got started.

He never played hide-n-seek or anything anymore, and every so often last summer when I would short-cut down the ditch I would see him in his back yard just sitting and staring. I felt sorry for the kid, and wondered with them selling their house, where they would go. Probably anywhere that they didn't have a constant reminder of Mr. Rickles.

*☺*

There were two ladies in the neighborhood who had converted one of their basements into a Beauty Parlor next door to Mrs. Rickles' house. The women would gather there under these huge, alien-head hair dryers to gossip, drink coffee and share stories. One of the ladies with CUTe-AND-CURL had three daughters, the middle one, the cutest, was my age.

I was just sitting in my room thinking about how dark mean Mrs. Rickles' house was. I could see her house from my bedroom window, and there was always just one light on in the house at night. Mom said Ryan has gone to stay with his grandparents for a few weeks while they tried to sell their house, and that he is really, really sad. I can't believe that he is just a few years younger than me and has already lost his dad. I don't know what I would do without my dad. I overheard Dad talking to some of the neighbors about the Rickles, and it made me feel really bad.

Mom and some of her friends down at the CUTe-AND-CURL hair shop have made meals for the Rickles, but no one is there to eat them. I feel bad that I have always been so mean to mean Mrs. Rickles. She is not nice to us, never has been, but that doesn't stop my dad from wanting to do things for her. As a matter of fact, the other day when Andy and I were heading up to the hill we'd be sledding on soon, I saw Dad over at the Rickles' house doing some yard work. It made me sad.

So here I am now in my bedroom drawing a card for mean Mrs. Rickles. Mom was talking at dinner about how everyone in the neighborhood should make an effort.

Carl just rolled his eyes and muttered under his breath. "I'm not doing anything for that mean old bat!"

Mom heard him, but pretended she didn't. She had a really hurt look on her face, like she was totally disappointed that he would feel that way about someone who had just had such a bad thing happen to her.

The truth is, I mostly agreed with Carl but didn't have the heart to tell Mom. So, to make Mom feel better, I am making this dumb card, and the more I worked on it, the better it is making me feel. I hope Mom likes it, and I hope Mean Mrs. Rickles likes it, too. It was all I could do not to write "Dear Mean Mrs. Rickles". After all, she tried to have Frisky taken away, and that is the lowest of all lows.

My card has pretty flowers on it. I was tempted to draw some corn on it, on account of the annual corn stomp we had all done to her to get her back for her meanness, but I didn't.

Dear Mrs. Rickles,

I am so sorry to hear
that you lost someone so dear
I think it is sad, I think it is bad
I hope this card makes that clear.

Sincerely,
Gabriel Peters

P.S.

I feel pretty rotten about the
stuff we used to do to you.

Sorry.

# CHAPTER THIRTEEN

# THE FROG FARM

My dad is a total weather nut, and he likes to try to predict what is going to happen, especially when it comes to changing seasons. This morning at the breakfast table he was talking about how by now we usually are spending more time indoors, but that we are having a very unusual Indian summer. That meant it felt mostly like summer instead of autumn.

We weren't the only ones feeling it. Dad was talking about the animals in the neighborhood, and how you could usually tell when seasons were really changing by how the reptiles responded. This year there were tons of snakes still darting around Dad's garden, and his peas were still growing. I thought about the way you usually didn't hear the frogs croaking across the road in the pond by now, but they were still busy over there and croaking into the night just like in summertime — which I knew because I still had my window open in my room at night. I liked the fact that it was warm, but sitting in a classroom when it still feels like summer is murder!

Later, I told Andy about my idea to have the World's Biggest Frog Farm while we were dangling our feet of the end of the tree house, both busy whittling sticks and watching the peelings float down to the ground like snow.

"I mean, how many frogs in one basement would it take to get into the *Guinness Book of World Records* Book?"

"In y-y-your basement?" Andy stared at me curiously.

"Yeah, you know, I got tons of fish bowls and stuff to keep 'em in."

Andy looked at me like I was losing my marbles.

"Come on man, I could really use your help!" I was so excited at my new idea that I was dancing around, wiggling my hips. I almost fell out of the tree house.

Andy reached out and caught my arm and pulled. "Y-You sure this could w-work? I mean, m-m-most of your ideas do, b-b-but..."

"Yeah, we could collect like ten thousand, get into the book and then sell them to the guy at the Pet Shop. We'd be rich!"

"Wh-Why would h-he buy f-frogs f-from us if he could j-j-just catch them?"

I laughed, "Can you see that funny guy chasing frogs around in the lake?"

Andy started to laugh, "W-Weren't you g-g-gonna do this with f-fish already?"

"Shut up! Fish are wimpy; the least little chlorine or something in the water kills them. Frogs are *tough*!"

"T-Tough?"

"Yeah, remember that one time that garter snake was eating that frog and I pulled it out of the snake's mouth, peeling half of its skin off its body? That frog lived the rest of the summer in the pond! I remember seeing it on the banks when we were drifting around on the inner-tubes."

Andy just looked at me like I was crazy, telling some weird frog story. "Yeah, s-so?"

"So, they're tough, like I said!" I barked. I pushed on Andy's shoulder, like I was going to push him out of the tree house, "You in on my frog farm or not?" I growled.

"Hey, knock it off!" Andy slapped my arm, "Wh-Where d-do you w-want to go frog huntin'? I m-mean, there are s-so many frogs at T-Tunnel Number Three this y-year!"

We spent so much time at all three tunnels under the railroad tracks, fishing, frog hunting and just hanging out. "I bet we could get enough out of the boggy field to do it! Let's go to the old barn and see if it's flooded," I said.

"Okay, I-I'm in!" he squealed. "B-But, I-let's do a l-little fishing f-first, okay?

"Okay..." I agreed, mostly because Andy is always game to do whatever, whenever. But the truth was I was pretty anxious to get going on the frog farm idea.

We folded up our pocketknives, climbed down the steps of the tree and then we were off to fish for a while. Then we would start to set a record, and then we'd get really rich.

Frisky and Friskier had been lying in the shade, and when they noticed we were on the move again, they both jumped up and started wagging their tails hard. Friskier shook really hard, trying to get wood shavings off her fur. They both cheerfully followed behind us, sniffing every inch of grass along the ditch.

Frisky took off after a jackrabbit, chasing it for a long time before it went under a fence and he couldn't get to it. He whined and scratched at the fence and then just gave up. He rejoined us and went back to sniffing.

We walked all the way down the ditch, past Mean Mrs. Rickles' house, which was now dark and empty. I never thought I would miss her crabbing at us, but I kind of did. Then we cut through a neighbor's backyard into this field that has this really cool old, spooky, broken-down barn right in the middle.

As I looked across the field at the barn that was presently sunk about one foot in the bog, it made me remember one night when everyone was down at the streetlight playing hide-n-seek. Finally we all collapsed in the yard next to the streetlight and started telling stories. That was the night I heard Jesse James and some other Old West cowboys had stayed in that old barn. The story went that there was a shoot-out in the barn, and the cowboys who got killed then are supposed to be haunting the barn to this very day, or actually night. So, at night you can see the cowboy ghosts up in the loft — or, at least that's how the story goes. I have a feeling sometimes the barn will play its way into a dare-off, that is if it doesn't get knocked down in one of the big tornado winds we get in the spring.

Sometimes when it rains really hard, like it has been lately, the whole field around the barn turns into a swampy mess, with about five inches of green-tinted water. I don't know where the frogs came from all of a sudden, but as we were sloshing through the marshy field I noticed that there were like a million little frogs, about the size of a quarter, everywhere. With all the water and the sun beating down, it was suddenly like a thousand degrees. The air felt thick, like there was as much humidity as there is in a closed-up bathroom when you take a really hot shower. I was sweating and so was Andy. The water didn't even feel at all cold, but kind of like bathtub water.

As we ventured across the flooded field, there were a million frogs all ribbiting and croaking at the same time. Every so often

a huge bullfrog would belch out its loud croak and the field would
go silent for a moment, then the little cheeps and ribbits filled
the air again. The sound grew crazy loud, the kind of loud that
fills your ears so much it ends up being kind of quiet. It's hard
to explain how something so loud can be quiet at the same time,
but I guess it's because it blocks out every other sound and kind
of puts your ears in a trance. Anyway, that's how it felt to me
— like my ears were in a trance.

These big white birds with really long legs were circling
overhead, and some were walking through the tall, wet grass
poking, poking, poking and then lifting their beaks straight up
high as the frog or minnow they caught slithered down their
throats. Then they'd call out to the other birds, BRAAAACK,
which is probably how birds brag when they do something better
than their friends. Frogs were jumping and hopping all over the
place, and then I saw several water snakes skimming across
the top of the swampy water. They were probably having frog
sandwiches, without the bread, for lunch. I felt little tickles and
bumps on my bare legs as water skippers, tadpoles and minnows
glided up and down these little river passages that cut through
the tall weeds flowing downhill toward our fishing lake.

Frisky was walking through the field, but lifting his legs really
funny because he didn't like the sticky, wet grass. He started
sniffing around with his nose low to the top of the water, and
then suddenly he gave out a little yelp and jumped straight up
in the air and splashed a little. A long yellow and black striped
snake was gliding away from where Frisky was crouching down
in the water rubbing his nose with his front paws. I figured the
snake must have snapped at him and clamped down on his
nose, but I knew garter snakes weren't poisonous. 'Come here
boy!' I called out to him, and he slowly moved over my way, but
he was still lifting each paw up high and it looked really funny.

Friskier wasn't bothered by the water or weeds or really
anything. She was hopping around the bog, curiously watching
frog after frog, her head darting with their every move, then she
started barking at the snake.

I was carrying my fishing pole and a fish bucket, which

I always keep the fish I want to take home to fry in, and suddenly a brainstorm hit me. "HEY, ANDY!"

He was sloshing about twenty feet away from me trying to catch a yellow and red snake. "Wh-What?"

"Let's start the frog farm now!"

"What...? Wh-Why?"

"To get in the record book and to make a million dollars, you dunce-orama!"

"H-How're we g-g-gonna make that m-much money?"

"I told you, the Pet Shop guy. He gives me twenty-five cents for every goldfish, and I bet he would give us double that for frogs!"

"Correction, he *would* give *you* twenty-five cents, *if*, you ever d-d-delivered a single l-live g-goldfish to him."

"Wow, you too, huh, Andy? The world is so full of pestimics!"

"What's a p-pestimic?" Andy wrinkled up his nose like he just smelled something terrible.

"Someone who's negative about stuff all the time, I think." I watched a pinkish-white bird with really long legs peck a frog out of the bog and head back up into the sky.

"P-Pestimic? Y-You sure th-that's the right w-w-word?"

"Duh, ya dummy! Pestimic, look it up if you don't believe me." I shook my head. I was passing by the ghostly barn, and even though it was the middle of the day, I walked way around it.

"B-By the way, I'm n-not negative! I didn't say I d-d-didn't believe you," Andy stammered.

"Come on, let's fill my bucket with these little frogs and see how many we can get today!" I pleaded.

"Nah, I w-want to go f-fishing n-now instead." Andy stayed firm.

"Fine. But when I have a million bucks, don't say I wasn't going to let you in on it."

"A m-million bucks for f-frogs? Give m-me a break." Andy shrugged and started walking toward the tunnels.

"Whatever... you'll see." I started filling my bucket about a quarter way with water so my frogs would feel like they were

still at home as I put them in my bucket. There were some tiny little fish trapped in the murky water in the bucket. Maybe the frogs would have them for lunch, or maybe I could put them in one of my fish bowls and see what they grew up to be if the frogs didn't eat them. I set the bucket down into the mud and started scooping up frogs. For every three I got in there one hopped out, so it took me a long time to get it filled up the way I wanted.

I saw a blur out of the corner of my eye as I was bent down trying to get a hold of a frog that was hopping along a long, green leaf. I stood up and stretched my back and watched T-Bone running pell-mell down the gravel road and heading out into the field. "Man that kid can run!" I said out loud to nobody but the frogs and snakes. I wondered to myself just what T-Bone was running from or running to. "HEY, T-BONE!" I yelled at the top of my lungs, but I guess he couldn't hear me because he just kept running in the same direction. I needed to talk to him about joining The Secret Brotherhood of Boys. I would have to stop off at the U-Pump-It soon to talk to him.

I was whooping and hollering and splashing around chasing down a hundred frogs when Andy came sloshing back through the foot-deep green water.

"Okay, so if I h-help, we sp-split the d-dough even, r-right?"

"Sure, Andy, whatever you say." I smiled, knowing that he couldn't resist trying his hand at making a frog fortune either.

When we had about a hundred in a bucket I covered the top of the bucket with the net I used to scoop the fish out of the water when we caught them. The water was sloshing the whole way home, and I had to keep stopping and switching arms on account of how heavy a hundred frogs and water are. Frisky and Friskier followed behind us slowly. They were really hot, and they were probably disappointed that we didn't end up at their favorite fishing hole, where they usually went a bit downstream and waded around looking at stuff.

Andy's brother Johnny met us on the road.

"Hey lamebrain," he said to Andy, "Mom wants you. You are in BIG trouble!"

"Yeah, f-for wh-what, J-John B-Boy?" Andy asked.

"For being an idiot! Don't call me that!" Johnny punched him on the arm and then walked on to no doubt meet my brother and the band of goons.

Andy swatted back at him, missing and muttering, "J-Jerk!" Then he said, "I'll c-come up to your house if I can, G-G-Gabe. D-Dangit, we should've j-just stayed with our f-fishing plan,

cause then t—that b-b-bonehead b-brother of m-mine wouldn't
have f-found us! B-But, I s-still get some of the m-money for
collecting, r-r-right?"

"Yuh," I answered, disappointed that Andy had to go home.
But as he headed off for home, I thought to myself, "I have
bigger fish to fry today than just fishing...." It was a goofy
saying, and even more goofy because I thought of it relating to
going fishing, but it made me laugh. I crack myself up so much
sometimes.

I sneaked into the garage, and then into the room where my
zoo is through the door leading in from the garage. The big empty
aquarium that Mr. Povich had given Dad when he was moving
was sitting there empty, hoping to have a box turtle or better
yet a long snake someday. Today though it was going to have
about a hundred froggies living in it.

I started singing this funny countdown song that I
remembered from preschool, "Ninety-nine little speckled frogs
living on a speckled log, eating the most delicious bugs, yum,
yum... One frog jumped in the pool, where it was nice and cool...
ninety-eight little speckled frogs...." It was really only five little
speckled frogs that you use your fingers to count down with,
but I liked singing it with ninety-nine on account of it taking
longer.

I had started to pour the bucket into the aquarium when
the little frogs all started hopping out and onto the floor. I set
the pail down and tried to catch two that had gotten loose and
were headed for the bathroom. My net fell off the top of the
bucket, and all of a sudden all of the frogs were jumping and
hopping out and across the downstairs floor. I didn't know what
to do. Every time I caught one and put it in the aquarium or
bucket, another one or two or three escaped. There must have
been sixty frogs going in every direction but the direction I
wanted them to go. Then suddenly Flop was running around the
basement floor chasing the frogs and stepping on them with his
big Flop feet and flipping them around with his mouth.

"Flopster, stop it!"

Flop ignored me and continued chasing the little frogs around the floor like he did his fake mouse toys.

Pretty soon Kitty was down in the basement catching frogs in her mouth and stepping on them with her paw. Then Friskier joined in. She started lapping a frog up and then started shaking her head and trying to spit it out, but pretty soon she was trying again to catch one with her mouth. Frisky was lying at the top of the stairs. He was the only one who had listened to me when I told him to stay, but he was whining and wanted to come down and eat the frogs, too. Pretty soon, there was frog mush all over the floor, for I had stepped on a bunch of them trying to keep the dog and cats away. By the time I was done, fourteen frogs were in the aquarium and the rest were frog squish.

Of course that was when Mom came down and saw frog guts and muddy water all over the floor. She yelled, "WHAT A MESS! GABRIEL, WHAT ON EARTH ARE YOU DOING DOWN HERE NOW?"

"Well, I was building a frog farm!"

"A what?"

"A FROG FARM!" I said, a bit more determined than I had meant to.

'Oh, never mind! Just clean up this mess, young man!' Mom said, her hands firmly on her hips.

After I was done mopping the floor and washing the walls Mom came down and inspected. She stood with her hands on her hips 'Well, you did a nice job cleaning up. What on earth are you doing with those little frogs in there?' Mom pointed at the end of the huge aquarium where the tiny frogs were huddled together, trying hard to climb up the slippery glass wall. 'Gabriel, those little frogs are wild animals. They won't survive in there. What do you feed them?'

I just shrugged, but with that I scooped the frogs into a large plastic cup and carried them out to the ditch to let them go.

I sang, 'Fourteen little speckled frogs, floating down the ditch today... I just watched my record swim away...'

And that was the end of my frog farm fortune plans.

Just then I heard a loud voice coming my way.

'What's up, G-Gabe? I'm back!' It was Andy jogging up the ditch.

'I'm going back to raising fish, Andy. At least they don't hop!' I threw the cup into the water and watched it float down the ditch, and then I started to follow it. I picked up a long, skinny branch that was on the side of the ditch and pushed the cup around, following the water. Andy kept following me.

'Wh-What happened?' Andy asked.

'I don't want to talk about it,' I sulked.

Andy looked at me curiously. 'P-Peters, you're w-weird!'

'Look who's talking, butt face,' I retorted.

Andy laughed, "B-B-Butt face? Okay, l-lame dunce."

"Oh, good one poopsquash!" I answered.

At once we both looked at each other and said, "Poopsquash?" Then we both broke out laughing really hard.

Andy grabbed a stick, jumped to the opposite side of the ditch and started moving the cup around, too. Pretty soon it was like we were playing a game of cup hockey in the ditch, calling each other ridiculous names and trying to move the cup from one side to the other and keeping each other from doing it. No one knew the rules, so we made them up as we went along.

After the cup got sucked through the grate on the side of Mars Boulevard, we ran across the road and waited for it to come out. We waited a long time and it never came out, so it must have gotten stuck on something in the ditch under the road. We got tired of waiting, so we walked back up the ditch toward my house, smacking each other on the back of the legs with the sticks and running after each other, trying to avoid getting hit.

We climbed up into the tree house and I told him the whole story about the defunct frog farm. By the time I was done it was even funny to me. Andy told me about how when he got home his mom wasn't even looking for him. His dumb brother made the whole thing up and Andy was planning on getting back at him. Speaking of revenge; we started planning how to sabotage our big brother's "secret fort" again.

"What if we dug up a huge red ant pile and put them down in the bottom again?" I asked.

"Oh man, by the time they figured out what was biting them...."

It went on like that for an hour, and then we really did go fishing. All the way down there we called out the red anthills when we saw them. We spotted five really big ones, and planned out how we would collect the ants without getting bit ourselves this time, and then we started laughing as we remembered the time Murph got all bit up and naked over the red ant prank. We also talked about when the Secret Brotherhood would finally start the Guinness record for the spit pool.

"Hey Andy, what do you think about T-Bone becoming an official member of our club?"

"I w-was thinking the s-same thing!" Andy smiled.

☺

That night Andy called me to tell me that "pestimic" was not a real word.

"Th-The word you're l-looking f-for is p-pessim-m-mistic. Let me r-read to you from the d-dictionary," he said, clearing his throat like he was being all official. "It's an adjective, a p-p-pessimistic outlook on l-life; gloomy, n-negative, d-d-defeatist, downbeat, cynical, b-bleak, fatalistic, dark, black, d-d-despairing, d-despondent, depressed, hopeless; suspicious, d-distrustful, d-doubting. I knew your d-dumb word p-pestimic wasn't a r-real word! T-Told ya!"

"Wow, you showed me, you poopsquash! Is that in your dictionary? Poopsquash?" We both started cracking up again. "Maybe you can have the world's record for being the biggest poopsquash!"

"G-Gabe, I'm g-going to squash y-you l-l-like a b-bug tomorrow!"

"I'm shaking in my boots, dude! See you then! Wait, Andy, why wait until tomorrow? Come down and sleep in my tent tonight!"

"I'll have to see if M-Mom will l-let me," Andy said sadly.

"Oh man, Andy, I forgot. I won't be around tomorrow. I'm going to that Anderman kid's birthday party. So you have to spend the night tonight!" I stressed.

"You d-dumb p-p-poopsquash! I'll ask M-Mom if I c-can sleep in your t-tent!" Andy barked and hung up.

I hung up and flopped myself down into the lower bunk and started to read Where The Red Fern Grows.

# OSTENTATIOUS?

I had been in Brandon's class at St. Joe's. He still went there, but I didn't. So I was shocked to find a letter to me from Brandon on the kitchen table. I figured 'out of sight, out of mind' as mom would say. It was for a birthday party.

The invite was in a small but very fancy envelope, with hand-drawn balloons and *YOU ARE INVITED* in primary colors written right under a fancy monogram on the stationary, which had ANDERMAN in bright blue letters. I had seen kids put these invitations on each other's desks at my old school, but this is the first birthday party invitation I ever received from a kid at St. Joe's school, and that includes *when* I went there! Wouldn't it figure I would get one when I didn't even go there anymore?

Brandon was always pretty nice to me at St. Joe's, even back in the time when the kids weren't too nice to me at all. I know Brandon had probably invited me since our dads work together at the college, but I really don't care why he invited me. I was just excited because it is a party at the country club, where all the rich, fancy people in town lived. I'd heard the Andermans had a maid and a full-time cook. They have to have a cook so Brandon's mom could work in her art studio, which is this really big building behind their house that is almost as big as my whole house.

The guys who live in Brandon's neighborhood and go to St. Joe's would always talk about going to Brandon's house, and how it's like being at a restaurant. They say you can choose whatever you want to eat, and the cook gets it out of these giant freezers in the basement and makes it for you. One time they were talking about a sleepover where they tested the cook by throwing out all kinds of wild ingredients and dishes they wanted to try from their past fancy vacations, and the cook was able to make it all happen! I'd felt so jealous when they were talking about that, because I thought I would never get to do that and here I had been invited to the BIG PARTY.

I thought about how one day, when I was in the crazy Batwoman's class and invitations were all over the place except for on my desk, I had been daydreaming that I had been invited personally to be the special guest of honor, which meant I didn't need a paper invite like all the other boys. I must have been daydreaming about this for a long time because when Sister Mary Claire came back into the room from getting some quiz copies, she flashed me a dirty look, which froze me in my spot. "Mr. Peters, aren't you supposed to be reading?" I turned my attention back to the boring textbook on my desk. A few of the kids were chuckling that I had been caught once again staring out the window, "lost in my own little world" as Sister Mary Claire always said.

Brandon Anderman was one of the most popular fourth graders (he's now in fifth) not just in my old school but everywhere in my hometown. His family is totally famous. He and his brothers always win the soapbox derby, the spelling bees, and the coupon contests (where kids go door to door to collect coupons for the big shopping trip, which is for the poor. Every grade gathers coupons and does bake sales, and the older kids do car washes and stuff like that. All of it is to earn money to spend on the poor people who need help. The coupons let us get like ten times as much stuff for the money we earn.) and at Field Day, the Anderman boys sweep the ribbons. They must have a room full of ribbons and trophies just to hold everything they win every year.

Brandon's family is always in the newspaper for doing something great. They are super rich on account that his dad is some kind of inventor and a teacher at the University, too, and his mom is an artist who was just on the front page of the newspaper with this huge sculpture that was going to Paris, France. She was going there, too, and I think the newspaper reporter was going with her to show us all what it was like. WOW, I cannot even imagine what it would be like to go to Paris, France, and to have all those people excited about your sculpture. The sculpture looked really cool, too! The newspaper picture of it made it look like this giant alien dinosaur that was eating a little man with a funny hat.

The other thing is that one time Brandon's mom was a model or something in New York City before she had kids, and that is why she is so pretty. My mom said that is why Brandon and his brothers are so good-looking. I never thought any boy was good-looking, but everyone else always talks about that when it comes to the Anderman family. When I was going to St. Joe's, all of us kids had to wear uniforms to school, but the Anderman boys always wore a kind of uniform even when they weren't in school. A kind of uniform, because no other kid wears fancy clothes to play outside games like them. Their mom shops in the big city, and their clothes look like the kind you see in the magazines. Their maid even irons their jeans, and they aren't ever allowed to get dirty, which if you ask me is sad. I wouldn't trade my fishing, hunting, and digging forts for all the money in the world. Mom even jokes about how dirty my clothes are. She says that she can't decide if she wants to wash them or just burn them in the backyard.

The photographer on Main Street downtown has this giant picture of the Anderman family hanging in his window with their dogs and horses and their big house in the background, which my dad says is *ostentatious*. I looked up the word in the dictionary and this is what my dad meant: **ostentatious** (adjective) characterized by vulgar or pretentious display; designed to impress or attract notice: *an ostentatious display of wealth*; showy, pretentious, conspicuous, flamboyant, gaudy, brash, vulgar, loud, extravagant, fancy, ornate, over elaborate; informal description: flash, flashy, splashy, over-the-top, glitzy, ritzy. Using that word

makes sense now; it seems like everything the Anderman family does is ostentatious, but even though it makes me jealous, I don't think of it as a bad thing.

Dad doesn't usually say too much about other people, especially bad stuff, but when the Anderman family came up because of the invitation he said, "I mean, who do they think they are, *royalty*? Anderman is so full of himself. He always brags in the faculty meetings and I get quite tired of it." I think Dad sounds a little jealous, too.

The Andermans live in their really big house out in the Country Club. It has giant pillars on the front so it looks like one of those mansions you see by the President's house in Washington, D.C.. I know it looks like this even though I haven't ever been in Brandon's house, because it is the house everyone in town drives out to see at Christmas because of the huge light display they have every year. You can see it glowing at the top of the hill from miles around. They have this wishing well with the elves and reindeer that move to Christmas songs, and a real sleigh in the front yard. On Christmas day their fancy prize Appaloosa horses pull all of the country club kids around the neighborhood in the sleigh.

Also in their yard are these huge sculptures. Mrs. Anderman has made all of these cool holiday sculptures that they put out in the yard that must weigh like a ton each to move around, but the Andermans are so rich they hire some company to decorate their house and move those things there.

Thinking about how incredible the Anderman's house looks at Christmas makes me think about how one of my favorite things during the holidays is to decorate the outside of the house with Dad and Carl. Even Carl is in a good mood when we do that! Dad brings his little 8-track player out. and plays corny Bing Crosby Christmas music while we hang strings of lights on the house and in the trees and put out the Santa and Frosty the Snowman figures that we made out of plain old plywood and paint. Ours doesn't look anything like the Anderman's house, but it's cool anyway. At night the lights glow and reflect off of the snow, and from my bedroom window the colors on the snow look just like they do on a Christmas tree. Mom and Dad sometimes joke about how the Andermans are on the other side of the tracks, which is weird because their house is in the opposite side of town from the railroad tracks. Somehow I think Mom and Dad mean something else, but I keep forgetting to ask.

All of Brandon's brothers are the oldest in their classes. Their parents hold them back so they will be the oldest, and can "be a leader," which is what the Anderman brothers brag about. Brandon's older brother thinks if they are older than everyone else, they can boss everyone around. So Brandon is turning eleven years old, almost a year before any of us. He was held back, but no one EVER teases him about it, because he is as big as the sixth graders and punches hard. I think even the biggest bully at St. Joe's is probably afraid of him.

I know about how bad Brandon's punching can be, because he's punched me on the shoulder a couple of times when he was trying to act real cool with his friends. But usually he's pretty nice to me.

The difference with Brandon was that one time he caught up with me in the boy's room at my old school and said, "You know,

I was just kidding with that whole arm punch thing. I was just trying to include you. We all just do that to each other all the time. You can punch me back if you want."

I just stood there with my mouth hanging open. Brandon Anderman had actually addressed me personally. He really was nice, sort of. And he was apologizing in his way — not that I would ever consider punching him back..

"Uh, nah, that's okay. It wasn't a big deal."

Just then this other kid, a big bully kind of kid named Trevor, and another stuffy Country Club kid, walked into the boy's room. "Hey, Brandon, what's up?" They all did this funny handshake thing, a secret handshake I wished I could learn, as ice filled my veins. I had never been anywhere close to this Trevor kid when he didn't say something mean to me or push me around. "Get out of my bathroom, you gimpy freak!" he suddenly yelled at me.

Brandon barked at him, "Hey, lay off Peters. He's cool."

Trevor stood there looking embarrassed. I think it was because he was trying to impress Brandon by being mean to me, because I wasn't big and tough like them, and it just backfired. I decided that day that I really did like Brandon Anderman, even if other kids thought he was stuck-up.

"I was just joking around, jeez Anderman, cool it!" Trevor finally shot back. And with that, Trevor punched Brandon in the arm, and Brandon punched me in the arm, just to show them I was just like them. I punched Brandon back, and he gave me this funny look, which I wasn't sure was a mad look or not.

Brandon was the town's primary school pull-up champion. He beat everyone all the way up to sixth grade in all four of the schools, except for his older brother Johnny. Also, Brandon's soapbox derby car had won three years in a row in the big Boy Scout/Cub Scout town jamboree, just like his brother's.

So this was going to be cool — to be one of Brandon Anderman's friends. I just wish it could have happened when I was still at St. Joe's.

CHAPTER FIFTEEN

# THE BIG PARTY

Mom was so excited when I got the fancy invitation to Brandon Anderman's party that she took me to the shopping mall right away to pick out the right gift. She made such a big deal about it. I wanted to buy him a few Hot Wheels cars, but Mom looked at the three cars I had picked out for Brandon and said, "Yes, Gabe, those are nice. Now, let's see, which track should we get with them?"

"What?" We were getting him the cars and a track, too? I didn't understand; that seemed like a lot of money, and Mom didn't even know Brandon. I mean, I could understand if the gift were for one of my really good buddies— though we had never spent anywhere near that much for them— but why would we get so much for someone we hardly knew?

Mom just grabbed the big track with the loop-to-loop and the motorized bridge. I had been saving my allowance for a year for this track, and Mom was just going to get it for someone who was almost a complete stranger and who I didn't even go to school with anymore? "Mom, what are you doing?"

Mom grabbed a few buildings that were made to set around the track, a filling station, and a garage that would hold up to ten cars.

Now I was getting steamed. I had asked for this very setup for Christmas last year, but Mom had explained that it was too much money. "Mom, what are you doing?"

"What kind of candy do you think Brandon would like?"

"What?" I couldn't believe my ears. Mom was getting ready to spend a fortune on Brandon Anderman's birthday. All of this for a kid who already had basically everything? It didn't make any sense to me... until I showed up for the party, in the neighborhood of mansions.

I was one of the only kids there who didn't belong to the Country Club, and man oh man, you should have seen those presents stacked up in the living room. Mine, though it was stuffed with the coolest things in the world, was the smallest box, and as

I would find out by the end of the party, the cheapest by far.

Trevor Jacobsen, that jerky kid from my old school, walked up the present table and looked around. "Which one did you bring, Peters?"

I proudly pointed at the box containing my dream birthday gift.

"That tiny box? Mine was so big we couldn't even wrap it. My old man got this train set that's like the size of a whole room. I whined so hard, he got me one, too. So, what's in that tiny box of yours, your old Barbie dolls?"

Trevor laughed really hard at his own insult, but I noticed none of the other guys who were standing around were laughing with him.

Just when I was going to tell him off, some of the moms walked up and told us to get ready to have some fun. Trevor put his arm around my neck like we were good old buddies, and then when they weren't looking squeezed as hard as he could. It really hurt. I never thought someone wouldn't think a Hot Wheels track and gear wasn't cool, but when you have everything and all you have to do is whine to get it, well, I guess it wouldn't seem very cool.

One kid brought Brandon this remote control truck that I know for a fact was advertised in the paper for seventy-five dollars. I calculated how long I would have to save up for it. Even if I kept my allowance, earned extra money cleaning the dog lady's backyard, sold tons and tons of newspapers and seeds and everything else my mail-in company sent me to go door to door with, it would still take me until next Christmas to come close to having enough to buy it.

Before the party, I had heard Mom and Dad arguing in the kitchen about how much Mom had spent for Brandon's presents. Mom was whispering, but it was loud and clear: "Honey, I don't want Gabe to be embarrassed. You know what kind of money the Andermans have. I mean, what would it look like if all the other boys showed up with fancy, expensive gifts and Gabe had three Hot Wheel cars? This is his chance for acceptance. You know how hard it has been on him."

"I'm not sure I want my son *accepted* or in with that crowd of highfalutin stuffed shirts..."

"Now, *you* don't even know them. They may be very fine boys, and it wouldn't hurt Gabriel to have friends other than the kids in *this* neighborhood."

"*This* neighborhood?"

"That's not how I meant it to sound. Let's just drop it, okay?"

I walked in to interrupt the fight. "What's highfalutin mean?"

Dad threw a dictionary my way and started muttering to himself, so as not to make Mom mad, but I heard him say something like Mom was always trying to keep up with the Joneses and it wasn't necessary. I didn't know who the Joneses were, but they probably lived in a big mansion like the Andermans.

I felt bad that my getting invited to this party was causing Mom and Dad to fight. I just thought to myself that if one of my friends brought me three Hot Wheel cars to my party, I would do a back flip, and if someone gave me that track and buildings and candy that Mom had bought for Brandon, I would faint right in my tracks. But if someone gave me the remote-control truck that Brandon got, I would scream so loud I wouldn't be able to talk for days.

I flipped through Dad's dictionary and found *highfalutin*. It means attempting to impress by affecting greater importance, talent, culture, etc., than is actually possessed. Actually, almost the same as ostentatious: affected, showy; overambitious, pompous, artificial, inflated, overblown, high-sounding, flowery, grandiose, elaborate, extravagant, flamboyant, ornate, grandiloquent, magniloquent, sophomoric; informal flashy, pretentious, la-di-da. (La-di-da? That one cracks me up. Who puts la-di-da in a dictionary?)

So, the party had really started now, and all of the boys who hang around together at school were clustered around the trampoline in the backyard near the pool that was closed for the season, which is near the tennis courts and the stables where the horses were running around. I couldn't believe how big the house was inside, and all of the fancy furniture and glass stuff on all of the shelves. It looked like a museum. You could fit my whole house, garage and all, into their living room. I guess in this neighborhood when you had a birthday party for a kid, the adults had a party at the same time.

Mr. and Mrs. Anderman seemed very nice, but I thought they were dressed too fancy for a kid's party. Mr. Anderman was wearing one of those all-black suits with the fancy shiny stripe going down the leg of his pants, and Mrs. Anderman was wearing a fancy dress, like the kind my mom wears when they go to some really fancy schmancy university party. She looked like a movie star, and everyone kept going on and on about how pretty her dress was.

All of the men seemed to crowd around Mr. Anderman listening to story after story. I heard Mr. Anderman talking to another dad about his famous invention: "Well, someday each house will have at least one. I had no idea when I was toying with the idea that it would catch on so fast. What a great patent. It should make a lot of people a lot of money, so you just let me know if you are still interested in investing. Don't wait too long...." The other man seemed really impressed.

Brandon was dressed up in a tie and everything, just like at my old school, and so were all of the other boys, except me and this kid named Izzy, whose family came from another country. I heard he had been invited because Izzy's dad worked in the same department at the university as Brandon's dad, and that Izzy and Brandon had never even met before the party.

I could tell Izzy felt totally out of place. I went up to him and introduced myself, but it was hard to understand what he was saying because of his accent, and he seemed to want to be left alone, so I did.

Izzy and I were wearing jeans and old t-shirts, which is what you are supposed to wear to a party where there might be food-fights or wrestling or running through the hose or whatever else usually happens in my neighborhood. Mom had come here with me too, and she was wearing a lot of makeup that she usually only wears when she and my dad go 'out on the town'. She was

wearing some new shoes, her favorite stirrup pants, which are
stretchy pants girls wear with a rubber band thingy that goes
around their foot, and a blouse I had never seen her wear before.
I always got a laugh out of her calling them 'stirrup pants', since
that was what you would wear to ride a horse. Maybe Mom was
planning on riding one of the Anderman's fancy horses?

After we were at the party though for just a few minutes, Mom
whispered in my ear that she was leaving and would be back
to get me later. When I asked her why she was leaving so fast,
she said something about being underdressed, and her face was
kind of red. That made me kind of sad, because I knew my mom
had been looking forward to going along with me to the fancy-
schmancy party. Dad had been invited to come too, but he had
complained that the last thing he wanted to do on his weekend
was spend it with 'a bunch of puffed-up, dressed-up, stuffed
shirts from the university.' I felt bad for Mom. I could tell she
really wanted to enjoy the party, but it didn't seem like she had
been able to do that at all.

*⊘*

The Andermans had hired a clown to paint faces, and a
reptile guy was back by the horse barn ready to put on a big
show. I planned to stay as far away from the clown as I could,
since the last clown I was near made me wet my pants at the
circus in front of million people, but I don't want to relive that
for even a minute. The reptile guy had cages full of snakes, lizards,
toads, and this really cool turtle with a long snout. There was this
big argument among the boys about whether turtles are reptiles
or not. I know they are because I might be a veterinarian when
I grow up and I would want to work with reptiles all the time, so
I know a ton about them. But I didn't join in on the argument,
because other times when I let on about how much I know, it
just made the other boys mad.

The reptile guy was showing all of us the toads and lizards,
and when he got to the green anaconda snake something really
funny happened. When he pulled it out, Trevor started backing
away and screaming. He was so scared of the snake. It was kind

of funny to see a kid who always acts all puffed up and tough being the one that is a scaredy-cat of a snake, especially one that isn't even venomous. I guess he could be acting this way on account of me telling Trevor and a bunch of the boys that snakes, like bulls, liked to attack the color red, and Trevor was wearing a red shirt. I told them how an anaconda squeezes its prey until it dies, and that an anaconda as big as this one could leap through the air faster than a bird and attack without any notice. I kind of made some of that up to sound like I knew something no one else did and to see if any of them got scared. I was making some low, gagging noises as if I were being strangled just to see what Trevor would do. It's mean, but watching bullies squirm is lots of fun.

When Trevor started making weird noises and backing away the other boys began to taunt him, which made him mad. The only thing he could do was lash out at me, since I was the smallest guy there and he might get whupped by the others. So he smacked me on the back of the head, "Stop making those dumb sounds, Peters!".

It didn't really hurt much, but Brandon snarled at him, "Back off! Just leave Peters alone!" Trevor stormed off saying under his breath that we were all going to pay. Everyone started laughing at him and one of the boys said "Sssssssseeeeee you later Trevie-poo sssssssometime sssssssoooon..." like a snake would talk.

When we went back to the backyard, there was this big tent set up on the grass in the back with tables full of food and drinks and huge pyramid of chocolates. The food there was so fancy it just didn't look like we were at a kid's party. People were dressed in these uniforms and serving the food like we were in the Country Club's restaurant. Everything seemed perfect.

There were more adults here than kids, and whenever Brandon would pass through the crowd around the food table one of the adults would hand him an envelope or just money. Brandon was bragging to several of the boys that the party had barely started and already he had over two hundred dollars. He pulled out this roll of money from his front pocket that was as big as my fist. "Now, I'll have extra spending money when we go on the African safari later this fall!"

I had never imagined having that much money in my whole life, and Brandon was getting it from people he didn't even really know, but people who knew his mom and dad.

But the saddest part for me was that Brandon's dad had these two really cool hound dogs, and they lived outside in kennels and were not allowed in the house. Brandon acts like he doesn't even know the dogs, and whenever he would get close to one of them his dad would remind him of his allergies.

I heard Mr. Anderman bragging about how the dogs were hunting dogs. My dogs were hunting dogs too, but they went everywhere with me when I was in the field hunting old cans and sometimes a rabbit. My dogs lived in the house with me, and were part of the family. Shoot, sometimes I liked them better than my brother. Well, most times, actually.

☯

Most of the kids at the party were A-okay, but some of the kids that lived in the Country Club were pretty stuck-up and mean. One kid, Franklin, just kept bragging about how rich his dad is and how he can go to Disneyland anytime he wants on his dad's company plane and blah-blah-blah. He asked me how many times I had been to Europe when he introduced himself to me as Franklin Wallace Prentice-The Third and shook my hand like I was a businessman or something. I pretended like I had never even heard of Europe. "Isn't that just north of California?" he looked at me like he wanted to choke me.

Brandon walked up to me and whispered in my ear when Franklin Wallace Prentice-The Third wasn't looking, "Stay away from that blowhard. He thinks he is the king of the Country Club. He'll play mean tricks on you if you give him the time of day."

When it was time to ride the horses, Mrs. Anderman brought out a bucket of apples so that we could feed them and then choose which one we wanted to ride. The horses were so beautiful. The kid named Franklin was feeding this one big shiny black Arabian horse in the stables when a brown-and-white horse nudged his arm, trying to get his attention. It made him jump out of his skin. He began to yell at the brown-and-white horse to leave him alone, and when he did he raised his arm really quick, like he was going to hit the horse in the face. The horse spooked and reared back with wide, scared eyes. Franklin kept yelling at the

horse to stop, which just made it more nervous. Then Franklin went on to feed the other horse again, and this time the brown-and-white horse that had nudged him before leaned out of its pen and bit Franklin right on the rear end. Franklin took this huge breath and then his face turned all red and he started to scream. He was crying really hard and jumping up and down and rubbing his rear end and saying some bad words he wasn't supposed to be saying, and out loud for everyone to hear.

Franklin was a jerk, and so even though I could tell he was in pain, I couldn't help laughing. It couldn't have happened to a nicer guy (me being totally sarcastic!). I tried to bury my face in my armpit so he couldn't tell I was laughing, but then all the other boys started laughing too, and I just couldn't stop. It was like when someone yawns and it makes you yawn. This made Franklin super angry, and he started yelling at me, "PETERS, YOU ARE SO DEAD! I AM GOING TO POUND YOU A GOOD ONE!" Tears were rushing out of his eyes, and like I said, even though I did feel bad for him, I couldn't stop laughing. The whole thing reminded me of a birthday party I had a couple of years ago when everything blew up because of Mean Mrs. Rickles.

Brandon put his arm around my shoulder and said, "Yeah, Franklin, really you're gonna pound him? You touch Peters and I will pound *you* into the ground! You shouldn't have yelled at my horse. He has a bad temper anyway, and you had it coming."

"Oh, yeah? Well, I hate your dumb horse and your dumb party," Franklin pouted.

"Well, why don't you leave, you loser. I didn't want to invite *you*, anyway," Brandon barked, loud enough for everyone around us to hear.

All of a sudden Franklin jumped on Brandon and started hitting him. Brandon looked stunned. He was sitting on his butt on the ground and his nose was bleeding. He jumped up and grabbed Franklin by the neck and they started rolling around on the ground. Some of the grownups were standing up by the house pointing and laughing. They thought Franklin and Brandon were just goofing around. They couldn't see that Brandon's nose was bleeding, and that Franklin's good shirt was torn

Franklin looked really embarrassed, because Brandon had gotten the better of him. "Let me go, you jerk!" Franklin screamed at Brandon. Some of the grownups looked mad now that the boys were messing up their good clothes.

"LEAVE!" Brandon sneered in Franklin's face and shoved him backwards.

Franklin was rubbing his butt, and didn't get his hands out to protect himself. He lost his footing and landed in this big silver metal bathtub-like thing that the horses drank out of. He came flying out like a wet dog and shrieking, "I'll get you, Anderman, and your stupid little friend!" Franklin nodded my way and then stormed out the backyard dripping water everywhere.

Brandon wiped his nose off and started to laugh. "I never did like that kid."

Somehow I knew a war in the Country Club had only just begun.

When Mrs. Anderman came out with this huge birthday cake covered with way more than eleven candles, everyone started singing "Happy Birthday." We all ran up to the fancy patio for cake and ice cream. When I got there, I couldn't believe my eyes. My mom was standing there talking to some of the other ladies, and she was wearing this really fancy black dress and her fancy black shoes with the heels that made her walk real funny, and she had her special dangly gold earrings and gold necklace on. She looked like she did the time she and dad went on their anniversary date to Denver to see a fancy-schmancy play and dinner. She winked at me and then went back to talking to the other ladies.

After downing the cake we rode the horses and played games and held reptiles and then, when the party was just about over, everyone got a bag full of party favors.

"Yo, Gabe, why don't you take Franklin's too, since he had to leave early, ha ha!" Brandon laughed.

"Geez, thanks, Brandon, are you sure?"

He nodded. I looked in Franklin's bag. It was full of candy and some joke gum and a few other great things. When I dug down to the bottom of the bag my hand seized something heavy. I pulled it out and couldn't believe it. It was a three-pack of Hot Wheels muscle cars. My heart leapt, and when I looked to the bottom of my own bag, there was a three-pack of Hot Wheels trucks. WOW, it was like I had had a birthday, too. Andy wouldn't believe my luck. Maybe I would give him one of them.

"Hey Brandon, d'ya think you would ever want to stay overnight at my house?" I asked Brandon. I fully expected him to say no.

"Sure, Gabe! That would be great!"

I wondered what Brandon would think about my tiny bedroom and my house that could fit in his horse barn. But for some reason I didn't really care.

# COUNTRY CLUB KID / COUNTRY KID

The very next weekend Brandon Anderman spent the night at my house. I wasn't sure a country club kid would want to do all of the things that we plain country kids did, but I figured we would just go out and try it. He showed up in his dad's fancy black Jaguar car that didn't look anything at all like my dad's Volkswagen bus. He climbed out of the car in dress pants and a dress shirt with some fancy shoes, the kind that he wears to school. Mr. Anderman waved at me and then at my dad, who was hoeing something in his garden in the side front yard. As he started backing up the car he yelled through the window,

"BRANDON, YOU BEHAVE NOW!"

"I will, Dad! See ya!" Brandon waved and carried his fancy suitcase to the front porch. By the size of it, you would think he was staying for the whole rest of the spring.

Then Mr. Anderman leaned across the passenger street and called out at my dad,

"Peters, you ought to join some of us next Saturday for a round of golf up at the club!"

Dad just nodded, which I thought was kind of rude. Mr. Anderman revved his engine and put his hands on the steering wheel. I noticed he was wearing really fancy leather gloves with holes all over the tops, which didn't make sense to me since it was warm outside. Brandon later explained that they were driving gloves. Mr. Anderman raced off down the road and then down the hill toward the highway. You could still hear his engine roaring as he shifted and turned out onto the highway. I listened for as long as I could until the sound disappeared and wondered how many of those fancy cars I would have when I was grown up and a millionaire. Brandon was just looking at me like I was a weirdo, 'cause I was staring off into space.

Frisky and Friskier started sniffing Brandon and his suitcase. Frisky licked his hand. Brandon bent down onto his knee and started petting Frisky and then Friskier, too. "Wow, your dogs are so cool!" He kissed Frisky on top of the head, and that was when I knew Brandon and I were going to be good friends.

"Hey, what about your allergies?" I asked him.

"I'm not allergic to dogs, my parents just think I am." Brandon dismissed the idea.

We went into the house and walked into the kitchen.

"Hello, Mrs. Peters," Brandon said cheerfully.

"Well hello, Brandon Anderman, and welcome to our humble abode!"

"Abode?" Why was Mom talking so formal?

Dad came in the front door, kicked off his garden shoes and said, "Welcome to the Peters' manor, Master Brandon. Your accommodations will be on the second floor. You will be sharing a bunk with Master Gabriel Peters."

Brandon started laughing at my dad's attempt at an English accent. "Thank you, Mr. Peters. You sound just like our driver in London last year!"

"Oy vei, the irony!" Dad said and slapped his forehead. "Did you bring other clothes in that steamer trunk of yours?"

"Abode; accommodations; irony?" I questioned. Why were my parents acting so weird?

"Uh, I have some pajamas and a robe," Brandon said.

Dad said, "Well, why don't you and Gabe haul that huge trunk of yours upstairs and I will bring you something a bit more suitable to the country."

Brandon and I looked at each other like we had no idea what Dad was talking about.

Brandon walked around my room commenting on my cool stuff. I knew, because I had been in his house, that my room was about the size of his closet, but he really seemed to like it. He called it "cozy," and said he wished he had a desk with a phone in his room. He told me he had to go down the hall to the "children's office" to do his homework.

He was flipping through my record collection, pulling out songs he wanted to hear, when Dad brought some of Carl's old clothes in and handed them to Brandon. "You might want to wear these if I know what Gabe has planned for you two."

"Thank you, Mr. Peters!" Brandon said enthusiastically, and he immediately started to change into a pair of well-worn jeans and a flannel shirt. I had never seen Brandon in anything other than fancy clothes. Even when we wore gym clothes at school, his were fancier than everyone else's.

We started heading down the stairs when Carl and Greg passed us.

"Who's your little girlfriend, chicken-puke?" Carl tossed at us.

"Who're you calling a girl?" Brandon sneered, standing as tall as he could. But he wasn't nearly as tall as Carl.

"I guess that would be obvious, fancy-pants country clubber! Hey, that's my shirt!" Carl barked.

"Oooh, Carl, I'd be careful! Isn't that one of the famous richy-rich Andermans?" Greg chided and laughed.

Brandon was used to brothers, but he wasn't used to being pushed around. "I'd watch my mouth if I were you, unless you want to fight a black belt in karate!"

"Yeah, right! I'm just so scared!" Carl exclaimed as he backed up a few steps.

Greg sneered and said, "Ohhh, yeah, we are so scared of a fifth grader!"

"You'll be the first one I destroy!" Brandon decided, turning his attention quickly from Carl and started walking back up the stairs toward Greg. He was clenching his fists and making a weird noise in the back of his throat, like you'd hear during karate or wrestling tournaments.

Greg's eyes grew really wide and he started backing up the hall and into Carl's room, bumping into Carl who was also retreating into his room. Greg scoffed, "Like I'd waste my time on a dumb fifth grader!"

But I could tell Greg was scared, and the weirder thing was, I think Carl was too. Brandon was pretty big for his age, but

I guess the threat of karate was more than they could take.

Carl's door slammed shut, but I could hear Carl talking to Greg inside. "I can't believe that megadork is wearing that old nerdy shirt of mine. I wouldn't wear that dumb thing on a dare."

It was weird Carl said that, 'cause I knew that flannel shirt was one of his favorites. I had been pretty surprised when I saw my dad had lent it to Brandon.

Brandon and I headed out the back screen door to the garden in the backyard.

"Oh my gosh, I can't believe you just stood up to my brother like that!"

"Years of practice, Gabe. I have brothers, too. Besides, I'm a guest, and your mom and dad are right here really close." He started to laugh. "Man, your brother's huge. How come you're so much smaller?"

"I dunno. I mean, we're adopted and..." I began to sputter.

"I didn't mean anything by that, Peters. Just forget I said it," he said suddenly, his face kind of red.

"Okay. But wait. You mean you don't really have a black belt?"

"HECK, NO! Well, actually, I have three. They all are in my closet at home!" Brandon started laughing pretty hard, and I laughed right along with him and the joke he had just played on those wise guys.

I stopped laughing though, thinking he might have said heck too loud, since Mom was right there in the kitchen. But I could hear through the back kitchen window that she was listening to the radio pretty loud to some corny song that went Midnight at the Oasis...

"Oh my gosh, did you see the look on their faces?" I said, laughing even harder at the thought.

The music came out through the window, Send your camels to bed... Mom was singing along and sounded really funny because she was way off key.

Brandon snorted, "Yeah, that was funny. Hey, what's that for?"

He was pointing to my tent.

"Oh, that's where I sleep in the summer, and sometimes even when it is warm in the spring, but only on Friday or Saturday nights on account of school the next day. That's where we'll sleep tonight if you want to."

"Are you serious? Your mom would let us sleep outside tonight?" Brandon's eyes were as big as saucers.

I thought it was cool that I had something Brandon didn't—mostly freedom, it seemed.

"Sure. It's a pretty warm day, so tonight it should be warm enough, at least in sleeping bags."

"My mom would never let me sleep outside like that!" Brandon scrunched his nose up.

"Sure she would; you just haven't asked her," I muttered.

"Huh? Oh man, you don't know my mom."

"You wanna sleep in the tent tonight for real?" I asked, hardly believing he would want to rough it.

"Are you kidding? That would be a total blast!"

You'd have thought I was offering a room at the fanciest hotel the way Brandon was so excited.

"Sometimes I even sleep up in the tree house, but you could roll off if you weren't careful." I laughed at that a little too loud.

"Uh, I think I'll stick to the tent. I kind of have a weird fear of falling out of trees in the middle of the night." Brandon laughed, all nervous-like. "Man, I can't believe your mom and dad let you sleep in a tent whenever you want to like that. They are so cool!"

"Well, it's not like we're going to get eaten by coyotes or anything."

"Coyotes?" There was a bit of fear in his voice.

"Heck yeah, they're everywhere around here. But Frisky and Friskier sleep out here with me and they would let me know if one was getting anywhere near and I have timed it. I can get out of my sleeping bag, unzip the tent and run in the back door in six seconds flat. No coyote is going to get close enough to beat me to the door. 'Course the bear that was sighted around here last summer could beat me."

"BEAR? Come on, Peters, you're pulling my leg. There aren't any bears around here."

"Ask my dad. Seriously, they live in the foothills, which is only about five miles from here, and they come down the creek beds when they get really hungry. Especially when they get really hungry for human flesh!"

"Get out of here, Peters! Now I know you're putting me on."

I noticed Brandon searching around the backyard with his eyes, following the ditch behind our house up toward the farmer's land to see where the bears would come down to our yard.

"Ask my dad, Brandon. Seriously."

"Hmmm, well maybe we should sleep on the bunk beds tonight instead," Brandon laughed nervously.

"You aren't going all chicken on me, are you, Brandon?"

He crinkled up his nose and stuck his chest out like a big mean muscle man. "Heck, no! Fine; then the tent it is!"

"Great!" I said.

Brandon was surveying the neighborhood now, at least the part you could see from my yard. "Hey Peters, anyone else around here sleep in a tent?"

"Yeah, all my buddies have tents in their backyards, and we just go from tent to tent on summer nights. You never know where you're going to end up sleeping for the night."

"Are you serious? You're only a fifth grader, so how does that work?"

"Just does. All the parents keep an eye on things, and we keep walkie-talkies in the tents in case we need Mom or Dad."

"Your parents use walkie-talkies?"

"Sure, but only as a safety measure. It's not like they talk on them all the time."

"That is the coolest thing I've ever heard!" Brandon exclaimed. "So, you guys can move from tent to tent anytime you want and you don't get in trouble?"

"Heck no, I didn't say we don't get in trouble! But not for

moving tents," I laughed, and swatted Brandon's arm playfully. He swatted me back, but in a friendly way the way Andy and the guys do. "Course, we stay up really late playing hide-n-seek all over the neighborhood every night in the summer, too!"

"Like how late?" Brandon said, looking around inside the tent.

"Mmm, usually some of the guys have to head in around midnight..."

Brandon's mouth hung open, "Yeah, right, midnight. You wish!"

"Ask my mom. She doesn't care as long as we're in boundaries."

"Boundaries?" he asked.

"Yeah, Mom drew a map for us that shows where we can and can't go after dark. It's on the side of the refrigerator."

"Seriously? Or are you joking?"

"No really! Basically, it's just no highway, no water, no railroad tracks, no farmer's land and no bothering Mean Mrs. Rickles or Killer!"

"WHAT? WHO'S KILLER?!" Brandon shouted too loud.

"Oh man, you do have a lot to learn about this neighborhood."

"Yeah, I guess. You know what?"

"What?"

"I have to be in bed at ten o'clock in the summer and nine o'clock during school."

"NO WAY!" I couldn't believe my ears. Did this kid ever have any fun?

"I never heard of a fifth grader who could stay out past midnight!"

Brandon was scratching his head like he just didn't believe me.

"We better get a move on if we are going to catch any fish!"

I handed him the shovel that was leaning against the back of the house and I grabbed a garden spade. We started digging and probably dug up a thousand worms, which we put in the rusty coffee can that I kept behind the big rhubarb plant. Brandon acted like he had never gotten his hands all dirty like that. He seemed to really like it. We got a couple fishing poles out of the garage, and a tackle box.

   While we were standing in the garage Carl and Greg were
coming out the front door and jumped down into the driveway
where their stingray bikes were leaning. I lifted my leg and
yelled, "HI-YAAAA!" and did a big karate kick in the air. Carl
and Greg rode off yelling something I didn't really hear because
Brandon and I were laughing so hard.
   We went back into the kitchen where Mom gave us each a
brown paper bag full of goodies and lunch. We headed down
the hill. I told Brandon about the tunnels and the lake, and he
said he wanted to try the lake because he thought it would be
fun to try to catch the famous ghost carp. When I told him the
legend of the ghost Indian he acted like he could hardly wait to
get there. We fished down at the lake for a long time and didn't
see either the ghost carp or the ghost Indian, but we did catch

a ton
of sunfish
and then went
to tunnel number
one to catch some bluegills. I
explained why the hill on the
west side of the lake was
all burned out, and Brandon
thought that sounded like the
coolest prank ever. When I told
him about The Secret Brotherhood
of Boys, he said he really wanted to join.

Later, we climbed the tree across the gravel road from my house and hung out eating candy in the tree house while spying on my neighbors. Then we walked down the railroad tracks hobo-spying. I showed him where the bloated, disgusting raccoon had been, but now all you could see was a little fur and a greasy spot where it had finally almost disappeared.

As we walked through the field we watched for the weird old lady who lives up on the hill, and I told him some of the spooky stories about her. We went to the cave and I showed him the weird drawings there and told him more about the legend of the ghost Indian in the lake and about Mr. Patchett.

We went down to the lake after dinner when it was dark with flashlights looking for the dead dog in the lake, and floated around in the rowboat under a full moon. Mr. Patchett was sitting on his back porch, so we had to be really quiet.

Brandon whispered, "You guys sure have a lot of dead stuff in this lake! You ought to name it THE LAKE OF DEATH!" When he said it, he used this scary voice and turned the flashlight up on his face the way I do when I scare Carl with my stories.

"Yeah, that's a cool idea!"

"Man, Peters, you got the life! This is the coolest place I've ever been!"

"WHAT?" I said too loud, "What? You've been all over the world; how can you say that?"

"I mean to live. Man, what I wouldn't give for the fishing holes you have! And sleeping out under the stars like the cowboys! Pranking your brothers and catching snakes, frogs and all kinds of stuff!"

Something moved in the water, and a few seconds later the rowboat started rocking on little waves.

"WHAT WAS THAT?" Brandon whisper-yelled.

Mr. Patchett's voice came booming across the water, "HEY, WHO'S THAT DOWN THERE IN THE WATER?"

"Oh no, that's Mr. Patchett. Keep quiet," I whispered.

"WATCH OUT FOR THAT GHOST INDIAN. HE'S BEEN SWIMMING AROUND FOR THE LAST COUPLE OF NIGHTS LOOKING FOR HIS NEXT VICTIM!" Mr. Patchett yelled from his back porch.

Brandon and I started paddling the water with our hands to get back to shore. Both of us were shivering a little, thinking about what was under there that had made the boat rock and when it might yank on our hands and pull us in.

"Come on, hurry up, man!" I begged.

We paddled for all we were worth, and jumped out on the opposite side of the lake. There we pulled the rowboat up onto the shore and took off running through the tall weeds up the sledding hill. When we got over the hill and could spy Mr. Patchett sitting out on his porch, we both lay down on our stomachs, huffing and puffing.

"OH MY GOSH, THAT WAS SO FREAKY!" Brandon was breathing hard.

"TOTALLY!" I whisper-yelled.

"Man, I am serious, this is the coolest place in the whole world, Peters! I mean it!" Brandon puffed.

"Hmmm, yeah, it is pretty cool. Wait till you see my zoo!" I teased.

"What?"

"Well, it's not really a zoo, but I have a ton of animals in the basement."

"In the house? Man, you are so lucky!" Brandon whined.

"You see that part of the hill?" I pointed down the sledding hill and told him about the monster jump, about Craig's dad's dune buggy and the crazy rides he took us on through the fields, ice fishing and hockey skating when the lake froze, and all of the other things we did in the winter. I just told him story after story about all the things that had gone on in this part of the neighborhood.

Brandon just kept saying over and over again he wished he lived here, which was weird because I thought he had it made living in that mansion out there in the Country Club. But I noticed he didn't have any stories to tell me, which was weird, too. What usually what happens when the guys sit around is that everyone plays top that story. Brandon didn't seem to have any to top mine.

I could hear voices coming from the neighborhood where everyone had gathered to play hide-n-seek, and I wondered what my buddies thought of my not being there. I felt kind of bad, but the truth was I was having so much fun with Brandon that I didn't really want to share him.

So, we headed back up to my house after walking for a mile or so down the railroad track throwing rocks and hiding in a hole as the train rushed by. We ate some late dinner, and then hung out up in the tree house just talking. A couple times some of the guys who were coming up there to hide almost found us, but every time someone was about to climb up into the tree the person that was "It" would yell out, "Ollie Ollie, in come free…" and they would go back hooting and hollering as the winners of the round.

When Brandon and I both got tired enough, we went across the street to sleep on the cots in the tent. Mom came out to see us and to kiss me goodnight, and the next thing I knew I was waking up in the morning to Frisky sniffing my face. I looked over to where Flop was, and he was curled up right next to Brandon.

After eating a ton of Mom's awesome pancakes and bacon, Brandon and I went back out for more adventures. We snuck up to the goons' "secret" fort, and I told Brandon all about the dare-off game we play. I showed him my zoo, and he decided he needed to start one too, that is if his mom would ever let him have animals in the house. I showed him where The Secret Brotherhood of Boys met for meetings when the big brothers were up in the tree house, and I took him up to the Bait Shop to meet Joe. We walked along the dirt road leading from the barns up the creek, skipping rocks and plunking them into the muddy ditch water. The whole time we were talking about all kinds of stuff. At one point Andy joined us for a little while, but he seemed kind of upset that I had another friend from my old school staying over and made an excuse to go home.

When it was about time for Brandon's mom to show up, it was weird to see Brandon change into school clothes when it was still the weekend. He and I were sitting at the kitchen table waiting for his mom to come, playing Go Fish and telling jokes. Brandon didn't want to leave. He kept saying things like, "Your mom is the coolest mom I have ever met. I love her cooking. I wish my mom cooked," and "That was so much fun playing Monopoly with your dad. My dad never plays games with us. He's too busy in his laboratory coming up with some new thing all the time… I'm going to see if we can get a tent. Then you can come stay outside at my house too!"

Brandon was petting Frisky and looking out the window toward my tree house when he muttered out loud, for about the millionth time, "Man, I really, really wish I lived here."

I started feeling sorry for him. It seemed like everyone wanted to live in a house like his, and it shocked me to hear him saying that.

"Hey Gabe, d'ya think I could come over again sometime soon? We didn't even get a chance to watch your favorite monster movies!"

My dad was sitting in his chair rocking Flopster and reading his newspaper. Suddenly he said, "Brandon, those clothes I gave you will be waiting for you. If I know what Gabe has in mind for your next sleepover, you're going to need them."

The smile on Brandon's face went from ear to ear. "Thanks, Mr. Peters! That's really nice of you!"

Brandon's mom showed up, and I was sad to see him go.

When their fancy car pulled slowly down the gravel road Dad winked at Mom. "You see, dear, kids are all alike. Sometimes it is the simplest things that they like the best."

Mom gave Dad a kind of dirty look mixed with a smile.

All I knew was Brandon Anderman, rich or not, was the kind of kid I liked hanging around with, and now I knew I was the kind of kid he liked hanging around with, too. I never thought I'd say this, but it made me kind of wish I was still going to St. Joe's. I think I would go to the very top of Brandon's best friend list if I did.

## CHAPTER SEVENTEEN

# A FUN ASSIGNMENT

We all rode the yellow school bus together on the first day of school. We all were wearing new clothes that felt itchy and restrictive.

I had picked my clothes from the Sears catalog so long ago that I had forgotten what I ordered. But I guess I picked out some red, white, and blue bellbottoms to go with an off-white shirt and a really cool leather belt. My toes already were killing me in my new shoes, 'cause they wanted freedom.

It was fun to see some of the kids I had gotten to know but didn't see over the summer. But the day ended on kind of a bad note, since the teachers didn't seem to think we would need more time to get adjusted to summer being over, and I went home the first day with twenty math problems and an essay to write about my summer vacation. Plus I had to come up with an idea for what I wanted to do this fall for the science fair.

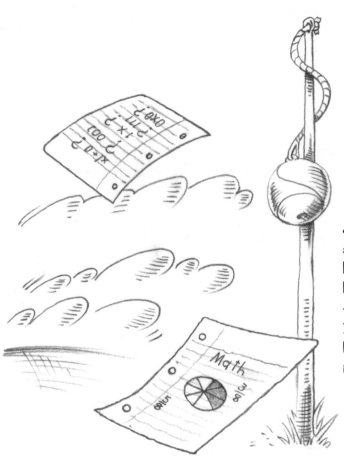

Still, the first couple of weeks of school went by pretty fast. I got my first real assignment in school, and have been working pretty hard on it for about two weeks. By now I would have had like ten assignments in my old school.

Mr. McCammon is teaching English to the fourth and fifth graders, and he is really nice.

He lets me write about stuff that interests me, like comic books. I told him about my gran giving me Where The Red Fern Grows, and he told me it was one of his favorites. So I actually liked writing my assignment for Mr. McCammon, because I could make it full of the kind of stuff I put in my journal, and I even get to add my funny drawings to it.

Here is the assignment that I turned in to him for my first essay, which Mr. McCammon said should answer a big question.

(Those are his comments, which are in his handwriting.)

Creative Essay Assignment
English — Mr. McCammon 1st
draft

*B+*

*Gabe, the comic book format is a great idea. What an imagination!*

# THE SEA MONKEY WHO ATE MY BROTHER

### THOUGH THIS IS A COMIC BOOK, THERE'S NOTHING COMICAL ABOUT IT, REALLY, BECAUSE IT HAPPENED!

By Gabriel Peters
Drawings by G. Peters and Flop
(Flop my cat kept bumping my arm while I drew, so the art looks like it does because of him.)

Hi there, my name is Private Eye Dirk The Smirk. Well the first thing you need to know about me is that I love comic books. I save my allowance to buy comic books, and I earn extra money for comic books to buy all the stuff in the back of comic books.

*(Try using a different word for comic. You used it three times in one paragraph. For example, the last reference could read simply— in the back of them. Also, expand on some of the description and use your vocabulary, I know you have a big one... I have heard it.)*

I have a huge collection of really cool stuff on my bookshelf that I got from comic books, like X-Ray glasses, gum that turns your mouth black, gum that tastes like fire, magic tricks, a lava lamp and a whole bunch of other really cool stuff.

I am going to become SUPER-HUGE because of Charles Atlas who was a bodybuilder long before the sport got popular. His advertisements are in my comic books.

When I ordered his program, I only weighed seventy-two pounds, just like the ninety-five-pound weakling (only twenty-three pounds lighter, $95-23=72$, Mr. McCammon always says to show your work, which sounds like a math teacher) that gets sand kicked in his face. Now, after only three weeks on the course, I am already at seventy-three pounds. So much of my life has changed because of comic books.

(That's a good idea, the comment about showing your work, and nice work on your muscle-building program. Keep it up and let me know your ongoing progress. Who knows, I might even try it.)

## THE BIG QUESTION: WHAT KID DOESN'T WANT A MONKEY? My brother laughed at me and told me that his science teacher told him that the sea monkeys I ordered weren't monkeys at all, just some kind of tiny shrimp that never really amount to anything.

Carlos (that's my brother) was laughing at me when he said, "The company just sends it to dumb kids like you who, after only a week or so, get bored and don't even care that they never got any real sea monkeys." He always rains on my parades, which is a funny saying, because I don't have any parades to rain on, but it means tries to spoil things on account of the fact that he is jealous of all the money I have and can spend on whatever I want.

YOU CAN replace ~~on account of the fact that~~ with 'because'. Also, you don't need to let us know that this answers a requirement of the assignment by stating that it is THE BIG QUESTION. Just work it into your narrative flow.

You see, in most of the comic books there are these companies that want kids to sell all their junk for them; like greeting cards and other crapola. I have a plaque that 'GREAT INVENTIONS CORP.' sent to me that says I am the number 103-ranked salesman in the whole country out of thousands and thousands, and with only $100 more in sales within the next six months I will be promoted to Junior Executive, which means my points and prizes double.

They have also offered for me as a Junior Executive to add my friends to the sales team, and their sales would become part of my points too. I already have a closet full of cool stuff that I have won from the contests-radios,  watches, X-ray glasses (they don't really work), t-shirts, key chains and a ton more stuff. My friends sometimes buy things from me with their measly allowances, never considering that there is a fortune to be made in the back pages of comic books.

So, I ordered the sea monkeys just to prove my dumb brother wrong. See, I am kind of a scientist myself. I have

been studying seahorses, and there are these marine biologists who can make seahorses grow ten times their normal size. I have a good idea to make my sea monkeys grow really really big, to prove they aren't shrimps.

My sea monkey came today. My brother was making fun of him, because you can barely even see him. I'll show my

brother. I'm pretty sure he made my sea monkey mad, because every time he walks into my bedroom Glenn the Sea Monkey, that's what I named him, bangs on the aquarium glass and shakes his fist at my dumb brother.

I have had Glenn for one week, and he is really growing, just like me. We are both on a body building program, you might say.

## GROWTH CHART
DAY ONE WEIGHT

ME     72 LBS
GLENN THE SEA MONSTER   1/4 ounce*
*estimated, based on comparison with a dime, which weighs about 1 ounce.

| WEEK ONE | | |
| --- | --- | --- |
| Day | My Progress | Glenn's Progress |
| Monday | gained 1/8 lb | gained 1/4 ounce |
| Tuesday | gained 1/8 lb | gained 1 ounce |
| Wednesday | gained 1/8 lb | gained 2 ounces |
| Thursday | gained 1/8 lb | gained 2 ounces |
| Friday | gained 1/8 lb | gained 4 ounces |
| Saturday | gained 1/8 lb | gained 8 ounces |
| Sunday | gained 2/8 lb | gained 1 lb |

Glenn's weight doubles every day. He doesn't mind me weighing him. Actually, he smiles when I hold him; he likes the human contact, and strangely seems adapted to either water or air. He reminds me of this monster thing that was on The Twilight Zone last night. That's because Glenn eats steak, potatoes and a small salad for his dinner. Plus I haven't seen my guinea pig for several days.

Glenn's weight continues to double every day. I have moved him to the bathtub; Mom hasn't found out yet. He still doesn't mind me weighing him, and now seems maybe more adapted to air than to water. But as far as I know, there are no air-breathing shrimp in the world, so that proves he is the real thing, a sea monkey, not a sea shrimp. He is eating steak, potatoes, and a small dinner salad three times a day now, and it looks like he is eating peanut butter by the jar (there are empty jars of peanut butter in a stack behind my dresser). My guinea pig is still missing, and so is one of the cats now. I think it is a simple coincidence, but just in case, I have moved my other cat Flop and the dogs to the garage to sleep at night.

| Monday | Tuesday | Wednesday | Thursday | Friday |

I stopped weighing Glenn, because the last time I did, I couldn't lift him to weigh both of us on Mom's bathroom scale. He is kind of slippery. Mom screamed when she saw him in the bathtub the first time, but I convinced her he was just a slimy toy I had won from a comic book contest. Then I moved him to the pond near my house. I haven't heard a frog croak since, and there used to be thousands, come to think of it. Except for my dogs (which I properly introduced to Glenn and told him to leave them alone OR ELSE), I haven't heard ANY barking in the neighborhood either.

More about Glenn later.

Gabe, this is very imaginative. Not exactly what I had in mind with the assignment, but if you keep at it and find a way to conclude it, I will count it for your grade. Perhaps sometime you could bring Glenn in for show and tell. I doubt many students have ever seen such a big sea monkey! I hope your animals are all safe. You might consider donating Glenn to the San Diego Zoo.

I thought it was cool that Mr. McCammon pretended to believe my story might be real, but how could I ever give Glenn away?

# CHAPTER EIGHTEEN

# A NEW BIKE!

"A NEW BIKE? I WANTED A NEW BIKE!" I screamed so loudly my ears were ringing.

Dad was standing in the garage with the biggest smile on his face.

I couldn't believe my eyes. Propped up in the middle of the garage on a kickstand was a candy-apple-red Schwinn Stingray with a four-foot sissy bar and a bright yellow banana seat, just like the one in the window at the bicycle shop, only this one had seemed to have custom metal-flecked paint, which made it extra, extra cool! Stuck to the seat was a Christmas bow and a note that read, 'FOR GABE, HAPPY BELATED BIRTHDAY *AND* MERRY CHRISTMAS!'

"It looks like the one in the window at the bike shop, Dad!" I squealed, still unable to believe my own eyes. I started thinking about what I could do on my new bike. Maybe I could even set a new world record for jumping.

"That's because it is the one in the window!" Dad laughed. "Now remember, it's from us and Gran and Gramps!"

I would see Gran and Gramps at Thanksgiving, and I couldn't wait to see them, especially my grandma, and thank them for the most awesome present ever. They didn't leave their farm in Kansas very often because there was always so much to do, but this year my uncle was living in their bunk house, which was the house Gran promised me I could live in too when I was old enough to come and stay in the summer to help with the farm chores.

I stared at my new bike. I couldn't believe that I actually had a candy-apple-red Stingray with the coolest banana seat known to mankind. There should be a Guinness World Record for this bike, just for existing! The tricks I could do on this bad boy were so many that it made my head spin.

"Check this out, Gabe!" Dad bent down and showed me how the locking bolts that held the long sissy bar twisted and popped right off. "This is so you can do your jumps down at the track and not knock yourself out with the bar. And you can also be stylin' when you are trying to impress the little ladies."

"Gross Dad, I don't like girls!" I snorted.

Dad just chuckled.

Carl popped around the garage door where he had been eavesdropping on our conversation. "Yeah, fat chance chicken-jumper could impress any of the ladies around here!"

"Whatever!" I growled, but I wasn't going to let Carl ruin my special day.

Mom popped her head into the garage. She looked at my dad. "You just couldn't wait could you?" she said, holding up her camera. "I had hoped to catch the surprised look on Gabe's face."

"Sorry, hon. I was sitting at my desk and tried to catch him when he came bounding downstairs and heading for the garage. Maybe you could fake a little surprise for Mom, huh, Gabe?"

Mom playfully hit Dad on the arm and aimed her camera at me.

"Gabe, you need to be careful on this bike. It has gears and can go really fast!" she warned.

"I know, Mom..."

"This chicken-rider couldn't go fast enough to hurt himself!" Carl growled, and grabbed his own Stingray and wheeled out of the driveway, "Come on squirt, I'll show you how a real man rides the jumps!"

I pulled my new red bike out onto the driveway, climbed on and took off on the coolest bike I had ever seen.

Mom took a picture of Carl and me heading out into the field toward the jumps.

θ

"Gabe, ten more minutes!" Mom called from inside the house.

I was checking my *Guinness Book of World Records* for any bike records in my tent with my flashlight. All of the other guys were down at the lake night fishing and looking for the Indian in the lake. But I couldn't pull myself away. My plan was to look at every page in the book to see the new what records were even possible for The Secret Brotherhood of Boys to set or break.

I wanted to get into the Guinness book more than anything, and now my plan was starting to take hold. Butch was in, and I knew Andy would be, too. With my new bike I was going to do something more daring than Evil Knievel. I was going to jump over the train.

There is this one-mile stretch where the train goes in between these two huge hills, in a canyon. We have tried to figure out how we could create a jump, to go from the top of one hill to the other. The problem is the hills go straight up and straight down with only about a two foot flat top and trying to get enough speed built up while riding straight up seems impossible. I tried it once, and ended up sliding down on my bike. I hit two yucca plants on the way down, and man that hurt bad. So this time we would have to build a rocket booster to wear on my back.

If we could figure out how to make a jetpack, I could fire it up right before I went off and if I wasn't going to make it, I could drop the bike and fly to the other side.

No way was I going to use my new bike. Now that I have a new bike, I can totally modify it better than my old one and maybe be able to fly.

☺

So, all the guys met at the tree house with our bikes, and we decided that we were going to start going everywhere on our bikes instead of walking. Everyone went back to their houses, and went through the decks of cards there, pulling out the jokers. We put them in the bikes' spokes with clothespins, and the loud clicking sound they made it feel like the bikes actually had engines.

When we rode by Mr. Stolz's house with six bikes and all those jokers click-clacking, he stood on his front porch with his hands over his ears. I could see his lips moving as he yelled at us about the racket, but I couldn't hear what he was saying over the noise.

"Where's the garden hose, Mr. Stolz?" Butch yelled, and then we all took off as fast as we could down to the railroad tracks.

We bumped along on the rocks next to the tracks for what seemed like a hundred miles. We came to this place where the older kids ride their dirt bikes. Motorcycles sound so cool when they are spinning up and down the hilly terrain. These two older teenage boys were sitting on their dirt bikes watching us as we pulled up.

"Hey, nice bikes!" one of them snapped sarcastically.

"Yeah, wow, those cards in your spokes really had me fooled! I thought you were all riding some dirt bikes!" the other kid said. He slapped his leg and almost fell off of his motorcycle, he was laughing at his own lame joke so hard.

"Wh-Wh-Whatever... j-jerks!" Andy sneered.

"What did you say to me, kid?"

"N-N-Nothing..."

"Yeah, I d-d-didn't think s-s-so!" the bigger kid said, laughing at Andy.

I could see that Andy's face had turned beet red. When you have red hair your face seems to show your embarrassment really well.

"Shut up, you dumb jerk!" I screamed before I could think

about what I was doing — yelling at a kid much bigger and
older than me.

The big kid jumped off his motorcycle so fast I didn't even
see it coming. He leaned it on its kickstand and then slammed
into me, knocking me off my bike. The other kid jumped off and
came at me too, and before I knew it they were holding me
down.

"Who you callin' a jerk, pipsqueak?" one of them growled.

"Leave us alone!" Butch yelled.

"Yeah, unless you want our big brothers to massacre you," I
chimed in.

Murph jumped off of his bike and jumped on the big kid's
back. "Yeah,-my-brother-could-tear-you-up-you-stupid-jerk!"
Murph punched the big kid right in the ear.

He whipped off of me and jumped on Murph, and they were
rolling around on the ground. Then he overpowered Murph and
pinned him down and raised his arm in the air like he was
about to smash his fist into Murph's face.

"Who's your brother, little man?" the kid sneered as he sat
on Murph's chest and beat on his chest like a drum.

"Boney-Murphy-and-he's-really-mean-and-tough-and..."
The kid jumped right off of Murph.

"You are Boney Murphy's kid brother? Oh, my gosh, kid, I'm
so sorry. I had no idea!"

It figures the big bully would be afraid now on account
of Boney being bigger, tougher and having spent time in juvie.

"Yeah?-You-think-you're-sorry-now?-Wait-until-I-tell-
him-what-you-did-to-me-and-my-friends!" Murph spurted.

"Please don't tell him, kid. I'll give you anything!" The kid was
stammering, his face bright red.

"Okay,-give-me-your-motorcycle!" Murph sneered at him.

A look of horror came over the kid's face. "Oh man, my dad
would skin me alive. How about this?" He pulled a pocketknife
and a twenty-dollar bill out of his pocket.

"Yeah-that'll-do...FOR-NOW!" Murph snapped the knife and

twenty off of his hand, and for good measure stomped on the big kid's right foot.

The kid started jumping up and down and screaming, "WHY'D YOU DO THAT, KID?"

"So-you'd-never-forget-Boney-Murphy's-little-brother.-And-if-I-ever-hear-you-came-anywhere-near-any-of-my-friends-again-I'll-tell-my-big-brother-to-whup-you-good." Murph laughed.

The kid limped over to his motorcycle and kick-started it. His friend climbed on watching us with a look of fear and anger. They left our neighborhood as fast as they could.

"EAT-MY-DUST!" Murph yelled, which was kind of funny because it was the mean kid who was making all of the dust.

"Wow, Murph, that was amazing!" I shouted.

"Tw-Twenty b-b-bucks!?" Andy laughed.

"That was fast thinking!" I said.

Murph just stood there soaking in the praise and feeling like a pretty big man right then.

All of a sudden setting, a world record on a bike, no matter how cool it was, seemed kind of puny, and after all, we didn't have a jetpack or really any way to build rocket boosters that would actually work. So, maybe just riding with my buddies and having fun on our bikes was enough... for now.

Back to the drawing board.

CHAPTER NINETEEN

# THE RABID RACCOON

Butch, Andy and I were down at the lake, wearing our Cub Scout shirts because we had just come from Deak Noble's house. Deak is our Boy Scout leader. He is a nice guy. He is some kid named Rocket's Grandpa, and Deak is always talking like we all know Rocket, but the kid lives in Wisconsin or someplace like that, and he's like five years old, so he doesn't sound that interesting anyway, except that he has the coolest name. Deak misses his grandson Rocket, and that is why he volunteers to be a scout leader.

Deak is really cool and knows a lot about just about everything. He was in one of the big world wars, and whenever Murph is around, he shows him some stuff that he brought home from the evil Nazis in Europe. That's like the only time Murph isn't going on and on about what *he* knows. He just listens and says, "COOL!" over and over at everything Deak says. I swear if there was a Guinness World record for being the most annoying kid in the world, Murph and my brother would be in a neck-and-neck competition.

One time when we were having a scout meeting, Murph asked Deak if he ever killed anyone. Deak looked at him like he was going to kill *him* and didn't say anything for a long, long time. The room was totally silent when Deak began to roll up his sleeve, higher and higher, until all of a sudden this tattoo of a lady who looks like the kind of ladies you see in the bathing suit advertisements in the Sears catalog showed up. She was riding a big bomb like you would a horse, and then with "U.S." in really big letters over some island appeared on Deak's skin. Deak just kept turning up his shirt all the way to his bicep.

Then he said, "You see this scar?" There was an angry purple rope of a scar that went all the way up his right bicep and stuck out about an inch from his skin. "That was something I got in a hand-to-hand, er... dagger-to-dagger combat when we were liberating one of those awful camps. You think this looks bad? You should have seen that nasty fellow I was wrangling with when I was done with him. They could have mailed him home in a manila envelope!"

Even though no one said a word, we were all thinking the same thing, "COOL!"

Deak rolled his sleeve back down, and went right back to showing us how to tie off flies for fly fishing like it was no big deal. I figured the box Deak keeps on the mantle with the purple heart next to this flag in a triangle frame had something to do with his arm.

After the meeting, I couldn't get that lady on Deak's arm out of my mind. Later that night I drew some tattoos on my arms like his. The funny thing is, when we all met up in the tree house again, I could see that Tony and Butch had been drawing tattoos on their arms too. They had tried to erase theirs, but I didn't. Mine was really cool — a slobbering wolf eating a Martian.

You can see pictures of Deak all over town, with his slogan, *To know Noble 'tis to know value',* because pretty much any house for sale seems like it is being sold by him. It looks like they took his picture a long time ago, on account of his hair is all black like my dad's, and not white like it really is now. And his face isn't puckered as much in the pictures. I guess when you spend all the dough to put your picture on metal signs, you don't just change the picture because your hair changes color. Still, I think Deak should rub charcoals on his head or something to make his hair look like it did in the real estate pictures. Maybe when people go to meet him to buy all those houses, they think he got really scared and it turned his hair all white or something. They probably think he saw God like that Moses dude on the movie after he goes up on the mountain and talks to the fake burning bush.

I think Deak should just show them his tattoo and his scar. That would make anyone buy a house from him.

Deak knows how to find the right rocks where all of the bugs hide on hot summer days, and he knows about how to calm a rattlesnake when it is shaking its rattle at you, and he knows so many more things. He sold most of the houses in our neighborhood when it was being developed, and my dad thinks he is really swell. Dad always says, "Deak is a true American hero!"

At our meeting, Mrs. Noble came in to say "hi," which made me remember one time, a long time ago before I was ever a scout. It was back when I had training wheels on my bike.

I had fallen while I was going around the block, and hurt my arm. Deak was sitting in a chair on the front porch of the house that Tony's family moved into after it was just built. He came out to help me, and then told me he was having an open house, which meant anyone could come in for a soda and some of Mrs. Noble's homemade cookies while he waited to sell someone the house. I kept Mr. Noble (that's what I called him until I was in his scout troop and he asked us to call him Deak) company playing card games like *Go Fish* and *War* until this family with three girls came to look at the house. That bummed me a little, because I was hoping more for a family with three boys my age.

Not long after that though, Tony and his dad came bopping in, and then his mom and brother and sister. Tony sat down at the table next to me and looked at the plate of cookies hungrily. "How old are you?" he asked.

I said, "Seven."

He said, "Well, I'm seven and a half. If we buy this house, do you want to be my best friend?"

"I can't. I already have a best friend, and I have a second best friend. But you can be my second-second best friend."

He asked, "Who's your first best friend?"

"Andy Epstein. He has four big brothers and talks funny, but he's a super kid."

"Talks funny?"

"Never mind," I barked, like I needed to defend Andy when he wasn't there.

"Okay, so what is a second-second best friend?"

"The same as a second best friend, just there is two second best friends; get it?"

"Who is your first second best friend?" he asked.

"Eddie." I said matter-of-factly, like everyone should know him. "So, what do you say?"

"I guess it's okay. Fine, second-second then."

He spit in his hand and held it out for me to shake. Spitting on a deal was something his grandpa taught him from the old country, he explained. Old country? I wondered where the country was that was any older than the country we were sitting in.

Not long after, a moving van pulled up to the house, and Andy and I rode our bikes down there really fast, since Mr. Noble had told us Tony and his family were moving in. When Tony came out of the house, I said, "This here is Andy. He is the great guy I told you about." I leaned close to Tony and whispered; "Don't say anything about him talking funny."

Tony just nodded.

"G-G-Glad t-to m-meet you," Andy smiled.

I said out loud for all to hear, "You can be Andy's second-second best friend, too."

I spit in my hand and held it out for Tony. He spit and shook mine. Then he spit and pushed his hand toward Andy.

"G-G-GROSS M-ME OUT!" But then Andy smiled really widely and spit in his hand, too.

Since then Tony and Andy and Eddie and I have been first and second and second-second best friends, but we don't tell the other guys that, and we don't spit in our hands when we make deals anymore either.

Anyway, Deak gave us all tasks to do, and we were picking our merit badge assignments when he told us he wanted us to check the trap he had put out to catch a rabid raccoon that had been sighted by several neighbors acting really weird and scary, and that way we could be "good citizens." Butch and Andy and I headed down to where it was, by the lake, but Deak sent me with this long pole to nudge the trap just in case there was a raccoon in it. "Don't you go anywhere near that crazy varmint, you hear?" He didn't have to tell us twice.

But when we got down by the lake where we had put the raccoon trap, we caught Carl and Denise together instead. They were on the other side of the lake, sitting so close to each other that they were practically in each other's laps. We watched them for a little while, and their voices were coming across the top of the lake. Carl was saying some really corny things to her, and I felt like I was going to gag if he didn't stop.

I broke the silence singing, "Carl and Denise, sitting in a tree, K – I – S – S – I – N – G, first comes love, then comes marriage..." I was wiggling my hips back and forth taunting them when Butch and Andy started to do the same thing. Andy looked really funny doing that since he is all arms and legs. He was moving his hips around like a hula girl, which made Butch laugh so loud he blew snot all over Andy's arm.

"Y-You dumb id-diot!" Andy screamed, punching Butch on the arm.

"Hey, you wiener, knock it off!" Butch whined.

"You are a t-t-total grossmeister! Y-You snotted m-me!" Andy jumped on Butch's back and wrestled him down.

"HEY, DON'T BE SUCH A JERK. OUCH, YOU'RE PULLING MY HAIR!" Butch screamed as he and Andy tumbled down the embankment towards the lake.

"Y-You're the j-j-jerk, snot face!" Andy yelped.

I just kept teasing Carl and Denise because Carl was staring across the lake at me with a look that could kill.

"Hey, lover boy, why don't you take a picture? It'll last longer!" I said, laughing really hard at my great sense of humor.

Carl jumped out of the little ditch next to the rowboat and started coming around the lake toward us. I screamed, "Holy Crapolee, guys, let's get out of here!" That's when I heard the snarling sound coming from the bushes right next to the lake, right next to Andy and Butch's heads.

"FREEZE, YOU GUYS!" I screamed, but they couldn't hear me because they were yelling at each other. Carl was running fast, and soon would be almost on top of me and wasn't going to stop for anything. I tried to figure out a way to get away, but that was impossible at this point. As he lunged toward me, I shoved the long pole I was carrying into his stomach.

"OOF!" He fell backward and just lay still holding his belly where I had driven the pole deep into his gut. "Y-You little jerk. I'm gonna k..."

"Carl, look!" I pointed to Andy and Butch, who now were fully aware of the fact that a very angry-looking raccoon was edging toward them.

Butch yelled, "It's foaming at the mouth just like Old Yeller!"

"It's g-gonna k-kill us!" Andy screamed

"HELP! HELP!" I screamed as loud as I could. "HELP! ANDY, BUTCH, RUN! GET UP AND RUN!"

Andy helped Butch to his feet, and they started to back away pretty fast but they were losing their footing in the mud, and the snarling raccoon was edging closer to them.

All of a sudden a loud report echoed off the water and down the canyon, echoing so loud it almost broke my eardrums. The raccoon popped straight up in the air and then, in what looked like slow motion, spun halfway around and started convulsing as it landed back on the ground. It then just flipped over onto its back, kind of spinning the way a turtle does when it's trying to turn over. The raccoon's legs were quivering and shaking all over the place, spraying rabies-infected blood in a circle around it. As it was dying, it let out the craziest scream I have ever heard. It sounded more like a crazy old woman than an animal, and the eerie sound echoed across the water too before it went pretty still. I watched its eyes roll up into the back of its head, and then all you could see was the white parts and this gooey slobber running out of its mouth.

Then Butch let out this crazy scream that kind of sounded like the raccoon. He was trembling, and all of a sudden Andy just busted out laughing really hard.

"GET AWAY FROM THAT DADBURN THING! NOW!"

I whipped around and saw Mr. Patchett standing on the dock with his rifle. He loaded another shell into the chamber and the clicking echoed across the water. Suddenly he shot again, just to make sure, and the raccoon stopped moving.

I looked over to the deep cover where the raccoon had come from, to see if there were any more rabid raccoons just waiting to pounce. Carl got up and grabbed my arm, twirling me into the lake.

"Hey! What the h..." I said as I went under.

When I got my head back up, I saw Denise. She had finally gotten to our side of the lake, but when Carl pitched me in the water, she threw up her arms, rolled her eyes and stomped away.

I could have sworn I heard Carl call after her, "Wait up, honey!" But it could have been the lake water that was in my ears.

All of a sudden Andy grabbed Butch's arm and twirled him into the lake too, and then jumped in behind him. I sloshed over, trying to land right on top of them. Then we all were splashing each other and cracking up.

Mr. Patchett stood on the dock laughing at the three of us while Carl was scrambling up the sandstone cliffs, desperately trying to catch Denise.

# CHAPTER TWENTY

# GOON SQUAD CHALLENGE

I was getting really dizzy, and felt like I might fall out of the tree. Eddie, Andy, Butch, T-Bone, Murph and I were dangling our feet out of the tree house, and with our heads down between our legs we were spitting into the baby pool down below for the hundredth time, trying to get it to fill for the Guinness record book. I think it was the first time Butch and Murph had been together in a long time when a dumb argument didn't break out, and I figured it must be because T-Bone was there. Butch usually started it with Murph, and Murph, having been the newest guy, seemed a lot more patient than any of us would be with Butch's constant ridicule. We were all waiting for the day that Murph let loose on Butch, but it didn't seem like today was the day. I had invited T-Bone to join us, and everyone but he knew that we were going to invite him into the club.

Carl and four of his Goon Squad buddies were walking with long sticks out toward Killer's house.

"Yo! What're you goons doing with the sticks? Playing little sheepherders, boys? HA HAHA!" Butch yelled and ducked behind a big branch, pulling his feet in quick.

We all pulled our legs in and lay still on our stomachs, huddling as close to the floor of the tree house as we could, trying to become invisible.

"How dumb was that? We are trapped up here, and you go and yell at the Goon Squad!" Eddie whisper-yelled.

"What'd you go and do that for, you lame-o?" I growled.

T-Bone looked at all of us like we were crazy or something, but he was smiling really big. I figured he spent so much time with his grandpa and out running everywhere, that when he hung out with guys his age, it must be really different.

"Y-Yeah, n-now they are g-g-going to p-pound us with th-their sticks!" Andy scowled.

"WHO CARES? They're a bunch of overgrown sissies anyway!" Butch said a bit too loudly.

Carl and his snarling Goon Squad had thundered up the small hill and were standing under the tree house.

"What the heck are you guys doing with that pool?" Carl shot up.

Mom was sitting on the patio and heard Carl. "CARL PETERS, LANGUAGE!"

"Sorry, Mom," Carl sheepishly said, loud enough for her to hear. But then under his breath he muttered, "I just said 'heck!' Why is that such a big deal?"

Greg looked at Carl and shrugged his shoulders. It seemed it was only in our house that 'heck' was considered a cuss.

Carl motioned with his head to Greg and looked at the pool. It was like my brother read his mind, 'cause they both grabbed

one end of the pool and started to lift it. They must not have
expected it to be as heavy as it was with a couple inches of spit
in it, because it started to twist away from them, and before
they could stop the pool's momentum, it came crashing down on
Johnny, who was on one knee examining a scab.

Johnny came up as mad as a wet cat,
covered in Secret Brotherhood
Detective spit. Even though
we were all really
mad that they
had spoiled
hours and hours
of our efforts, it
was almost worth
it to see Andy's big
brother covered in
disgusting, gooey spit.
"YOU IDIOTS!"
Johnny started
screaming at Carl and
Greg, and looked
like he was going
to punch their lights out.
Then all of a sudden he started to gag. The reality of what was
covering him was more than he could take. He threw up and the
projectile hit Carl, soaking his t-shirt.

"Gross, Johnny, you are sooo gro...." All of a sudden Carl
started to gag from having a ton of warm vomit on his chest,
and then released his own projectile vomit, hitting Johnny and
Greg with his spray.

Greg started making noises from deep in his throat like a
wild animal, and with one forceful push launched his own vomit
river right back at Carl. The other two goons, Jeremy and Jimmy,
backed up against the fence around the pond, staying out of
firing range.

It was both one of the strangest and funniest things I had

ever seen. Watching what was going on below us was like having a front-row seat to the best show you could ever imagine. I was so astonished I couldn't even laugh or speak. All three of the goons were yelling and puking and heaving, and it was kind of like when someone yawns and it catches on, and pretty soon everyone is yawning. Only this time it was with vomit.

All of a sudden Andy started making gagging noises, and the thought of him throwing up in the tree house make me feel a little queasy. I wondered if filling a wading pool with puke would make it into the Guinness book, but hated the idea immediately.

Carl and Johnny ran around to the pond's gate and jumped into the pond, whipping off their shirts and splashing each other. Pretty soon Greg jumped in too, and then Jimmy and Jeremy, even though neither of them had gotten gross. Soon they were all whooping and hollering and having a great old time, and that's when we started really get mad about what they had done to spoil our Guinness record. My mouth was sore from spitting so much, and the other guys felt the same, and we weren't wasn't sure we could start all over again. That meant all that film in my camera documenting our progress was a waste, and I wanted revenge.

The Goon Squad climbed out of the pond and came back to the tree. They all lay down on their backs looking up at us, daring us to just try spitting on them as they were drying off in the sun. Through his squinty face Carl growled up at us, "You boys have just entered the total dare-off zone." The look of evil crossed every one of the goon's faces. We all looked at Butch with the look that kills for being so dumb to call the Goon Squad over.

The next thing we knew, a REALLY big deal dare-off was going to happen because of Butch's big mouth. A total dare-off is when all of the guys you are hanging out with have to participate in the dare-off against all the guys the other group has, and you can't recruit anyone else to help. Carl's Goon Squad had just as many people as ours, but they are older and bigger so they had the advantage. We weren't about to back down, but one of the problems of this particular total dare-off was that T-Bone was with us and had never done a dare-off, but the total dare-off was going to require that he be a part of it. We would have to convince him that he had to do it, but with what the Goons were probably going to cook up, it might be hard to get him to go along.

So the first part is you play rock, paper, scissors, one on one to see how many from each team is left standing. When you win a battle, you get to lick two of your fingers and hit the underside of your opponent's wrist as hard as you want with just those two spit-soaked fingers. It stings like you can't believe when you connect right. Then the winners from each team battle the same way until only one person is left standing and that person's team wins, meaning they get to make up the dare-off for the other team.

Here's how we paired off: if your brother was on the other team, you went up against them, because of the unwritten law that a big brother can hurt his little brother but no one else had better even think about it. So Carl and I began, with it being two out of three, and the count of one – two – three - go. I had scissors, he had paper, and scissors cut paper. So I won the first round. Then, one – two – three - go. He had rock, I had scissor, and rock smashes scissor. Then one – two – three - go. He had paper, I had rock, and paper covers rock. Carl had won, and he wet his right index and middle finger and left a two-finger welt on my wrist that immediately swelled up, telling me it was planning on being a great bruise. I danced around but would not call out or cry or scream.

The rounds went the same way until it was Carl and Andy left. Carl beat Andy three out of three with a rock every time. When Carl went to smack Andy's wrist, Andy's big brother stepped forward and gave Carl the stink-eye. Carl let Andy off with a wimpy little smack, and all I could think of was how bad my throbbing wrist felt and how now I doubly wanted revenge. I decided right there and then that I was somehow going to get Carl really good — and the rest of the Goon Squad too, if I could.

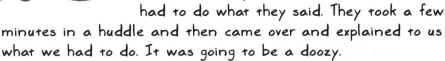

They won, so we had to do what they said. They took a few minutes in a huddle and then came over and explained to us what we had to do. It was going to be a doozy.

Before anyone could say a word about it, T-Bone yelled, "I'm in! You ain't gonna scare me!"

I figured with what the Goons had come up with, we could count it as T-Bone's initiation into The Secret Brotherhood of Boys.

# THE SUPER-DUPER TOTAL DARE-OFF

Andy, Butch, Murph, T-Bone, Eddie and I walked up the railroad tracks for about three miles with our backpacks on our backs and our sleeping bags tied on. It took a lot of convincing on T-Bone's part for his grandpa to let him come with us for an overnight, but I guess I had hung around the U-Pump-It with T-Bone enough and his grandpa thought I was a funny kid, so he let him come along for the overnight. Of course T-Bone left out one small detail about the fact that the place we were going was haunted.

Frisky and Friskier were following along with all of us, but they kept stopping to smell the ground and wandering off. At one point they found a dead animal that got so smashed by the train you couldn't even tell what it had been. It smelled like crispy death on account of it being all crackly, and almost all of its fur was gone. Frisky started to roll on it, and I yelled him away. He looked kind of ashamed of himself, but Friskier looked jealous that she hadn't gotten a chance to roll on it. My stuffed squirrel Deeden was in my backpack just in case. You never know when a vampire squirrel might come in handy—especially when your dumb big brother, who is afraid of the squirrel, might try to pull a prank on you with his dumb, goony friends.

Before we headed out down the tracks, we stopped by Deak's house and explained to him what we had to do. Deak told us the overnight stay in the "haunted" schoolhouse would qualify us all for a bravery merit badge. I wasn't sure if there was such a thing as a bravery merit badge, but it sounded good. Deak suggested a different place we could earn our bravery merit badge though — a cool cave near tunnel number three where we could spend the night, but we had heard about the Indian legends from that cave. Andy and I had spent some time in the cave even, but never, ever at night. I wouldn't say it out loud, but I just wasn't *that* brave, and the truth is I don't think any of my friends were either. We'd rather take our chances in the haunted schoolhouse, I guess because we figured it was bigger and had more places to hide. A cave had only one way out, and if you are inside, you aren't getting out.

On our way out, Deak invited T-Bone to join our scout pack. He was really becoming one of us, and fast.

The truth was, we didn't really have a choice where to spend the night, since the dare-off was specific about the haunted schoolhouse. We had convinced our parents to let us sleep in the old abandoned schoolhouse up the railroad tracks three miles — it's next to the ditch where Mom and Dad go asparagus hunting — because it would let us earn our merit badges for bravery. What we didn't tell our parents was that it was probably one of the scariest places on earth, and the real reason we were doing our bravery badge time there was because we had lost the dare-off.

The schoolhouse is an old one-room schoolhouse that's half falling down. It was once called the Fossil Creek School. It was white at one time and, according to Deak, could be seen from all over town. In its day it had a school bell up in the belfry. Now there were just bats up there.

Today the old school is a weathered gray-looking wood, and seems to have shrunk into the little valley it was built in. It looks spooky even during the day. The bell has been gone for decades, but some people claim they can still hear it clanging in the middle of the night when the old witch-teacher is mad. It was a school where kids as young as kindergarteners spent

time in the same room as kids who were old enough to be in high school; they all got taught there by the same teacher. The teacher lived upstairs when school was in session, and she is said to still haunt the schoolhouse. We would be staying in her old bedroom.

We were all a little bit afraid to go up there because of all the things we had heard about the schoolhouse. We had certainly explored it during the day enough, but never at night, which is when everyone says it's haunted all the time by an evil witch-teacher who taught there when people were still driving wagon trains. They say at night sometimes you can hear her yelling at the kids that were trapped in there with her during the famous blizzard. Trapped so long they all starved to death, and after that she panicked and hid the bodies between the walls of the old classroom. When the wind is just right you are supposed to be able to hear the ghost kids wailing and screaming and trying to escape.

The starving was supposed to have happened during a huge blizzard, in which the students would have just spent the night or nights in the schoolhouse until the weather cleared enough for people in their horse-drawn wagons to come pick them up. When it was clear enough, the townspeople came looking for their kids, and when the teacher confessed to what she had done, they hung her right in the middle of the schoolhouse.

Now legend has it that inside the schoolhouse at night, you can hear the loud scratching of her fingernails along the blackboard and see messages from beyond that show up mysteriously on the blackboard. The story also is that all of the people who were present at the teacher's hanging — there were seven in all — mysteriously died within a year and within a mile of the old schoolhouse. When one of them would die, the bell in the belfry would start ringing over and over by itself, one peal each for each of the kids that she had hidden between the walls.

Every Halloween, groups of people go to the haunted schoolhouse to see if they can make it a whole night inside without chickening out. My dad told me that every year, some of his college students try it, and they almost never spend the entire night.

The guys in The Secret Brotherhood of Boys and I have looked in the schoolhouse windows before, and the only thing we saw was the bird poop all over the wood floors and something written on the blackboard that gave me a chill.

### BEWARE OF THE CHAIR THAT GOES FROM HERE TO THERE, IT IS BEING RIDDEN BY A WITCH-TEACHER, SO ENTER IF YOU DARE.

There was a chair, all broken up and sitting in the corner. It had been there all those years.

It was the chair they had made the witch-teacher stand on when they put a noose around her neck, then kicked it out from under her. I guess no one had ever dared move it out of the dunce's corner. When we saw that writing on the blackboard and the broken-down old chair we had run away so fast even T-Bone wouldn't have been able to keep up with us.

I was angry. Carl and his Goon Squad would probably be too chicken to stay in the schoolhouse *or* the cave for that matter, but they were making *us* do it. So I was really starting to focus on revenge. After all, we didn't really have the time for their dumb dare-off with all the Guinness record work we had to do.

Right across the highway, near the abandoned schoolhouse, there is a neighborhood where a bunch of really mean teenagers hang out by this big lake we like to go to sometimes because of the big raft in the middle and the two awesome rope swings that catapult you way out into the lake on a hot summer day. We've seen them go into the schoolhouse before, and I wondered if they would be stopping by as we tried to make it through the whole night.

☺

Whenever the teenagers were near the schoolhouse, we would stay down in the ditch where there are tall weeds to hide beneath, watching them with our binoculars until they left. But if they came up this night, we would have nowhere to go because we would be trapped upstairs.

The teenagers think they are really tough, but they are kind of gross because sometimes the boys are over there with their dumb girlfriends acting all stupid and goofy, like older guys do when a girl is around. Sometimes we see them kiss. The boys all try to act really tough to impress the girls, but my mom says girls don't think that is so great and that it usually doesn't impress them at all. Girls don't seem to like the same stuff boys do, and they kind of get bossy when you call them "your girlfriend." Who wants that?

Mom told me about bossy girlfriends after Carl was bugging me really bad the night Denise ate dinner with our family a couple weeks ago in the backyard, and Denise started bossing Carl around and he seemed to listen to it. I didn't mind that because she was mostly telling him she thought I was cute and he ought to be nice to me. But she *was* pretty bossy.

Dad says Carl and Denise are an *item*, and that she has a ring in Carl's nose. I don't really know what that means, and

I am not sure I want to know. How a girl could like my big brother is beyond me anyway; since he is hairy, scary and mean.

Carl got really mad at me because he said something about how ugly I was at dinner to Denise and she said, "I think he is a cutie!" (I know I already mentioned that, but I kind of like that part of the evening the most.) She even winked at me. Carl then just stamped on my foot under the table, and the bite of cheeseburger I was eating ejected from my mouth because of the pain in my foot. It isn't like I just go spitting cheeseburgers all the time, but Mom told me that it wasn't funny and to stop showing off.

I am not sure how spitting your cheeseburger across the table is showing off, but I wasn't going to argue and make a big scene because it might embarrass Denise and she seemed really nice. Still, I was glad it wasn't me she was bossing around.

                                    ☺

The dare-off at the schoolhouse turned out to be different than what we expected, except that we didn't get much sleep and I felt really tired the next day.

I would admit that there were a few moments during the night that I felt pretty scared. Once I heard a strange scraping sound that made me sit right up, until I realized Murph was moving his foot in his sleep and it was his army boot that was scraping against the wall. But the things we feared most didn't happen, and we were talking about it as we walked down the railroad track back to our neighborhood.

"The teenagers never even showed up like you said they would, Butch," Tony murmured.

"Yeah, and we never even heard the screeching on the witch-teacher's chalkboard," T-Bone chimed in.

We all stopped over Tunnel Number Three, and started throwing the pink railroad rocks down into the water, competing to see who made the biggest splash and KEPLUNK. All of a sudden, thousands of small swallows flew off their mud nests which clung to the inside of the tunnel. They blackened the sky above us.

Murph said, "That's-because-it-was-a-weekend-night-and-even-ghost-teachers-take-the-night-off-on-weekends,-don't-cha-think?"

Andy answered "We n-n-never heard the tr-trapped k-k-kids screaming. B-But I swear I heard a v-v-voice in the m-middle of the n-night and it was c-coming through the wall!"

That kind of made my skin crawl.

"Andy, you better close your mouth if you are going to watch those birds, or they'll poop right in your mouth," Eddie chuckled.

Andy was watching the birds darting about overhead, but now he slapped his hand over his mouth.

"The most amazing thing was that the Goon Squad never showed up like we thought they would to torment us!" Tony said, squinting really hard to see if there were any big carp milling around in Tunnel Number Three's waters.

We had a couple old fishing poles stashed nearby in the weeds in case we saw a big run of fish from the top of the tunnel.

"Yeah, wh-where were those w-w-wussies?" Andy stammered.

"Oh, like you would have done anything to them if they had come, Epstein. You are such a huge chicken!" Butch jeered.

"Shut up Butch!" I growled.

We went on like that for a long time, and then we were all lying in the steep embankment that led from the tracks down to the water just looking up at the clouds and calling out what we saw in them. Every so often someone recounted details of the night before, and then as usual everyone tried to top the other with details and, before you knew it, it sounded like it had actually been a pretty terrifying night.

"So, how does someone join your secret club anyway?" T-Bone asked.

"Just like you just did!" I exclaimed, and all at once everyone put their arms into the middle of a human circle and made hand pancakes.

"That's it? I'm in?" T-Bone asked excitedly.

"That's it. You are official," I said.

T-Bone was smiling from ear to ear.

"W-We have t-to go b-back on a weeknight and tr-try it again," Andy muttered.

"Why on the weeknight?" several of us asked at the same time.

"B-Because, g-ghost teachers m-must t-take weekends off like r-regular t-teachers!" Andy insisted.

We all just laughed nervously and changed the subject quickly.

☺

Mom was on the back patio, soaking in one of the last days that would be warm enough to sit out there, when I walked in through the gate. She asked me the usual twenty questions about what happened, and I went through the whole experience with her again. I told her the whole story, and I told tell her how the dare-off worked, and I even mentioned how weird it was that the Goon Squad never even showed up to make sure we were sleeping in the haunted bedroom.

Mom explained that Carl and his gang were otherwise occupied on account of something else coming up, which involved Denise and two of her girl cousins who were visiting her family from San Francisco. Again, girls this and girls that... girls, girls, girls! Sheesh, I will never understand why they are such a big deal.

"As a matter of fact, they are in the living room right now." Mom nodded her head toward the house.

To avoid them, I climbed up the steel patio lattice, crossed the roof and snuck in through my bedroom window. I crept out into the hall and spied on them instead.

The Goon Squad and the girls were downstairs in our living room watching *The Brady Bunch* and you would think Denise's cousins were some kind of movie stars the way the older guys in the Goon Squad were acting. They laughed at everything the girls from California said, and acted really squirrel-y. Carl and Denise were sitting right next to each other on the couch.

I got bored listening to their dumb conversation after about two seconds, and army-crawled back to my own bedroom to make more plans about how we were all going to get into the Guinness book and how I was going to ask Andy not to mention us all going back to the abandoned schoolhouse without looking like a chicken. The thought of spending another night in there made my skin crawl.

*

I sat at my desk drawing and reading and thinking about the night before and how safe I felt in my room. I put my favorite Partridge Family album on my phonograph, and I pulled a Space Food Stick out of my desk drawer, peeled the wrapper back and chewed on it.

I guess the schoolhouse wasn't so scary because there were five of us and we had locked ourselves in the small bedroom upstairs and pushed a huge branch from a tree that had crashed into the window some time back against the door, so there was no way anyone could get in the room we were in. But the more I thought about those kids being inside the walls, the more I realized no branch could keep them from floating out into the room where we were. Besides, when you are with four other guys, it's not like staying alone in a scary place.

I hope Andy's suggestion that we go back up there on a school night to test Murph's idea about the teacher would pass right on by. Maybe next summer, but as the President I would have to insist that we get back to the task of setting a world record. The truth I would never tell the guys was that I was C-H-I-C-K-E-N to go back and spend another night.

The day after the dare-off at the old schoolhouse, the guys and I went to our scout meeting and described to Deak our night of bravery. We all exaggerated a lot, and it seemed the more he laughed and the wider his eyes got the more we added to the story. We got merit badges, and Deak made us all hotdogs and macaroni and cheese for lunch. Then we had a contest to see who could fit the most marshmallows in his mouth. Andy won of course on account of having the biggest mouth I have ever seen.

# CHAPTER TWENTY-TWO

# OPERATION ESCAPE

I thought Mr. Lattimore was this nice man who used to remind me a lot of my grandpa. At least, he did until I found out more about him and he stopped talking to me, but that is a long story. So here goes....

One day Mr. Lattimore was riding his bike up the hill by my house on his way to go fishing when he came over to my little snack shack and bought three cups of grape Kool-Aid and a couple bubblegum balls from me and sat in the shade of the lilac bushes talking to me.

"So, Gabriel, you seem to be a very enterprising young man. This I have noticed about you. You don't let the grass grow under your feet."

"Uh huh," I said dumbly in response. At first I wondered what I had to do with the grass growing because we were near the curb where there wasn't any, but then I guess since my snack shack was nowhere near our grass that's what he must have meant. And I thought he must mean I was like the people on Star Trek because they were enterprising all over the galaxy.

The great thing was that he chewed the gumballs and drank all three cups of Kool-Aid while we talked. Sometimes I see adults pouring the Kool-Aid out after buying it, like I am some kind of charity to support. If they just tasted my grape Kool-Aid, they would gulp it down like Mr. Lattimore and come back for more. He asked me tons of questions, which I noticed were mostly about how I felt about animals. That was easy for me since animals of all kinds are my favorite.

By the way, I add a secret ingredient to the grape Kool-Aid. It is the juice from the maraschino cherries Mom keeps in the fridge door, but I can't tell you how much I add because then I would have to go back to charging ten cents a cup instead of a quarter on account of anyone being able to make my secret formula. I am telling you, even Butch who says he *only* likes the green Kool-Aid comes back for more of my grape. There just isn't a more delicious cup of Kool-Aid anywhere.

Mr. Lattimore told me all about his wife and kids, and how since his wife was gone to heaven now and his kids lived with their own families, all he had now were his furry little friends.

"What kind of furry friends?" I asked.

"Oh, you have never petted an animal like these. Come down to my house this evening and I will introduce you to them. As a matter of fact, if you would like to have a job, I could use some help. You really do seem like a very enterprising young man. It seems every time I go by here, you have some kind of a grand sale going on from your humble stand. While all the other boys fritter their time away, you are making an honest buck. You will be the millionaire from this group," he promised.

I liked the way that sounded. "What are they? These soft animals of yours?"

'Oh, you will see. I promise, you will feel like you are petting furry butter."

I actually thought that sounded kind of gross. I had spit enough fur off my tongue from my animals to think that a whole stick of furred-up butter might be the sickest thing I ever heard of. One time when Flop was sitting up on the fridge and went into his narcoleptic seizure while Dad's head was poking around in there, he landed half on Dad's neck and half in the butter dish. It was funny listening to Dad trying to wash my big old cat in the sink afterwards, which was tough on account of how fat Flop is. The cat wash went okay as long as Flop was out cold, but boy oh boy when he woke up he gave Dad fits. I wasn't sure who was howling louder, Dad or Flopster. I could have told Dad that cats don't like water, but hey some people have to learn the hard way.

Dad walked funny for about a week after that. His neck had gotten stiff from fat Flopster landing on it..

☺

Later, I rang Mr. Lattimore's doorbell. He met me on the doorstep and then followed me out like he didn't want me in his house.

"Follow me, young Gabriel."

It was funny how he said everything so formal-like.

We walked around to the side door of his garage. He used a key to get in, which was kind of a weird thing to do at your own house. We never lock any of our doors, so he must have something pretty valuable in there.

When we walked into the garage, I couldn't believe my eyes. The garage was all fancy, with carpet on the floor, the walls painted a pale orange, and this giant rectangle of cages in the middle that went from the floor to the ceiling with about a hundred floor lamps and small warming machines. In each cage there were these cute little furry creatures he called chinchillas. I had never seen anything like a chinchilla before, except for some big mice; my guinea pigs weren't exactly the same.

"What's a chinchilla?" I asked as I wondered if they bit like my friend Craig's hamster.

"They come from South America, and are said to have traveled on ships from Spain at some point."

He pulled one of the babies out and put it in my hand. He took my other hand and guided it to the baby chinchilla's back.

"Will it bite?" I asked.

"Not unless you squeeze it, startle it, or if you are named Master Gabriel."

I looked at him and frowned, not sure what to make of that comment. Then I noticed he was smiling. "Master? Like on *I Dream of Jeanie?*"

He rolled his eyes, and I could tell he had no idea what I was talking about.

"I am joking you, young man. They will not bite. Feel that soft fur? That is a valuable, eccentric commodity you are holding in your palm."

What the heck is "eccentric" and "commodity," I wondered. And why didn't Mr. Lattimore just speak regular English? I mean, my dad was an English professor, and for the most part he spoke English that pretty regular people could understand. I stroked the little chinchilla's fur, and couldn't believe it was even real. The baby's back was so soft it did feel as soft as furry butter. It looked at me with its little beady eyes, and I looked around the room again. "HOLY GUACAMOLE! How many chinchillas do you have?"

"I didn't know avocados could be religious."

He chuckled into his hand a little too hard if you ask me, and I just tried to figure out what he thought was so funny.

"Right now I have over two-hundred, but I have had as many as four hundred at a time. So you see why I could use some help?"

I nodded, handing the baby back to him. He pulled a big one out of a cage to set it in my hands.

"WOW, he is so soft! Why do you have so many pets?"

A strange look crossed Mr. Lattimore's face that I didn't like. It was kind of like the look Count Dracula gives people to convince them that he is just part of the village, when really he is planning on sucking all of the blood out of their veins.

He shrugged his shoulders, and started scooping these pellets out of a huge bag on the floor. He used them to fill the little trays hanging on the wire cages. When I saw what he was doing, I grabbed a little scooper that was near the bag and started to do the same with the cages opposite of where Mr. Lattimore was standing.

"I am going to be having some new arrivals within the week. About twenty of the mommies are going to have little babies, and then it will be pandemonium around here."

"Pandawhatium?" I asked.

Mr. Lattimore just gave me a blank stare, shaking his head as he kept putting pellets of food in the small trays that hung on the cages.

"Wow, I bet the new babies are cute!" I squealed, thinking of all of those soft little babies crawling around in the cages.

"Actually, they look a bit like little rats. Soon enough their fur comes on, and they kind of grow on you," Mr. Lattimore said under his breath.

"HUH?" I imagined a bunch of hairless butter rats growing all over your body, and got grossed out. I grabbed some of the feed out of the big bag and followed Mr. Lattimore's lead. "Do they all have names?"

"Er... actually, none of them does. Now, how about you and perhaps your brother come down a few afternoons a week and help me feed, water and change all these pans? Of course I will pay you well."

I thought that was weird not to name your pets, but I guess with that many it would be really hard to remember all those names. "How 'bout my best friend instead of my brother?" I begged.

"Fine. I will pay you both three dollars a week for coming three times."

"ARE YOU KIDDING ME?" I got between fifty cents and a dollar a week for allowance, depending on what all I did. "I would do it for free! These guys are so cool!" I squealed, and then I got mad at myself. What if he said, *okay, then you will do it for free.* What a knucklehead that would make me, when I could have made good dough doing it.

'No, I will pay you both; it's a lot of work! Here is a key to the side door. Come Monday and Wednesday after school and Saturday by ten o'clock in the morning. Bring your friend down here tomorrow, and I will show you both all of your duties. If you do a good job, I will give you both a raise your second week.'

'WOW! Okay, deal!'

I wondered if there was a world record for feeding, watering and changing four hundred cages, but just then I heard my brother out in the street calling my name really, really loud.

'I gotta go, Mr. Lattimore! Thanks, I'll be back tomorrow with my buddy Andy! Seeeeyaaaaa!'

I bolted up the hill. I saw Carl going the other way, and I wanted to beat him home. No doubt Mom had sent him looking for me. I was going to try to climb up onto the roof and slip into my room without anyone knowing, and then I would come down the stairs like I had been there all the time, just to make my brother look like an idiot.

*θ*

After Andy and I had been working for Mr. Lattimore for a week, he told us we would each get three dollars and fifty cents a week as long as we did a good job. I sat at the dinner table explaining my job to Mom and Dad.

'So, he is paying me and Andy a ton for spending time with his chinchilla pets, and you should see the new baby butter rats!'

'What?' Mom and Carl said at the same time.

'Hmm...' Dad hummed.

'I meant...' I started to explain, but realized I was interrupting Dad by the look on his face, so I stopped talking.

'Hmmm, I guess your fifty-ish cent a week allowance doesn't have much impact any more...' Dad muttered.

'Give it to me then; it's not fair. I want a job like that!' Carl snarled.

I felt kind of bad that I had taken the job away from Carl then, but not bad enough to include him.

'Mr. Lattimore said he might have as many as five hundred Chinchillas by the end of the summer.'

Mom and Dad looked at each other in a way that made me suspicious that they knew something they weren't telling me.

A few weeks after Andy and I started working for Mr. Lattimore, I was talking about it at dinner again.

"He gave over one hundred of the adults away, so it is a little bit easier now. I guess he decided having five hundred pets was too much! The babies don't make much of a mess and their moms feed them mostly, so we don't have as much to do now. But Mr. Lattimore told us he was really happy with our work, so we would make the same amount even with less of them."

"Well, Gabe, he didn't *give* them away," Mom said.

"What do you mean?" I asked.

"He sold them, Gabe... er, he..." Mom paused here.

"Who would buy that many chinchillas?" I asked.

Mom and Dad looked at each other in that way parents do when they are going to tell you something you might not want to hear. Mom started to talk first.

"Gabe, do you know why Mr. Lattimore raises the chinchillas?"

"Because he's lonely. When his wife died, he was all alone in the house, and he needed more to do."

"Well, that's probably true, but there is a bit more to it than that."

Dad looked kind of sad all of a sudden.

Carl looked at me with a pained expression. "Uh, could I be excused?"

Carl always seemed to know when things were going to take a turn, and almost always figured out how to get out of it.

Mom and Dad nodded, and Carl bolted for the door. Mom and Dad explained it all to me, and I swear I think I cried for two hours straight. I felt like a criminal. I had been feeding and watering those cute little animals, never knowing I was getting them ready for something so sinister.

All of a sudden, I didn't like Mr. Lattimore at all. That's when I decided he was nothing like my grandpa. I mean, sure, Grandpa has a farm and all, and I know that some of his cows and pigs and chickens get eaten in the end — that is, all except for his three-legged cow — but that is for food, not some dumb lady's coat. I was so sad and so mad all at the same time that I went

upstairs and hit my pillow so many times it exploded and feathers
went all over my room. They fell from the top of the bunk bed,
where I always slept when I was mad or sad (otherwise I slept
on the bottom bunk, since Carl had moved out into his own
room). The feathers floated down like snow, and poor Flop started
sneezing so much I think it knocked him out, because he fell
face-first off the top bunk and landed next to his pillows below
with a sickening thud. This night was the worst night of my life,
and I just had to do something about it.

I had seen 101 Dalmatians twelve times last summer at the
summer movie matinee on account of the nice lady that lets you
sit there all afternoon watching all three shows as long as you
have good manners. So for four days in a row, me and Andy and
Butch rode our bikes down the railroad tracks to the Fox Theatre
and sat in the cool dark eating Hot Tamales, tubes of chocolate
drops, and red licorice while watching the evil Cruella De Ville
get hers from the much smarter dogs. Having seen that movie,
there was no way I was going to stand by and watch my little
Chinchilla friends get turned into someone's coat.

I picked up my phone and dialed Andy.

"Hello. Hey, go somewhere where no one can overhear you,"
I instructed.

"Wh-What's up? D-D-Do you have a n-new record to b-beat
in the b-b-book?" Andy whispered.

"Not about that," I whispered into the phone, just praying that
no one was listening in on our party line.

"Okay, wh-what's up?"

He was in the basement now where he could use his normal
voice.

"Andy, you know how Cruella De Ville was planning on making
Perdita and Pongo's puppies into a fur coat?"

"Yeah, s-so?"

"What do you mean by 'so,' you dummy? That's like the worst
thing in the world! Did you know her last name spells Devil?"

"It's just a m-m-movie! It's not l-like she's real, G-Gabe!"

"Yeah, well, what if I told you we had a Cruella De Ville in our
neighborhood?"

I went on telling Andy all the stuff
that Mom and Dad had told me. It
seemed like he was getting every bit as
angry as I felt thinking about the evil
thing that was happening down the street.

"H-He tricked us, G-Gabe!"

"Well, he never said anything about it, that's for sure!"

"So, what're w-w-we g-going to do about it?"

We spent the next half hour coming up with a plan.

*☺*

I called Andy with my plan. I had it all drawn out on a map
of our neighborhood.

"Wear as much black as you can, and
wear your ski mask — you know, the one
that covers your ugly face."

"Sh-shut up, you ugly b-butt face. I'm n-not
w-wearing a ski m-mask on a nice autumn n-n-night."

"Well, I am. If you want to get caught, that's your
business, but I'm not getting in trouble on account of you!"

"All r-right already."

"I'll meet you at 9:30 sharp tomorrow night at
Mr. Lattimore's side door. Be on time!"

"Y-Yes, s-s-sir."

Andy and I snuck down to Mr. Lattimore's
house on Wednesday night. Having worked
for him now for weeks, we knew that he
would be downtown playing bingo at
the Elks Club.

I opened the side door with the key Mr. Lattimore had given
me. Andy and I snuck into the garage and used our flashlights
only.

"Pssst, okay, I will hand them to you, and you
put them in the wagon and wheel
it across the road to the field, just
like we planned."

"I c-can't d-do it... M-Man
this hat is s-so hot!"

"Duh, I'm opening all the cages. Stop complaining. Think of the mission. Man, where is Murph when we need him? He'd know how to run this like a military operation. Get movin'!"

"Okay, b-b-but I-let's h-hurry! If w-w-w-we get caught, we'll g-get skinned."

I began to spring open the doors and tried to load them into the wagon, but they were jumping around, and a couple of them splatted out of the wagon and ran across the floor. I could imagine them all screaming "FREEEDOMMMM!" in squeaky chinchilla language that just sounded like a bunch of squealing to us.

All of a sudden Frisky came running into the garage and started chasing the Chinchillas that were scurrying across the floor.

"Frisky! BAD DOG! GO HOME!" I yelled, and he looked at me like I had hurt his feelings and cowered near the door. I felt bad, but this was hard enough. "I SAID, GO HOME!"

Frisky turned to go, but then saw a chinchilla heading out the side door and started to chase it across the street. I shook my head and made a basket with my shirt for the little furry animals. I had about eight of them in my shirt when I ran to the other side of the road and put them down in the field. They scurried this way and that, and then started following each other out into the darkening night.

Andy saw my success, and ran across the street and into the garage, opening cages and using his shirt to carry the animals too. Every so often one of us would yelp or yell because we got scratched or bit, but Operation Chinchilla Freedom was worth the sacrifice. We ran back and forth and back and forth until every cage was empty, and then we closed up the garage and got out of there as fast as we could.

"Hey, Andy, do you feel bad about what we just did?"

"I th-think it w-was the r-r-right thing to d..."

Andy stopped talking because car lights were turning onto Milky Way, where Mr. Lattimore lived, and we figured there was a good chance it might be him.

"DUCK!" I yelled, and we got down under a car that was parked along the curb. Both of us shinnied our bodies under the car, and then the car that had turned sped past Mr. Lattimore's house and down the hill.

"RUN FOR IT!" I screamed as I scrambled out from under the car and headed across the road into the field. I thought I saw about a thousand little eyes reflecting blue from the hundreds of Chinchillas that were looking for a warm place to spend the night. I wondered if the jackrabbits and cottontails would be their friends, or if they would be bullies.

We hid behind cars, trees and houses and then ran up in the ditch, past my house were I could see Mom and Dad sitting at the breakfast table having some ice cream. Then we crossed the gravel road and climbed up into the tree house where we perched ourselves with my binoculars and waited for Mr. Lattimore to come home.

Andy fell asleep, but I kept an eye out. My body felt all tingly, and then I really started realizing what we had done. Mr. Lattimore was going to come home and find a whole garage full of empty, open cages, and we were the only ones who had keys. It made me feel kind of bad, but then I started thinking of him as a real-life Cruella De Ville again, and I got angry all over again. Then I saw Mr. Lattimore's pickup truck coming up Venus Avenue and turning onto Milky Way. I watched him get out of the truck, stop and look at something in the grass. Then the spookiest thing happened. He turned really slowly, like Frankenstein, and looked up the hill toward our house. And then it looked like he was looking right at me.

Then he bent down and picked something up. I couldn't see what it was because it was too dark. He slowly walked around the side of the garage and I saw a bright light flood through the three windows on the front of the garage door like an evil three-eyed jack-o-lantern lighting the front driveway and lawn. Then I saw what he had picked up and set back down. It was one of the little chinchillas, and it wasn't moving.

"FRISKY, YOU BAD DOG!" I said aloud to no one in particular.

It seemed like an hour passed, but it could only have been minutes when I heard our phone ring across the road. The night was quiet except for Andy's soft snoring and the constant sound of crickets.

Dad leaned out the back patio door and yelled, "Gabriel!"

I froze in my place. Everything seemed to be moving in slow motion.

"GABRIEL! ARE YOU BOYS UP IN THE TREE HOUSE?" Dad yelled.

I felt bad, but I simply couldn't move. My mouth was frozen. I could tell by the tone of my dad's voice that we had done a very bad thing.

All of a sudden my walkie-talkie started to crackle, "GABRIEL PETERS! THIS IS YOUR FATHER. I WOULD SUGGEST IF YOU CAN HEAR MY VOICE THAT YOU GET HOME PRONTO!"

Oh man, this was going to be worse than I thought. This was going to be worse than the time I cut up my brother's underwear and buried it. This was going to be worse than the time.... My mind stopped working. I looked over at Andy, and was suddenly angry with him for being able to sleep. I wondered if I was ever going to be able to sleep again. Dad is not the spanking kind of dad, but the sound of his voice made me think he might be tonight.

I had to think fast; what was I going to do? I could run away. It was only about two hours before the next train would be coming through, and if it was going slow enough I could hop it and live in Mexico for the rest of my life. Then just when I thought it couldn't get worse, I saw something moving up the road toward my house. I whipped my binoculars up and OH MY GOSH, I couldn't believe my eyes. Mr. Lattimore was heading up my driveway toward my front door. I wondered if I was going to have to go to prison. I suddenly could see my face in one of those black-and-white photos in the post office.

I could hear our doorbell and then the low murmuring of two angry men. All of a sudden my walkie-talkie started to crackle again, and I was surprised to hear Carl's voice whispering through it.

"Gabe, come in... it's an emergency!"

Carl's voice sounded really scared, which sent a huge chill up my spine.

"Gabe, come on, I really need to talk to you!"

"What do you want?" I whispered back.

"Oh man, thank goodness I got a hold of you. What in Sam's name did you do this time?"

"None of your business! Just leave me alone!"

"Gabe, I am trying to help you."

"WHERE ARE YOU?" I whisper-yelled.

"I'm in my bedroom, but I was at the top of the stairs listening to Dad and that old guy talking about something you did."

"Mr. Lattimore?"

"Yeah, if that's the guy with those chinchillas."

It struck me as strange that Carl was speaking to me, and not calling me a chicken-so-and-so. "Why are you trying to help me?"

"Keep it down, little brother. I am upstairs and hearing all the arguing downstairs. You got that Lattimore guy good and steamed. What were you *thinking?*"

"He was going to turn all of those chinchilla babies into fur coats!" I started to cry, realizing I was in big trouble.

"Oh man, Mr. Lattimore just told Dad those things were worth a thousand dollars."

My heart sunk.

Andy woke up and asked, "Wh-what's g-going on?"

"We have to run away!" I told him frantically.

"Hang on, Dad's coming up the stairs." Carl whispered.

"What's he doing?" I asked desperately.

"SHUT UP!" Carl said in the loudest whisper I have ever heard. He kept his finger on the button so I could hear Dad asking him if he knew where I was. Then all of a sudden Dad's voice crackled on Carl's walkie-talkie, "Gabe, if you know what's good for you, you will be heading to our house as we speak, OVER AND OUT!"

"Andy, it was all my idea. You go home and don't ever say a word about any of this. No one will know you were involved," I said.

"N-N-No way! W-We d-d-did this t-together..." Andy whispered.

"Just go. I mean it!" I insisted. I guess it was the tone of my voice that convinced him. He just looked at me like he felt sorry for me and then shinnied down the tree and ran down the ditch toward home. Things were sometimes tough enough for Andy at home. He didn't need to get in trouble for my hair-brained idea.

When I walked in the front door, Mom was sitting on the couch with Mr. Lattimore, showing him some pictures in one of our family albums. Mr. Lattimore stood and walked over to where Dad had met me by the front door. I saw Carl slip out the back door into the dark, and I envied him more than I ever had.

"You need to start explaining yourself, young man," Dad said in a stern voice.

"Oh, I'm not sure any explaining is necessary. I think we know very well what he has done." Mr. Lattimore smiled, but it was more like an evil leer, and I swear his teeth looked more like a vampire than human.

Mr. Lattimore put his hand on my shoulder and said, "Gabriel, did you simply let the animals go in the yard?"

"Oh, no."

"Well then, where are they?"

"Uh..." I could feel a huge lump forming in my throat, "We... I mean, I carried them across the road into the field."

"Ah, domesticated chinchillas in the wild fields with fox, coyote and the Indian in the lake... what a divine idea."

Mr. Lattimore winked at my dad, but Dad just gave him a strange look.

"I'm sorry, I just..."

"Gabriel, there is no excuse for what you have done," Mom chimed in.

"I know, I just..."

We stood there in a strange circle discussing what an idiot I was when a loud commotion at the front door startled all of us.

Andy, Carl and four of his Goons came busting in the door. All of them had a ton of squirming, furry chinchillas in their shirts.

Carl said excitedly, "They are all just sitting in the field, like they are frozen in place, all huddled together. Some of them tried to get away, but we got all these and more. We rounded up the other kids that were playing hide-n-seek and they are out there collecting and filling the cages back up with them. How many were there?"

Mr. Lattimore looked shocked to see all the chinchillas squirming around in the shirts. "I had perhaps one hundred and eighty of them."

"Okay, well we'll go put these back in the cages and go back out for more. Andy, you count the ones in the cages when we get back there."

All of a sudden the chinchillas in Greg's shirt squirmed out, "OW, THAT LITTLE RAT JUST BIT ME!" Greg started sucking on his hand while five chinchillas went bounding across the living room floor.

"Greg, don't put that in your mouth!" my mom said, "You don't want whatever was in the little critter's mouth in yours, do you?"

Greg started to sputter and spit.

"Greg! Don't spit on the carpet!" Carl snarled.

Greg's upper lip started to tremble like he was going to cry, "Oh man, now I have rabies and will have to get shots in my gut!"

"Don't be so melodramatic!" Mr. Lattimore scowled, his butt stuck way up in the air as he tried to reach the chinchilla under the couch. "My chinchillas are disease-free! There is a greater chance of you giving it a disease than the other way around! OW!"

Mr. Lattimore pulled his hand back quick. He had been bitten, too.

One chinchilla ran to the top of the stairs and started tumbling down the stairs. Frisky and Flop were pouncing, hissing and running after it. I saw one go under the couch, and Flop got a hold of one in his mouth.

"CAN I GO HELP?" I squealed, afraid I was going to be grounded for the next fifteen years.

Dad looked at Mr. Lattimore and mom and said, "Well, it would be the right thing to do. But you and Andy are still in a heap of trouble.

Right before I headed out the door, I looked at the three of them and lied straight to their faces. "Andy had nothing to do with this. It was all my idea and I did it alone," I claimed.

I turned and ran out the door and joined the other kids who were gathering the chinchillas to save my skin. I knew we had to do it, but I still hated the idea of those furry little creatures being made into someone's coat.

⊘

As it turned out, we found one hundred and sixty-eight of the chinchillas, which Mr. Lattimore seemed fine with. But Dad made me work for Mr. Lattimore for free for three months after that to learn my lesson. After that, Mr. Lattimore and I didn't talk like we had.

I didn't have much to say to Mister Cruella De Ville anymore.

The only positive thing that came from the whole thing was that my big brother defended me and went to a lot of trouble to keep me out of really bad trouble.

## CHAPTER TWENTY-THREE

# INDOOR GARAGE SALE

Since I lost my paying job with Mr. Lattimore and my candy concession always closed down in the winter months, I had to figure out a way to make some money. Carl got a bunch of money for Christmas that he had been holding on to for a long time now, so I figured it was a good time for me to set up my indoor garage sale like I had in the good old times. I grabbed several items from my closet, priced them, then set them on my television tray in my doorway and waited.

Last year I took a bunch of the stuff that Carl had sold me at one of our indoor garage sales and wrapped it up in boxes and put them under the tree for him. It was funny. I kind of started it as a joke, but when we were unwrapping our presents on Christmas Eve, it turned out that he was really excited every time he opened one, and it was already his once.

Ever since Carl and I got our own rooms, we have been having these sales in our doorways right across from each other. We set up television trays in our doorways and put stuff on them with price tags made out of brown tape and pen and then begin a kind of indoor garage sale without the garage. I always put gumballs, atomic fireballs, lemonheads and any of the other candy I got at the Bait Shop that was still leftover on the tray because those were automatic sales.

It's kind of funny when Carl sells me something he really still wants, because he begs me to put it back up for sale after he starts to miss it and I always charge more than he sold it to me for (what are little brothers for?) He has, or should I say had, and now has again, a record album of Pete Seeger that Dad had for ages. Seeger's this corny folksinger, and Carl really likes his music. I convinced Carl to sell me that album once at one of our doorway sales for fifty cents, and then played it in my room so quiet that Carl could barely hear it, but loud enough that I knew he knew I was listening to it. He would yell across the hall for me to turn it up, but I sometimes can be mean, so I would just close my door, making it even harder for him to hear. That's what he gets for pushing his weight around all the time.

So, we were having this sale and I had a bag of marbles that Carl wanted in the worst way. In the warmer months, he and his buddies would sit under the tree house tree and play marbles all the time. My bag has three of the best steelies you have ever seen, and a cat-eye peewee that is supposed to be some kind of collector's marble worth maybe hundreds of dollars. I got it from Joe up at the Bait Shop in a marble tournament. I won it fair and square, but I still felt bad about taking it off of Joe on account of the fact that he's a nice grandpa kind of a guy. Oh, and just in case you don't play marbles, a steelie is actually a small ball bearing, which is a bearing between a wheel and a fixed axle, in which the rotating part and the stationary part are separated by a ring of small solid metal balls that reduce friction. But man, can they knock a whole bunch of glass marbles out of the ring!

So I set up my television tray in my doorway with a bunch of cool stuff displayed for Carl to see when he got home from one of his friend's house. He walked up and stared at the pile of Atomic Fireballs that I listed for a quarter apiece.

"What gives with that? Twenty-five cents for one? That's ridiculous! No one's going to buy those for a quarter!"

"Uh, you mean no one as in you?" I asked, giving my best innocent look.

"That's highway robbery!" he snarled.

That was another thing everybody said that made no sense to me; what highway were they talking about?

"What?" I said with as little interest as I could manage.

In my room my turntable was playing Gordon Lightfoot, another one of the albums my brother wanted back so bad. The volume was so low that you barely caught the lyrics of *The Edmund Fitzgerald*, my brother's all-time favorite song. And I had the album cover propped up on my dresser so he could see it from my doorway.

"Give me *five* fireballs for a quarter!"

"NOPE!"

"Four?"

"NOPE!"

"Three? Come on!" he pleaded.

"NOPE!" I sneered at Carl as if it was the most ridiculous thing to think I would part with them for that amount, even though I bought them from Joe at the Bait Shop at twenty for a dollar.

"Fine! I'll just go up to the Bait Shop tomorrow," Carl said, thinking he was being clever.

"Closed on Sundays," I sneered.

"Fine, you little chicken-weasel. I'll give you a quarter for *two*!"

He leaned toward me and clenched his fist, trying to scare me.

"NOPE! ITS ONE FOR A QUARTER OR NOTHING!" I popped an atomic fireball in my mouth and started making sucking and *mmmm* sounds. "Man, these are *sooooo gooooo!*" I rolled the fireball around in my mouth, clicking it against my teeth. "I may just eat them all myself instead of selling them at all!"

"You chicken-jerk!"

Carl was so frustrated his face was turning all red. He stormed into his room and grabbed his piggy bank. He turned it upside down and a pile of change fell onto his bed. He threw a quarter at me, demanding a fireball.

"FINE! GIVE ME ONE, YOU BIG CHEATER!"

"NOPE, price just went up." I taunted. "You argue with me, I raise the price. It's fifty cents for one now!"

"I'll tell Mom!"

"I don't care. They're my fireballs, and I can sell them for whatever I want to!" I sneered and sucked loudly on the fireball.

"YOU GOT 'EM FOR A NICKEL APIECE! *TWO* FOR FIFTY CENTS!" Carl demanded, clenching his fists.

I quickly calculated my profit and said, "SOLD!"

He threw another quarter at me and I threw two fireballs into his room. They bounced off the wall, making a loud cracking sound.

"You chicken-jerk! I'll never buy another fireball from you, EVER!"

"Oh, that's too bad, because they *just* went on special... THREE FOR A QUARTER!" I yelled like one of the carnival barkers.

"YOU CAN'T DO THAT!" Carl's voice was all whining.

"OH, REALLY? OOPS, THE SALE CHANGED BACK BECAUSE YOU ARGUED. NOW THEY'RE TWO FOR A QUARTER AGAIN! SOON GOING BACK TO ONE FOR A QUARTER, GET 'EM WHILE THEY'RE HOT!" I looked at Carl's desperate face, "Get it, *hot?* They're *atomic* fireballs, get it?"

"No, explain it to me, you big chicken-rip off, " he growled, looking like he was ready to crash through my TV tray and throttle me.

My sense of humor was totally lost on Carl as he grabbed another quarter that had dumped out of his piggy bank and threw it at me before I could change the sale again. I threw two more fireballs at him. I still had fifteen fireballs, and since he just gave me seventy-five cents for four of them, that meant I had fifteen fireballs for a quarter or less than two cents apiece, including the one in my mouth. Not a bad day in the candy sale world of Gabriel Peters, if I must say so myself. Now if I could convince him to buy two more for a quarter, I would have recouped my entire dollar spent and still have a ton of atomic fireballs for myself to show for it, and all for F-R-E-E!

I pushed the other merchandise on my television tray forward to keep Carl's interest. I started the song *The Edmund Fitzgerald* back up on my phonograph and turned it up a bit, knowing that Carl couldn't resist even the smallest sales pitch.

Carl barked from inside his room, "How much for the Gordon album?"

"NOT for sale," I muttered.

"Come on, man, I'll give you back the dollar you gave me for it!"

"No way, Jose, it's a collector's album."

"Two dollars?"

"Nope!"

"Three?"

"Uh, no!" I could hardly believe my ears; I'd make two dollars profit and I really didn't like the album that much. I was going to hold out, though. I know how Carl gets, and even though he threatens never to buy things at my high prices, he can never stop himself once it is in his mind.

"I'm gonna tell Dad that you *took* it from me."

"I didn't though!"

"I don't care. He doesn't know that and I'll..."

"Here's the deal. The album is four dollars, BUT..."

"WHAT? FOUR *DOLLARS*. DO YOU THINK I AM SOME KIND OF A MORON? THAT'S FOUR TIMES WHAT YOU PAID ME FOR IT!"

Carl sure knew his math and I did in fact think he was a moron.

"As I was saying before I was SO rudely interrupted, that includes the album *plus* FOUR atomic fireballs, TWO super-sized lemon heads *and* ONE chewy Marathon bar! The sale only lasts for one minute! ACT NOW!"

I had heard the radio commercials on KIMN radio and they always told me to "act now" if I wanted their deal. I looked at my Timex watch on my wrist and followed the second hand.

"Forty-five seconds!"

Carl was desperately trying to pull dollar bills he had stuffed into his piggy bank out with a pencil. "OKAY! HANG ON!"

"THIRTY-SECONDS!-CHANCE-OF-A-DOLLAR-INCREASE-LIKELY!" I said as fast as I could, to add suspense.

It looked like every time Carl almost had the dollars coming out of the bank's bottom hole, he lost his grip, and they went

back inside. He had so much money stuffed in his piggy bank
that none of it was coming out easily.

"Fifteen seconds!"

"HANG ON!"

"Ten seconds!"

"HANG OOOONNNN! GABE, I'M GONNA POUND YOU ONE
IF YOU DON'T SHUT UP!"

I whispered tauntingly, "Uh, we aren't supposed to say shut
up!"

Carl flashed me a look-to-kill look. I knew Dad was
downstairs, and if I screamed for him he would rescue me from
any beatings, so I continued the countdown.

"Five, four, three..." I slowed down a little, seeing that he had
finally had a big explosion of dollars on his bed, as they all had
come out at once. I couldn't believe my eyes; he had fives, tens
and tons of ones. He was totally loaded, and I wanted that
wad of bills.

"STOP! I GOT IT!" Carl grabbed a bunch of cash in his fist
and rushed to the door.

"Two..." I just kept counting down.

"Here!" He threw a five-dollar bill at me, but it fluttered to
his feet.

"ONE, BZZZZZZZZZ!"

I made the bzzzzzzzz noise like at the end of a period in
basketball to signal the end of the sale. Carl's face was a mix
of panic and anger as he bent over and picked up the fiver and
slammed it down on my television tray. Now his face was so red
I knew not to push him any further.

"SOLD, ladies and gentlemen, to the big ugly Carlio Peters!"

Carl glared at me and growled, "Hand it over, chicken-thief!"

I looked at his five-dollar bill and said, "Now sir, instead
of giving you your dollar in change, I could throw in four more
Atomic Fireballs, four extttttrraaaa large grape bubblegum balls
AND...you won't believe the level of my generos..." I paused to
increase the tension. "...ity!"

Carl leaned his big face into mine and growled, "Get on with
it, if you know what's good for you."

I retreated back behind my television tray into the safety of my room and pulled the tray securely into my doorway, blocking Carl from coming in. "Yes, ladies and gentlemen, you won't believe what I am willing to part with for this measly extra dollar... a huge almond-filled CHUNKY chocolate bar!"

"FINE!" Carl shouted.

"Wow, Gabriel, you should go into advertising or sales."

Dad was at the bottom of the stairs. All the yelling must have gotten his attention. He looked at Carl standing in the hall and me ducking my face through the doorway to see him.

Carl twisted my ear as I leaned out.

"OW, you jerk, what was that for?" I yelped.

Carl just leered.

"You boys have fun and be nice to each other now. Carl, I'd watch it. Our little salesman will have your entire piggy bank by the end of the day if you let him."

Dad walked back into the kitchen laughing, and I called after him, "HEY DAD, YOU WANT TO BUY A BAG OF MARBLES?"

"I'll pass!" Dad laughed from the kitchen.

Carl eyed the bag of marbles I had brought out.

"Hey, how much for the marbles? Are your steelies in there?"

"Yuh..." I said, acting totally disinterested

"What about the cat-eye? Is it in there?" Carl asked greedily, and I knew from that point on I had him on the hook, no matter what I charged.

"Yuh..."

"How much?"

"A hundred dollars!"

"Yeah, okay, a hundred dollars! Let me just write you a check chicken-butt! How 'bout we trade something?"

Carl's mouth was all red from the atomic fireball he had started eating; it looked like he was wearing Mom's lipstick. I wiped my lips hard on my sleeve because mine probably looked the same.

"You don't have anything I want," I said snottily.

"Oh yeah, well that's what you think. Check this out."

Carl walked in his room and grabbed his own television tray. He set it in his doorway and then threw a huge brick of Black Cat firecrackers onto the tray, followed by some bottle rockets, a bunch of snakes and a single M-80. "Don't tell Mom," he said with a leering taunt

"Don't you think I've gotten in enough trouble as it is with firecrackers this summer?" I asked in a way that I thought would make Carl think I wasn't interested and then he would bring the price down.

Carl puffed up really big and looked across the hall at me. "Yeah, and don't think we have forgotten about your stupid prank on us that night. We *will* get you back, and good! These would be a nice addition to your collection..."

My eyes must have grown really big, because I saw by the look in Carl's eyes that he knew he had me. I felt all panicked inside. I wondered if he had found my stash in the crawlspace. Was pulling the same trick on me, selling me back my own stuff — stuff that I had stolen from him that he had stolen from my uncles? I felt kind of sick, thinking that there was even a possibility that my big lug of a brother could outsmart me at my own game. "WHERE *DID* YOU GET THOSE?"

"Doesn't matter! What does matter is that I have them and you don't!" Carl snarled, turning my sales tactic right back on me. "Now, how about trading me back my money and another five bucks for these?"

I wanted those firecrackers in the worst way, and more than anything right then I wanted to know if my brother had somehow outsmarted me. The Secret Brotherhood of Boys thinks it is the coolest that I have those fireworks, and oh man, we had planned to do such cool things with the firepower to torment our older brothers when the smoke had cleared from the last time. I couldn't even imagine what the club would think of me if they knew somehow I had been outsmarted. The only way I could see to keep that from happening is to buy all of them back.

At that point Carl could probably trade me for everything in my room, but I remembered something Dad had told me about poker faces and not letting on, so I acted like I really didn't want them at all.

'Eh, Andy's brothers can get me more, I mean some firecrackers, any old day.' Which I knew wasn't true because we had tried to talk them into it before and they said no way — that they weren't going to go to juvie for giving a bunch of little kid punks illegal firecrackers.

'Oh yeah, well Andy's brothers are my friends and I will just tell them not to.' Carl snarled at me.

So, Carl and I went back to bartering back and forth, but the whole time I had an eye on his or was it really my firecracker collection, and when he wasn't looking I saw in his closet that he had a whole bunch more. By the end of the sale Carl had all of his records back and I had a huge pile of firecrackers (including a second brick of Black Cats and a brick of Ladyfingers, which made me wonder if Carl really had found my stash in the crawlspace, because I didn't have any Ladyfingers) and I knew just what I was going to do with them. I also put two and two together, and figured Carl and his buddies must have been the ones who blew up Mr. Patchett's ceramic garden frog (which I only knew about because Mrs. Parsons had included it as big news in the *Skyview Newsletter*, which she put in everyone's mailbox once a month), and when I needed to, I would use that info as blackmail to get Carl back *and* to get my/his money back.

The funny part was I had only bought all of those dumb records off Carl so I would have something he really wanted when he had something I really wanted, and it had worked like a charm.

Sometimes big brothers aren't nearly as smart as they think they are!

I walked over to my phonograph and put the greatest record of all on and turned it up; *Indian Reservation* by The Raiders. I walked around my room waiving a tomahawk that I had bought when we went to the Grand Canyon.

"Hey, give me my record back!"

"Next sale maybe!"

The truth was, I wasn't going to sell it to him at all. I liked it too much.

"I'll get that album! You watch!" Carl barked and slammed his door.

The sale was over. We both went back to our own business, and I waited until Carl was in his room with the door closed. Then I snuck downstairs and, as quietly as I could, unlatched the crawlspace door and secreted myself inside, pulling the door shut behind me. I crept to the Christmas box where underneath I had hidden the firecrackers. I knew right away that Carl had been there by the way the box was moved. I lifted the box and there was a note that said: 'HO HO HO, Chicken-Dumbo, you can never fool this big brother. Better luck next time, loser!'

I ripped his note up into little pieces and stuffed it into my pocket.

I turned the light off and slowly opened the crawlspace door. As I was putting the door back into place, I noticed Carl, out of the corner of my eye, sitting at my dad's desk on the other side of the room just waiting for this moment.

He laughed like an evil monster. "Booo ha ha, I guess we know who's smarter now, huh chicken-dummy?!"

Oh, we'd just see about that.

# CHAPTER TWENTY-FOUR

# BUDDIES

The Secret Brotherhood of Boys decided it was time to get back at the Goon Squad for their dumb dare-off plan. When it was starting to get dark, we were fishing for sunfish and bluegills down at the lake for the first time of the season, because finally we would be able to break through the thin crust of ice to fish. Just a few weeks before there had been an arctic blast that lasted for about five days and it had been too thick to break through without a fishing drill, and we wanted to skate and sled over the fish instead of catching them. Now we were in front of a cave on the sandstone cliff side with our lines, all fishing in the same large hole we had broken out. As we sat there, we were planning the records we were going to try to beat to get into the Guinness book over the spring, as well as planning how we were going to get back at the Goon Squad for all of the stuff they have done to us in the past year.

Suddenly my brother and his Goon Squad popped out of the high weeds on the other side of the lake where they had obviously had been spying on us.

"We can beat you pukes at any world record challenge!" Carl snarled across the lake.

"Yeah, any day!" Jimmy agreed

"STOP LISTENING IN ON OUR PRIVATE CLUB MEETINGS!"
I shouted, completely insulted that they would eavesdrop like that.

"Yeah, we totally could break any record you tried to set!" Greg
yelled.

Carl snarled, "We'll listen to any meeting we want to. Think
*you* can stop us?"

I rolled my eyes at the other guys, knowing that trying to fight
with the older kids wasn't going to work. We had to outsmart
them if we were going to beat them. That's how it always is with
bullies, especially big brothers.

One after another, the Goon Squad chimed in about how
great they were and what pukes we were as they popped up from
the weeds like army men.

Murph snorted while he was looking at them. He was holding
up an imaginary rifle, probably pretending he was in some war
and had them in his sights. He whispered too loudly, "Yeah,-like-
maybe-the-most-ant-bites-in-a-fort-caused-by..."

"SHUT UP!" Butch screamed at Murph, clamping his hand over
his mouth. Then he whispered, "You idiot, you want them to know
we did that?"

What Butch wasn't counting on was that a voice carries across
water as if you rowed it over in a boat.

"Did he say red ants?" Carl asked his friends, "What did you
say, you little puke, about ants?" Carl snarled toward us. "So they
*did* dump those ants in our fort. Man, you little jerks are going to
pay for that!"

"Yeah, let's go get those little twerps!" Greg screamed.

"We need to get them back for the pop-bottle rocket night
anyway!" Carl cried out, and all of the Goons started running
from their hiding place, whooping and hollering at the tops of
their lungs.

All at once we all started reeling our lines in, and so our
sinkers and bobbers were getting into a big tangled mess. I
motioned for everyone to just drop their fishing pole into the
dense bushes right below the cave that was only about five feet
above the ground and scramble. We could come back for the poles
and gear later, but this was looking to be a danger zone.

As the Goon Squad ran toward us, their banter about what they were going to do to us if they caught us went on and on until Mr. Patchett turned on his back porch light and yelled across the lake, "WHAT IN TARNATION IS ALL THE YELLING ABOUT OUT THERE? YOU COULD WAKE THE DEAD! NOW SHUT UP!"

Andy stammered, "D-D-DEAD?"

"Did-he-say-wake-the-*dead*?" Murph squeaked.

The neighborhood streetlights and back porch lights were popping on, because now the sun was totally gone and the shadow of the mountains had darkened the land.

A shudder ran up my back as I thought about all of the dead legends surrounding the lake. The dead Indian, the dead dog, the girl who had drowned there once; there were so many things to scare you at night down at the lake. One by one, each of us in The Secret Brotherhood of Boys made kind of lame excuses to pack it in and go home.

Mr. Patchett was laughing at something really loudly. I suppose it was us and the way we scrambled to get out of there so fast. He would be the first house we would doorbell-ditch later, and then on to the Spitter's and Mr. Stolz's house.

"Well,-no-way-we-can-get-any-planning-done-with-those-losers-around!" Murph said loud enough so they could hear him. "Man,-I-wish-Boney-was-around.-He-wouldn't-let-those-lameos-pick-on-us!"

"Yeah, hehheh..." I laughed nervously, trying to think of what our best escape plan was.

This time of year, some of the water from the neighbors' backyards flowed down the cliffs, forming ice sheets at night that you wouldn't want to get into since it was like a thirty-foot drop onto hard boulders below. Our best way out of the canyon was to go up before the Goons got around the lake. Leading up the side of the cliff were five caves that you climbed to and out of to get to the next one. But this time of year they could be treacherous on account of the ice, and some of the kids in the neighborhood had fallen trying and broken their arms and noses. But at this point we didn't really have much of a choice if we didn't want to get pounded on. Otherwise we would have to slip down and creep along the river and then up one of the passages that wasn't so steep to get out of here. But that gave them a lot more time to catch up.

Murph and Butch had shinnied up to the next cave and were still climbing toward the next one. I whispered, making sure the Goons couldn't hear me, "Murph, test the cliff above your cave. We need to know if there is any ice there."

"YESSIR." Murph saluted me and continued his crawl upward. He got to the top of the cliff and waved his arms like a bird against the sandstone. "All-clear-General-Peters."

"Oh brother," Butch snarled, following so close to Murph that they both almost took a topple off the top.

"WATCH-YOURSELF-PRIVATE!" Murph barked to Butch.

"Oh, shut up already, army-man idiot!" Butch answered as he clung to the sandstone, crawling past Murph upward.

Murph turned away from Butch and asked, "Next-order-General-Peters?"

"General?" I asked.

"Well,-actually-as-the-President-you-would-be-the-Commander-in-Chief,-like-Ike-Eisenhower,-who-was-a-General-and-then-became-the-President-because..."

"Murph, we don't have time for a war story. Come on guys, follow Butch and Murph and let's get out of here!" I commanded and started shinnying up the cliff.

"W-W-We ought to g-g-go see wh-what's going on up at the streetlight!" Andy said loud enough for the Goons to hear, but acting like he didn't want them to. He was thinking kick the can, doorbell-ditch or hide-n-seek would beat anything going on down in the dark lake right now. And even though there were probably ten streetlights in our neighborhood, we all knew which light he meant. There was one central meeting place for all kids.

As I climbed up the cliff last following the guys, I noticed Carl and his buddies were coming around the lake pretty fast as we were all cresting the top of the cliff and went dashing up the path that ran along the top of the cliff toward home to get away from the goons.

We ran into the open field toward home and stopped in a huddle, no one sure which way was the safest to get away from them.

I whispered, 'Come on guys, let's hide out in the tree house until those lamebrains find something better to do, since Andy just let them think we were heading for the streetlight.'

But Carl and his friends were hot on our trail, and there was no way we would get up into the tree house without being seen. So we all ran up to my house and then dashed down the ditch behind my house. Oh, what I wouldn't give for a few of those firecrackers right now!

We ran for a while, and then jumped down in this dark place under a huge cottonwood tree, where the roots stick out over the ditch and kind of make a bridge we could all hide under. We held our breath as the Goon Squad ran by. We could hear them talking about us, and what they were going to do to us if they caught us. I guess Murph mentioning the red ant incident was all it took to get them pretty steamed.

As we were hiding down in the ditch, I started thinking about how this one time in this ditch last summer we caught the monster crawdad. The cottonwood trees are really thick down where the ditch is, and someone a long time ago tied a rope swing to a big branch, so we decide to swing off it and see who could make it across the ditch by holding on only with their hands. I went first and sailed across, barely making it to the other side. Murph went next, and of course started pretending he was on a Green Beret mission, crossing the King Kong Delta or something like that. As he flung his body across the ditch the rope snapped about five feet above his head, sending him suddenly down into the ditch's fast, rushing water. He sprang out of the muddy water and started screaming like he was drowning or something, even though he could stand up and the water only came up to his chest.

Everybody made fun of him for screaming that he was drowning, and he's never lived it down. Then, as all of us were pointing at him and laughing really hard about the shocked look on his face, suddenly he started hopping around and screaming like a kindergartener, 'OW, OW, OW, they've got me.'

Of course, we all assumed Murph was just in one of his war fantasies. But when he held one of his feet up over the ditch water, there was the biggest crawdad I have ever seen pinching his big toe through his tennis shoes. He started screaming about it taking his toe off, and what shocked us was that Butch was the one to jump into the rushing water and grab the monster crawdad off of Murph's foot. Butch took his prize monster crawdad home, and told us later that it was really good with butter and hot sauce. He also told us he sucked the brains out of its head, but none of us really believed him.

Anyhow, now we had to find a good place to hide, because no doubt the Goon Squad would be back looking for us soon. As I looked up into the canopy of the tree for a place to climb and hide, I saw that someone had tied another rope to the same spot right above the center of the ditch. I noticed it at the same time Murph did. I guess he wanted to do it right this time, because he ran backwards about twenty feet and then sprinted to the lip of the wide ditch and flew through the air, with the rope in his hands. He was sailing toward the other side when all of a sudden the rope snapped just like last time and he plummeted down into the now icy waters. It was so cold where we were standing, I couldn't imagine how cold the water must be.

The wind was whipping, and you could feel the unseasonably early chill of spring in the air as Murph scrambled up the muddy side of the ditch and screamed like a little kid again. Murph's teeth were chattering, and as he got to the side of the ditch, he looked like he was about to cry. I think he was afraid that the waters were full of monster crawdads. I felt bad for him, and then something happened that I didn't think would happen in a million years. Butch took his own coat off and gave it to Murph on account of feeling so bad for him. Now, that could be a world record right there!

# THREE SECRETED GRAVESTONES

Some spring days feel exactly like some fall days, which reminded me of last Halloween when it was right around the corner, the chill in the air and all of us had spooks, ghosts and goblins on our minds when we weren't trying to figure out just how in the world we were ever going to get into The Guinness Book of World Records. We all pretty much decided we would try a lot of things, but the idea of the world's largest spit pool still seemed to be our best chance. Those houses that usually just had the black-hand silhouettes in the windows that meant it was a safe house to go to if you were in trouble, now had pumpkins, witches, skeletons and all kinds of decorations to welcome the spooks that soon would be trick-or-treating at their doors. I always imagined the black-hand silhouette was the hand in the box on The Addams Family show.

Those kind of days in fall are just like this spring they're hard times of year up in the tree house. In the summer it is really hot and you can just jump down into the pond. In the winter it is always cold, so you wear a ton of clothes to stay warm. But on these days sometimes it's hot, sometimes it's cold. Usually it is both in the same hour, but we love being up in the tree house anyway. My friends and I passed around the bottle of Elmer's glue® and one by one squirted the sour-smelling glue on to our palms and spread it out thin.

Then we just sat there in a circle telling dumb jokes and blowing on our hands to dry the glue.

Tony's cousin, who was visiting from out of town, started telling jokes he might have read out of a book somewhere.

Since Tony was an official member of the Secret Brotherhood of Boys, he got to invite special people into the group like anyone else. So his cousin Tucker got to be in the Secret Brotherhood for the weekend, which meant he could come to our secret meetings in the tree house.

Tucker's a couple years younger than us, but he's a really cool guy. Tucker was telling us about the time his cub scout troop got to go to the fire station and ride in an old-fashioned fire truck that one of the guys' grandpa owned, which sounded so cool that we all decided to ask Deak if our troop could do the same thing.

Tucker squirted a bunch of glue on his palm and said, "Hey, you guys want to hear some jokes?"

"Sure," Tony said right away to put his cousin at ease and to let us all know that we should include him.

"What do you get when you cross a cow with an earthquake?" We all just shrugged. It's always kind of weird when someone hangs out with you that you aren't used to, but Tucker was great and fit right in without being a pain.

"A milkshake!"

That got a few chuckles.

"Hey, how about this one?

What do you get when you cross a centipede with a parrot?" Tucker continued.

"What?"

"A walkie-talkie!"

Then it just went on from there.

Eddie chimed in, "Why did the skeleton not go to the dance?"

"Why?"

"He didn't have no body to dance with."

A groan filled the tree house.

Eddie thought it was funny that he could make us all groan, so he continued, "Why didn't the skeleton cross the road?"

"Why *didn't* he? Don't you mean why *did* he?" Butch scowled.

"Don't ruin my joke. If I meant to say *did*, I would, wouldn't I? SO, why didn't the skeleton cross the road... as I was saying."

We all shrugged.

"He didn't have the guts to. Get it?" Eddie rolled around like he was the funniest guy ever.

"LAME!" Butch growled.

"You-come-up-with-a-better-one-Butchski!" Murph barked back.

"Don't call me that!" Butch growled.

Andy jumped in, "Wh-What d-d-do you c-call a c-cow with n-no legs?"

Everyone just shrugged and blew on their gluey hands in a disinterested way, but I said, "I dunno, what?"

"G-G-Ground b-beef!"

Andy's smile showed me how much it meant that he had stumped us with his joke.

Tony added, "Hey, I know another centipede joke!"

"Oh yay for centipedes," Butch muttered.

"G-Go home, ya b-b-big grouch!" Andy growled.

Butch just rolled his eyes.

Tony said, "Hey Butchski, what do you call a centipede who lost all ten thousand of his legs?"

"A-REAL-SORE-LOSER-WHO-NEEDED-TO-GET-A-LEG-UP!" Murph chuckled.

"How dumb is that? They don't have that many legs," Eddie snarled.

"DON'T CALL ME THAT!" Butch snarled.

"Sorry, Butchski," Tony said sarcastically.

Butch rolled his eyes and started laughing, starting to catch on that everyone was sick of his attitude.

"Oh yeah, speaking of legs, what do you call a man with no arms or legs standing on your front porch?" Butch threw at us.

"How-can-he-stand-on-a-porch-without-any-legs?" Murph scowled and talked fast like usual, and it was funny watching Tucker watching Murph talk. I guess we were just all used to him by now and could keep up with him.

"Shut up and don't ruin my jokes, Warboy!" Butch scowled, so quickly back in a bad mood.

"I-was-just-asking-a-logical-question..." Murph just went back to blowing on his hand.

"Okay fine, what do you call a man with no arms or legs on your front porch?" Butch asked angrily.

"That's-more-like-it.-Geez,-everybody-knows-this-dumb-joke," Murph murmured into his hand. "Matt?"

"Thanks a lot for ruining my joke, you moron." Butch punched Murph on the shoulder, but not too hard, actually kind of playfully. It was obvious to everyone that Butch and Murph were becoming better friends, even though it never looked like Butch was going to accept him as one of us.

Murph smiled, "Those-jokes-had-a-beard-when-my-grandpa-was-a-boy-in-a-treehouse.-What-do-you-call-the-same-guy-with-no-arms-or-legs-in-your-bathtub?-BOB!"

A collective groan filled the tree house.

"SLOW DOWN, MURPH, IF YOU ARE GOING TO INSIST ON TELLING YOUR LAME JOKES!" Butch growled, but it was funny because we all knew he just wanted to be able to remember them, even though he was trying not to let us know that.

Murph just kept rattling off his jokes.

"What-do-you-call-the-same-guy-on-your-wall?-ART!

"LAMER!" Butch growled.

Murph ignored Butch.

"What-do-you-call-the-same-guy-in-a-pool?-BOBBY!

"LAMEST!" Butch growled.

"What-do-you-call-the-same-guy-on-the-ice?-PUCK!"

"LAMESTER!" Butch growled.

"Lamester?" Murph continued. "What-do-you-call-the-guy's-one-legged-wife?-ILENE!"

"LAMESTEST!" Butch growled.

"What-do-you-call-the-same-guy's-one-legged-wife-in-China?-IRENE!"

"NOT COOL!" I yelled. "I hate jokes that make fun of the way people talk!"

I glanced at Andy. He just nodded while Murph grunted.

"And I hate jokes that make fun of people who are different than you..."

"Wow-relax-Peters-it's-just-a-joke!" Murph complained.

"ANYWAY, MURPH, THAT WAS THE LAMESTEREST!" Butch growled, but he was laughing all the same.

Tucker joined in again, "What do you call a chicken with his head cut off? DINNER!"

"Ha ha!"

For that one, everyone kind of forced a laugh.

Tucker smiled, "What do you call a skinny chicken with its head cut off? THINNER DINNER!"

That got a bigger chuckle.

Tucker frowned, but kept going.

"What do you get when you cross a frog with an icicle? A Frogsicle!"

"That's just dumb!" Butch growled.

"Says who?" Tucker asked.

"Says me!" Butch glared at him.

Tucker didn't seem to care.

"Why did the star get up in the middle of the night? To twinkle!"

The loudest groan yet rose from the tree house.

"That-is-so-dumb!" Murph laughed

"Kind of funny though, huh..." Tucker said, smiling ear to ear.

One by one we each peeled the dried, tacky glue off of our palms and set all the pieces on the garbage bag on the floor of the tree house. Soon we would connect them all and smash them into the world's largest dried palm-glue sheet. We hadn't found anything like that in the book, so there was a good chance that we could make it into the book as a first. Maybe even the Elmer's® glue company would pay to fly us to Ireland to accept our prize, if there is one, because we were using their glue and just making them more popular. We had each agreed to spend some of our allowance on a big bottle of Elmer's® glue, so we would have enough to make the sheet of glue big enough to cover every inch of the floor in my house. We figured if we had a catchy record name like, 'Glue peeled from six boys' hands that covered the entire kitchen floor in a house,' it would get someone's attention.

Tony started laughing at something and said, 'Hey, how many Polocks does it take to screw in a light bulb?'

Butch said, 'No Polock jokes!' on account of both of his sets of grandparents were from Poland.

To which we all just said, 'OkiedokieButchski!'

He didn't think that was funny, especially when Murph started talking about the war in Poland.

Tony snorted and laughed, 'One-hundred, ninety-nine to turn the house, and one to hold the light bulb!'

Eddie spouted, 'There's these two muffins, and they are in the oven. One of the muffins looks at the other and says. 'Hey, is it getting hot in here or what?' The other muffin looks at him and says, 'Oh my god, a talking muffin.''

I said, 'Like we haven't heard that one a million times.'

Tucker said, 'You shouldn't say 'God.' Say 'gosh.''

Andy blew on his palm and said, 'M-My d-dad says it's the same th-thing. You j-just say g-g-gosh, but you mean G-God and He knows it anyway!'

'Shut up, that is so dumb. God has more important things to worry about than you saying gosh or not!' Butch growled.

'You saying my d-d-dad is d-dumb?' Andy glared at Butch.

'OKAY, STOP ARGUING AND BLOW ON YOUR GLUE!' I growled. Being the President meant that people had to do what you said.

Andy looked at me blankly and asked, 'D-Do you w-want to h-hear a funny g-g-girl joke?'

"Uh, do we have a choice?" I asked. For some reason, usually when Andy told a joke it was really, really long and with his stutter even longer. The way he told it usually wasn't at all funny, but he's my best friend and I wasn't about to say no. I poured more Elmer's® glue onto my palm and laughed to myself, wondering if it would be dry by the time Andy was done.

"Okay, th-there's these t-two g-girls and they are having a smart-off. Th-that's when th-they try to d-decide wh-who's the smartest."

That was one of the problems with Andy's jokes. He always explains things that we all understand already.

"So anyway, th-they have b-b-been at it f-for about a w-week and they are b-b-both g-getting r-really t-tired of it when one of the g-girls l-l-ooks at the other and says, 'H-hey, I've g-g-got it! Wh-Which is cl-closer, F-Florida or the m-m-moon?' The other g-g-girl says, 'D-Duh, c-can you s-see F-Florida?'"

I started laughing, not to make Andy happy but because I thought it was funny and because Butch and Tony both said at the same time, "I don't get it."

"That's because you two are girls!" I laughed into my shirt.

"SHUT UP PETERS!" Butch whined.

"Make me," I snapped.

Butch made a farting sound on his arm. "PHHHHHHT, you're made."

"Sooooo funny I forgot to laugh," I said out of boredom.

"Then remember next time, you moron!" Butch growled.

"Butchski, you are a major Pollock jerk!" I yelled.

"Hey, watch it, wiener," he snarled.

"Make me, WHINER!" I answered.

Butch blew on his arm again. "Told ya before, PHHHHHHT, you're made!"

"Wow, how original." I said, rolling my eyes.

The whole time Tucker was watching everyone, trying to make it all out. I think he was probably wondering why it sounded like

we didn't like each other, but that's just how we talked. I think
if you aren't getting kidded with, then there's something wrong.

I peeled the thin, dried glue off of my palm and while it was
still kind of tacky, pushed it together with another piece and
sealed it with my fingernails along the edge. I pulled the piece
up off of the plastic bag; it was now about the size of a large
pizza.

☉

Meanwhile, the early spring air was whipping through the
branches of the tree and making us shiver up in the tree house.
We were no longer as secreted as we had been since the leaves
were all but gone and winter was hanging on as long as it
could, even though by the calendar we were supposed to be
having spring weather. We got tired of the glue project, and went
back to trying one more time to set the Guinness World Record
with spit and the wading pool. We knew the spit was still
going to freeze a little at night and then thaw during the day.
Spitting off the tree house would be stupid if our spit turned
into icicles on the way down.

Murph had finally had it with all of Butch's constant
ridicule, our world record attempts and our obsessions with
playing football, fishing and swimming in the water holes. He
thought we were all a bunch of sissies. I knew that because
when he stormed away from our tree house where we had all
been spitting in the wading pool below, he stomped his foot
and screamed, "YOU-ARE-ALL-A-BUNCH-OF-SISSIES!" As
he stomped off toward his house, waving his arms around and
marching like he was in a war, he looked back one more time
and yelled, "BUTCH,-YOU-ARE-THE-BIGGEST-SISSY-OF-
ALL!"

"Oh, yeah?" Butch yelled loud at Murph. "What did I do?" he
asked us.

"YEAH!" Murph shouted.

"Say it to my face," Butch growled.

Murph turned around like he was going to head back. Then he put his hands on his hips, and with an angry look on his face screamed really loud for the whole neighborhood to hear, "Come-down-and-I-will.-Not-only-that-but-I'll-smash-your-face-in!"

"Whatever." Butch just sat there and rolled his eyes like he couldn't be bothered, but if you ask me, I think all of a sudden he was kind of scared of Murph because neither was budging.

When Murph realized nothing was going to happen, he turned and stormed off toward home.

About a half an hour later I watched in my binoculars as Murph, dressed like he was heading to a war with black face paint and green camouflage fatigues, moved sneakily out into the fields with a canteen and a big buck knife on his belt and what looked like a pellet gun in his hand.

Butch saw him too. "I think I hate that kid. Can we vote him out?"

I spun around and looked right in Butch's eyes. "How would you like to be left out? Do you know what it feels like to have everyone have friends except for you? You bug him way too much. I like Murph. I think he is sometimes kind of annoying, but not as annoying as you are. So just shut your mouth once in a while and give him a break."

Everyone looked at me like I had lost my mind.

I think I feel so strongly about it because of how lonely I was when no one at school would be nice to me. I thought Murph was annoying a lot of the time, but mostly he's all right. And sometimes I get really sick of Butch always being so negative.

T-Bone came running up the hill, waved at us, and ran right past us toward Killer's and the old lady's house. He was wearing a funny outfit — combat-style boots and all black, including a funny looking hat. And it looked like his face was covered in dirt or something.

"M-Man, that k-kid can r-r-run!" Andy laughed at the sight of T-Bone, the blur, running past so fast.

"What's with the outfit?" Eddie asked.

"Dunno," Craig said, and we all shrugged and agreed.

I watched T-Bone with my binoculars as he disappeared down the hill by the railroad tracks.

Tony looked at his watch. "Tucker, we have to go. See ya guys!"

"Th-Thanks for the spit, Tucker."

"I hope you guys make it into the Guinness book. See ya!" Tucker said, and they climbed down out of the tree and walked toward Tony's house.

After a while of spitting, my mouth was too dry to go on, and I was really starting to feel the chill in the air. Summer was right around the corner, But this day felt like winter and I was soon to find out how the sense of dread and fear can add to that chill.

Murph had circled all the way around us, and was now demanding we all put our arms in the air. He was pointing his pellet gun straight up in the air. T-Bone was standing next to him with a stick that was bent kind of like a rifle, pointing it and looking down it like he had us in his sites.

"YOU-WON'T-BELIEVE-WHAT-I-FOUND!" Murph said once he had our attention.

"Keep your voice down, Murph!" I demanded, thinking if he really found something cool, the last thing we wanted was for one of the older brothers to overhear.

"There's-a-spooky-graveyard-up-on-the-south-field-of-the-cattle-farmer's-farm!"

Murph whisper-yelled.

T-Bone nodded furiously.

"Yeah right! Big deal!" Butch growled, still sore that he had been challenged by Murph and that we had all seen him back down.

"No-really,-there-are-three-gravestones-and-they-aren't-for-animals!-There-is-a-really-weird-haunted-shack-there-too.-There-is-a-big-gravestone-and-two-small-ones.-It-is-so-spooky,-like-they-are-for-kids-or-something.-Isn't-it,-T-Bone?"

T-Bone just nodded and kept us in his sights.

"How far is it from here?" I asked.

"It's-just-on-the-back-side-of-the-farmer's-field!" Murph was so excited.

"That's bull. I've lived here all my life, and I would know about it if it were that close," Butch snarled.

"You-don't-know-everything-Butch!" Murph barked.

Butch squinted and snarled, "More than you, WARBOY! I'm an insider, you aren't."

"SHUT-UP-BUTCH!-I-MEAN-IT,-YOU-BETTER-SHUT-YOUR-STUPID-MOUTH-OR-I'M-GOING-TO-SHUT-IT-FOR-YOU!" Murph was shouting, and T-Bone was looking at him like he had gone completely crazy.

"Murph, come up here and say that," Butch said, but pretty quietly.

I think he wasn't sure he wanted Murph to hear him.

Murph put his pellet gun down, leaning it up against the tree. Then he punched the air.

"I'm-not-dumb-enough-to-fight-in-a-tree.-You-come-down-here-and-I-will-pulverize-you!"

"Go, Butch; you push him around enough. Go show him who's boss around here," Eddie said.

Butch had no choice; he was the one who had challenged Murph, and to keep face he was going to have to back it up. He started down the steps. Murph moved closer to the tree.

When Butch stepped off the last step, Murph raised his hands in fighting position. "I-tried-to-be-your-friend,-but-all-you-ever-do-is-make-me-feel-stupid.-I-don't-know-if-I-can-beat-you-up-but-I-am-going-to-try!"

T-Bone climbed up the tree house steps to get a better view and probably to make sure he didn't get any of the wild punches. Butch raised his fists, and they started to circle each other. All of a sudden Murph threw his right arm right around and his fist came crashing down on Butch's nose. Butch's nose exploded with blood, and then Murph threw his other arm and his fist came down on the side of Butch's head. Butch went down on his back, and Murph jumped on him and pinned his arms to the ground.

"Ow man, you broke my ear!" Butch started to cry.

Murph said, "You-had-enough?"

His fists were still up high in the air and looked like they were ready to do more damage.

"COME ON GUYS, THIS IS SO STUPID. I MEAN, WE ARE ALL IN THE SECRET BROTHERHOOD. WE AREN'T SUPPOSED TO FIGHT EACH OTHER, JUST OUR DUMB BIG BROTHERS! IF YOU BOTH WANT TO GET KICKED OUT, KEEP IT UP!" I yelled.

Butch looked pitiful. I couldn't really blame Murph though. Butch did ride him hard, and there is only so much a person can take.

"UNCLE?" Murph asked.

"Uncle," Butch squeaked.

Murph jumped off Butch, who just lay there on the ground holding his ear.

"Say-sorry!" Murph snarled.

"Sorry," Butch said so quietly you could barely hear it.

Murph reached his hand down and helped Butch to his feet.

"Friends-now?" Murph asked.

Butch looked at him curiously, "Yeah. I guess."

"B-B-Best f-friends?" Andy laughed.

"Don't push it." Butch snarled, but he was looking at Murph in a way that you could tell things were going to be different between them from now on.

After Murph and Butch climbed back up into the tree, Murph said, "Let's-tell-Deak-at-our-scout-meeting-tonight-about-the-graves!"

"T-Bone, would you like to become an official member of our Secret Detective Brotherhood?"

T-Bone just nodded, stunned from what he had just seen. He stared at Butch, whose face and shirt were covered in now drying blood.

θ

Later, after our regular scout meeting, Deak rubbed his chin and had a weird frown on his face.

"What did you say the name on those stones was, Murphy?" he asked.

Murph raised his eyebrows as he said, "Just-Murph,-please!"

Deak nodded, "Okay, *Murph.*"

Murph smiled and continued reading the note he had written in his little notebook where he draws all of his tactical maps and war strategies. "On-the-big-one-it-said-'Here-lies-my-beloved' —SAMUEL-STROH-1889/1941-and-on-the-little-ones-it-said-SARAH-STROH-and-STANLEY-STROH,-but-I-didn't-write-down-the-dates,-cuz-we-got-scared-off-by-this-weird-moaning-sound-coming-out-of-the-haunted-

shack!"

"Well, I'll be. Those are Grizelda Stroh's kin," Deak said, scratching his chin.

"Who?"

"She lives up there in the old house on the hill overlooking the lake," Deak muttered.

"Oh,-weird.-How-do-those-people-fit-in-with-her-and-why-are-they-buried-on-the-farm-then?" Murph asked.

Deak's phone rang.

"Excuse me, gentlemen." Deak got up and answered the phone, then cupped his hand over the receiver. "I have to take this, boys. It's a client who is closing on a house this week. You can show yourselves out. Take those uneaten cookies with you!"

As we were leaving Deak's house, we all walked together up the hill, munching on the freshly baked chocolate-chip cookies and dropping off one by one until we walked to Butch's house, where he and Murph both turned to go in.

"Where you going, Murph?" I asked.

# CHAPTER TWENTY-SIX

# PEN PALS

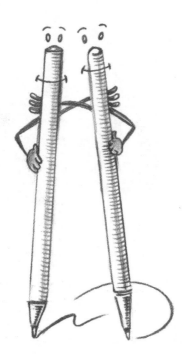

Mr. McCammon gave us another assignment. This time we had to include correspondence. We had to write a story and include a letter in it that we would write to the person we were telling the story to. Mr. McCammon told us he would give us a grade, but if we were writing a letter to someone special, we should tell him that and then he wouldn't read the letter, because letters were personal. Boy, this assignment was really on the honor system.

I wanted Mr. McCammon to read my letter and my story even though in my story I mentioned that I almost cried, and then did. Somehow I knew Mr. McCammon wasn't the kind of person who would make fun of someone for having feelings.

Creative Essay Assignment
English - Mr. McCammon
1st draft

## LETTERS TO AND FROM MY FRIEND TYLER
### By Gabriel Peters

I decided to write about one of my friends who had moved away. My friend Tyler moved to Iowa, and as I was writing the story I thought about how I felt when I first found out.

I was sitting in my room, and I felt like I could cry when Tyler came in to my room to tell me. I stopped myself just in time. I didn't want him to make fun of me, and I didn't really want to talk to him about it. There are just some things that are hard to put into words.

Tyler was a good friend and I was going to miss him, especially because I knew I may never see him again. And, I felt sorry for him, because the reason they had to move was to get away from his mean dad.

Finally, when Tyler left the room, I let myself go and started to cry. My dog Frisky began to whine. He didn't like it when people felt bad. He jumped up onto my bed and started to lick the salty tears off my cheeks.

Tyler came back over later for dinner. My mom wanted to have his favorite dinner as a way of saying goodbye. She made hot dogs, macaroni and cheese, and canned fruit. Tyler really appreciated it. At dinner Mom suggested that Tyler and I become pen pals. She said we should write each other every other week, with one letter from Tyler one week answered by mine the next, and so on. Since Tyler and I had always made up stupid poems about everything after reading a Dr. Seuss book, we decided to write to each other in rhyme.

A month later I got a letter from Tyler. I recognized his handwriting on the envelope and was excited to tear into it. I slid my finger under the sticky flap and pulled out a sheet of paper from his Big Chief notebook, which is a lined notebook with a real Indian chief on a red cover.

Tyler's first letter read:
    So how's it all going?
    I hope you are fine.
    Iowa is hot
    Mom said I just whine

I first wrote down my response on his letter, so I would remember what I sent him. Then I copied it down onto another sheet of paper later:
    Things are okay
    Not as good without you
    Sorry you are so hot
    Move back here, please do

Tyler wrote back:
    I wish I could come back
    I don't much like this place
    Being so far away
    Gives me a mad face

I wrote back:
    Well your face is so ugly
    No matter where you living
    I am just kidding
    To you my jokes I am giving

Tyler wrote back:
    You talk about ugly
    Go look in a mirror
    If you're looking for ugly
    It couldn't get too much clearer

I wrote back:
    So, how's your sister
    Is she still really mean?
    Tell her I said
    Her teeth are all green

Tyler wrote back:
   My sister says "So what?
   Who cares what he said!
   Your ugly friend Gabey
   Smells just like he's dead."

I wrote back:
   So she hasn't changed
   Do you have any friends yet?
   I'm one of your best friends
   So don't you forget.

(I didn't have the heart to tell him that Andy and I are really the best of best friends.)

Tyler and I sent a couple more letters, and then when we were both back in school we pretty much stopped writing. Mom told me maybe sometime I can call him, but it is long distance and that is really expensive, so maybe I'll write him back next summer. But I had already written this letter, so I sent it, even if it didn't rhyme.

Dear Tyler, you don't have to feel like you always have to write me. Things around here are good. We are having tons of fun and the Brotherhood is growing. We have two new members; one is a kid named Keith Murphy. We call him Murph. He is really into war and stuff. He is kind of a dork, but like they say, there is strength in numbers. The other kid is this really fast runner named T-Bone, and he is funny. I miss you. GP

I sent that last letter and never heard back from Tyler. "Out of sight, out of mind," as Dad always says.

Still, Tyler is a good guy. Maybe someday we will get together and laugh about the good times we had together in the neighborhood. I wonder if he thought that in my letter I was telling him that Murph and T-Bone had replaced him, and that he wasn't important. I sure hope not, because Tyler was one of the best guys I've ever hung out with.

# CHAPTER TWENTY-SEVEN

# BEST FRIENDS

Andy and I headed down to the pond to fish for bluegills and sunfish and for the millionth time Mr. Master, who was the five-hundred-pound carp who lived at the bottom of the pond.

We knew Mr. Master was down there because he had bitten one of Andy's big brothers' foot when he was swimming. I saw the bite marks with my own eyes, and those must have been some huge teeth, like on a great white shark. My dad said Andy's brother had just caught his foot on some weeds or something, and the whole carp story was just another fish story, which sounded weird to me. Since carp are fish in the first place, what other kind of story could you tell about them?

Andy and I talked about Jonah and the whale. Andy was cool that way. He knew some of the stories I learned up at Camp Saint Malo. I mean, you could ask Andy about Moses, Noah and all those guys in the Old Book, but if you got too into the New Book he got all confused. He wasn't allowed to read the New Book, which I thought was kind of weird. Just because you read it doesn't make you believe it. It's like saying if I read too many Archie comic books, I would end up being Archie. But really I would be Jughead, since I'm dorky and really, really like hamburgers.

Andy and I talked about how in warmer weather we liked hanging our feet off the raft in the middle of the lake. The cool water felt good on my feet on those hot days, but it must have felt better for Andy because his legs were so long both his ankles and feet were underwater. I always started thinking about the giant carp, and pulled my feet out of the water. That wouldn't be a problem now since the water was so icy.

"Let's fish from the rowboat," I said.

I decided for some reason to talk about the bullies at my old school to Andy. I had never told anyone but my family about what they had done to me. I guess since so much time had gone by now, it somehow didn't seem like I was such a wimp on account of it. I started to tell Andy about this bully named

Ronnie who was really mean to me for awhile, but then ended up kind of liking me. And then there was Sister Mary Claire and this kid named Eric who didn't like me at all for some reason.

Anyway, we were floating in the lake in this little rowboat that someone put down there for anyone to use, just drifting along with the flow of the river that flows in and out of the pond. We had caught about one hundred bluegills that day, on account of how lazy they get when the water gets colder, when I told Andy about Eric.

"Andy, I had my own personal bully," I started.

"Wh-What's a 'personal b-b-bully'?"

Andy looked up at me like I had two heads from watching these three ducks paddling along in some tall waterweeds, pecking at minnows or something.

'There was this really mean guy at my school named Eric.'

'Why d-did you c-c-all him your p-p-personal bully?'

'I didn't until one day he told me that. He said, 'I'm your new personal bully.' He liked to push me into the wall when I was walking down the hall, and he would get the other guys at my school to call me things like 'gimpy' and 'stupid' and other meaner things too. But I didn't care that much!'

I turned away so Andy wouldn't see that my eyes got a little wet. My dumb eyes always do that when I get embarrassed, mad or sad about remembering something bad. 'I couldn't tell anyone about it at school, or it would have just gotten worse!'

'M-Man, that stinks!'

'There was this other kid at my old school that some of those guys were pushing down on the playground, and he ratted them out to one of the nuns. Man, he got it bad after school a couple days later. Telling just makes it so much worse. Adults never seem to figure out a way to get jerks in trouble without dragging the poor kid that's getting picked on into it.'

Andy got a really mad look on his face. 'I w-w-wished I w-went to your school l-l-last year, G-Gabe. I would have b-b-beat that j-j-jerk up for you!'

Andy's face was really turning a weird color of red.

I thumped Andy in the arm. "Heck, you big dummy, I can beat *you* up! How could you ever beat *him* up?"

Andy is seriously the best, best friend a guy could ever have! I mean, how many guys would get so mad about you getting picked on that they would almost get a brain hemorrhage?

"L-Like heck you c-can!"

Andy smacked me harder, and we started to rock the rowboat. We almost went in.

"M-Man, those j-jerks were l-lucky your b-big b-brother didn't go there! H-He would have k-killed them f-for d-doing that t-to you!"

"Yeah, and what if your four big brothers would have been there?"

"My b-brothers don't like y-you enough!"

Andy laughed so hard at himself he tipped back and splashed into water! He came up like a drowning dog, and I just started rowing away from him, even though I could see his breath.

"Come on, tough guy, and see if you can catch me!"

Andy swam up and grabbed the boat. He worked his way around the side and then grabbed me and pulled with all of his weight. I went crashing in on top of him into the freezing water.

I looked down and shiver-screamed, 'HERE C-C-COMES THE M-MONSTER C-CARP!'

I don't know who got to the shore first, but I am sure if someone had timed us, we would be in the Guinness book for fastest swimming. Then we both started shivering really hard and dripping with icy cold water we ran home to hot showers.

*θ*

I was thinking about The Secret Brotherhood of Boys and all the stuff we had done this past year. Things were going to change next year.

Things were bound to change next year on account of Eddie going to junior high. Even though he claimed nothing would be different, I knew there was no way a junior high kid was going to hang out with a bunch of elementary school kids. I had seen older kids pull away from their friends who were just one year younger. Now there would be two different schools, and Eddie had told us at our last meeting that he was done with scouts on account of being a junior high kid now.

I think that is only the first change.

The thing is, the guys in my club are the greatest group of guys I have ever known. They are my best friends of all time, though Andy and I had made a secret pledge to each other to be very best friends for life. The seven of us have been in air rock bands together, joined the Scouts together, lived in a tent for a month together (in my backyard, not really living there, but we spent almost every night of July last summer in it together, though usually I ended up sleeping under the stars next to my own tent on an army cot with Andy because Craig and Butch not only snore, but they both gas up the tent real bad all night, and that, in a five-man canvas army tent, is too much even for me).

Speaking of bad smells: we have this little cement incinerator at the end of the path leading out to the garden where people used to burn trash. I'll bet the whole neighborhood stunk when everyone was burning trash from the house all day. Dad lets us roast wieners and marshmallows in it, so we feel like we are really camping out and all and the colder it gets the more we like to huddle around the warm fire.

Most of us in the club are younger brothers to the gooniest band of brothers to walk the gravel roads of our neighborhood. Our brothers are all getting a lot bigger now, and seem more like an army of special forces looking to slaughter the enemy. And of course we are always the enemy. The goons try out all of their special force tactics on us younger brothers, but we have gotten them back some this past year, and will next year too. But sometimes five or six of them, depending on who is grounded at the time, will kidnap one of us, and then the rest of my club has to figure out ways to get our friend back.

So, all in all, even though Andy is my best-best friend, all of the guys in my club are my best friends, and there are no better friends than mine!

I am going to call another meeting in the crawlspace. I have been doing some work down there to clear a special space for us to meet when we really need to go top secret, but I think I'll take one of the space heaters from the garage down there.

# CHAPTER TWENTY-EIGHT

# GLENN THE SEA MONKEY FINAL DRAFT

The last assignment before school is out was to turn in our revised papers as realistic fiction to Mr. McCammon. I had to check my punctuation, change some words, add some detail, take out some things that at didn't matter and exaggerate some of the story to make it more interesting (the exaggeration idea was mine, not Mr. McCammon's, but he did want me to expand my vocabulary, so I looked up some better verbs in my dad's verb dictionary, and I used cool words like 'monsterific,' and I added a bunch of pictures, kind of like a comic book. I was having so much fun, I kind of forgot it was an assignment! I wish all of my teachers would make assignments fun and let us kids decide what we wanted to do for them.). The coolest part of this assignment was that Mr. McCammon told me mine was the only one he showed around to the teachers in the lounge, and he said they all liked it.

My librarian, Mrs. Van Edda, even stopped me when I was in there checking out books to tell me how much she liked it. She had Sea-Monkeys© when she was a girl, and thought maybe she would get some for the library. She said, 'I just hope they don't grow huge like Glenn!' and then laughed. I thought it was cool that she even remembered his name. Then she said something that I thought sounded cool too: 'Gabe, I just bet that before I retire as a librarian, I will be shelving books by you!' That just made me want to really improve my story so Mr. McCammon would share it too!

I took all of the notes and ideas about Glenn the Sea-Monkey© and turned in my paper. As you can see, I got an A-. Mr. McCammon told me that my creative writing is some of the best he's ever seen from a kid my age and that I should keep at it. So... I did, and I have, and it's great!

Creative Essay Assignment
English - Mr. McCammon
Final draft

A-

# THE SEA MONKEY®
## WHO ATE MY BROTHER

THE STORY YOU ARE ABOUT TO READ IS BASED ON ACTUAL EVENTS.
By Gabriel Peters        Drawings by G. Peters

As a private eye known worldwide as Dirk The Smirk, it is important that I keep myself informed and have all the latest gadgets. Much of the best spy gear can be found in the back of comic books, and some of the messages in comic books are used to keep us private eyes informed of what is going on around the world and allow private eyes and spies to communicate. If you look closely, you can often see that the superhero you are reading about is giving clues to certain ones of us on specific cases. Most of the time I am buying spy gear from the back of these books, but sometimes something else catches my eye to buy like Sea-Monkeys® and trick gum. This is a story about a magical, monsterific Sea-Monkey® and what happened when he took over my neighborhood.

    I was reading my Superman comic when an ad caught my eyes (So I don't get in trouble, these words were copied right from the ad): OWN A BOWLFULL OF HAPPINESS - AMAZING LIVE SEA-MONKEYS® - THE WORLD'S ONLY INSTANT LIVE PETS! You will gasp with AMAZEMENT when you see adorable baby Sea-Monkeys® actually being BORN ALIVE before your very eyes in just ONE SECOND FLAT! Sea-Monkeys®, a unique laboratory-developed variety of Artemiasalina, are in fact SO EASY TO RAISE AS PETS, even a six-year-old can do so without help. A THRILLING LIVE SEA-CIRCUS IN YOUR HOME!

    And the description goes on and on with stuff like: Watching them harmlessly "clown around" in their bowl of water while they scoot and play provides ENDLESS hours of FUN and LAUGHS for you and your whole FAMILY! You can even utterly astonish your friends by making your Sea-Monkeys® appear to do TRICKS and STUNTS at YOUR COMMAND! SO absolutely FANTASTIC, this genuine NEW MIRACLE OF SCIENCE has EVEN been GRANTED patent # 3, 673, 986 by the UNITED STATES GOVERNMENT itself!

FREE with each kit we include:
1. 1-YEAR SUPPLY of Sea-Monkey® GROWTH FOOD.
2. WATER PURIFIER.
3. LIVING PLASMA.
4. A magnificent, fully-illustrated manual of Sea-Monkey® care, raising, training & Breeding.
5. Our famous LIFE and GROWTH GUARANTEE CERTIFICATE! ALL FOR ONLY $1.25 Copyright © 1972 Transcience Corporation.

I have a huge collection of really great things on my bookshelf that I got from comic books like X-Ray glasses, gum that turns your mouth black, gum that tastes like fire, garlic, onions and dirt, putty in a plastic jar that makes really funny PHHTTTT sounds, magic tricks, a lava lamp and a whole bunch of other really cool stuff.

Also, because of comic books, I am going to grow SUPER-HUGE muscles like Charles Atlas who was a bodybuilder long before the sport got popular. His advertisements are in my comic books.

I ordered my Sea-Monkey® Glenn and the bodybuilding program on the same day, and they arrived on the same day. When I ordered the program, I only weighed seventy-two pounds, just like the ninety-five-pound weakling (only twenty-three pounds lighter, 95-23=72) who gets sand kicked in his face. Now, after only three weeks on the course, I am already at seventy-three pounds. So much of my life has changed because of comic books, and now I am going to be so huge my brother and his friends won't mess with me anymore. But that is nothing compared to what happened, because I ordered my very own Sea-Monkeys®!

# WHAT KID DOESN'T WANT A MONKEY AS A PET?

A monkey is great, but a monkey that lives in the sea is even better. Like on that commercial on television; 'Ask any Mermaid you happen to see... What's the best tuna? Chicken of the sea!' So, I made up a rhyme like that one, "Ask a Merman you happen to sea (get it - sea, not see?)... What's the best monkey? Monkey in the sea!" Hah hah, I crack me up!

But a monster Sea-Monkey® is no laughing matter. They start out cute (not cuddly), and they grow into monsters like the ones on my favorite television show, Creature Features. If I hadn't seen it with my own eyes, I wouldn't have believed it.

Another interesting fact about all of this is that what you are about to read kind of felt like it was a movie - almost to the point where it seemed the world around me turned into black and white, just like those old movies. Like somehow adding a monster to your life makes all of the color disappear, and everything gets all eerie and stuff, and if you listen really hard, you can hear that weird, eerie violin music in your head like when things are getting spooky on the movies and then the music builds and builds and suddenly the monster jumps out at you - although in the case of a Sea-Monkey®, it kind of slithers and slips around more than jumping. But then, when he becomes full-grown, the dude can move really, really fast!

My brother laughed at me and told me that his science teacher told him that the Sea-Monkeys® I ordered weren't monkeys at all, just some kind of tiny shrimp that never really amount to anything. "Kind of like you, chicken-shrimp," he went on to say.

Just wait until I am a Charles Atlas muscle-bound monster dude! My brother won't be calling me a "chicken-anything" anymore (but this may never happen on account of Glenn, the Sea-Monkey® eating my brother, after all).

Carlos (that's my brother) was laughing at me and he said, "The company just sends it to dumb kids like you who after only a week or so get bored and don't even care that they never got any real Sea-Monkeys®." Carlos always rains on my parades, which is a funny saying, because I don't even have any parades, and he can't make rain to rain on them if I did. But it means tries to spoil things because he is jealous of all the money I have and can spend on whatever I want.

You see, in most of the comic books there are these companies that want kids to sell their junk for them - like greeting cards, posters, magic tricks and other crapola. I have a plaque that 'GREAT INVENTIONS CORP.' sent to me that says I am the number 103-ranked salesman in the whole country out of thousands and thousands, and if I break into the top 100 my prizes and commissions will double: BIG WINNER'S CHOICE OF PRIZES JUST WAITING FOR YOU! They sent me a page of items I could win, including a Hi-Riser fun bike with a cool sissy bar (assembly is required, four more orders), a full-sized wood guitar (two more orders), two-piece luggage set (four more orders, and maybe this would be good for Mom and Dad for Christmas), Tyco lighted race car set (I like Hot Wheels tracks better, but maybe I could get it for Carlos for Christmas, if he hasn't been eaten by then, three orders), and one really cool thing is a Voit Skin Diving Outfit (eight orders). BUT, what I am going to get first is the coolest thing I have ever seen on their prize page; drum roll please... An Electronic Treasure Detector (for only thirteen orders). I would be rich if I could use this to find treasures in all of the old dumps down by the railroad tracks near my house.

I already have a closet full of cool stuff that I have won from the contests - radios, watches, X-ray glasses (they don't really work), t-shirts, key chains and a ton more stuff. My friends sometimes buy things from me with their measly allowances, never considering that there is a fortune to be made in comic books if they just sold the stuff in the back of their comic books themselves.

So, I ordered the Sea-Monkeys® just to prove my dumb brother wrong. See, I am kind of a scientist myself. I have been studying seahorses, and there are these marine biologists that can make seahorses grow ten times their normal size. I have a good idea to make my Sea-Monkeys® grow really big, to prove they aren't just shrimps.

My Sea-Monkey® came today, with his own enclosed jar, some pebbles on the bottom and a stick that is supposed to look like a fan coral, but you can even read PRINTED IN CHINA on the bottom through the glass. There were three other Sea-Monkeys® in the jar with Glenn, but when I looked again, they were gone. I think taking him out of the package and into the light made him come alive like a zombie Sea-Monkey® and made him start to eat everything in sight.

Okay, I kind of admit at first it was a bit disappointing because Glenn is tiny and has these funny feeler kind of legs, so I guess he kind of looked like a shrimp, only much, much smaller. The thing is, since the other Sea-Monkeys® disappeared, he seems to be about four times bigger than he was when he first arrived, and that was just a little bit ago. Now he seems to be eating the pebbles in the bottom of the bowl and maybe even chewing on the fake plastic coral.

My brother was making fun of him, because at first you could barely even see him. I'll show my brother. I'm pretty sure he made my Sea-Monkey® mad, because every time he walks into my bedroom Glenn the Sea-Monkey®, that's what I named him, bangs on the aquarium glass and shakes his fist at my dumb brother. I had to rub my eyes to make sure I wasn't seeing things, but sure enough that is what he did.

Now, I have had Glenn for one week and he is really growing, just like me. We are both on a bodybuilding program you might say.

# GROWTH CHART
## DAY ONE WEIGHT ME = 72 LBS
## GLENN THE SEA MONSTER = 1/4 oz *

*after he ate most of the pebbles in the bowl and the whole stick of plastic coral, not to mention his other Sea-Monkey® traveling companions. This weight is estimated, based on comparison with a dime, which weighs about 1 ounce.

| WEEK ONE | | |
|---|---|---|
| Day | My Progress | Glenn's Progress |
| Monday | gained 1/8 lb | gained 1/4 ounce |
| Tuesday | gained 1/8 lb | gained 1 ounce |
| Wednesday | gained 1/8 lb | gained 2 ounces |
| Thursday | gained 1/8 lb | gained 2 ounces |
| Friday | gained 1/8 lb | gained 4 ounces |
| Saturday | gained 1/8 lb | gained 8 ounces |
| Sunday | gained 2/8 lb | gained 1 lb |

Glenn's weight doubles every day. He doesn't mind me weighing him; actually he smiles when I hold him. He likes the human contact, and strangely seems adapted to either water or air. He reminds me of this monster thing that was on The Twilight Zone last night. He is eating steak, potatoes and a small salad for his dinner now. I haven't seen one of my guinea pigs for several days.

Monday　　　Tuesday　　　Wednesday　　　Thursday　　　Friday

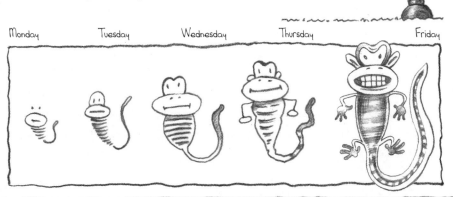

Glenn's weight continues to double every day. I have moved him to the bathtub; Mom hasn't found out yet. He still doesn't mind me weighing him. Since as far as I know there are no air-breathing shrimp in the world, that proves he is the real thing, a Sea-Monkey® not a sea shrimp. He is eating steak, potatoes and a small dinner salad three times a day now, and it looks like he is eating peanut butter and pickles by the jar (there are empty jars of peanut butter and pickles in a stack behind my dresser, and I am not sure where he is finding them). My guinea pig is still missing, and now so is one of the cats. I think it is a simple coincidence, but just in case, I have moved my other cat Flop and the dogs to the garage to sleep at night.

I stopped weighing Glenn, because the last time I did, I couldn't lift him to weigh both of us on Mom's bathroom scale. He is kind of slippery. Mom screamed the first time she saw him in the bathtub, but I convinced her he was just a slimy toy I had won from a comic book contest, and I moved him to the pond near my house. I haven't heard a frog croak since, and there used to be thousands there, come to think of it. And, except for my dogs (which I properly introduced to Glenn and told him to leave them alone OR ELSE), I haven't heard ANY barking in the neighborhood either.

The neighbors had a meeting the other night to talk about where all the dogs and cats in our neighborhood were going. Mrs. Morris said she hasn't had any bunnies chewing on her garden, and everyone is worried about the cows in the pasture across the street. Panic is starting to grip the neighborhood.

The farmer up the hill has reported that he is missing sheep, pigs and a whole flock of chickens. He found slime coming out of the ditch and a trail leading right through his pasture and into his barn. The most chilling thing he told my dad was that there were bones lying in heaps all over his wheat field, and the heaps were made up of his livestock with the bones still connected, like they were skeletons in a museum without any flesh at all. It seems there is some kind of wild animal loose (only I know who it is, and I think I am about to be in big, big trouble!)

My cat Flop, who is never afraid of anything, and my dogs Frisky and Friskier won't even leave the house. They shake and whine and just want to sit up in my bedroom all the time. Last night all of the water in the pond spilled over the banks and flooded the gravel road. When my friends and I climbed up into the tree house we could see where Glenn had been, and that the pond was completely empty of water, though it was flowing in from the ditch again. But there were no frogs, snakes, lizards, fish or any of the normal stuff we could see lining the pond's banks, except for tiny skeletons all over the bottom of the pond. Right by the front gate we spotted a coyote's skeleton all intact, just stripped of fur and flesh, like he was eaten in one gulp, digested and his entire skeleton burped out in one piece. In his jaws was a bunny rabbit skeleton, and in its jaws was a carrot skeleton.

I couldn't believe my eyes. I was going to have to tell the other guys so they could help me. The sad thing is, we were going to have to destroy Glenn the magnificent Sea-Monkey® before he ate every living thing in our neighborhood.

The board that makes decisions about our neighborhood has asked some of the university professors to come and examine the carnage left by Glenn. I have to find him, move him or destroy him before they show up and before he ends up eating a human.

I heard a huge commotion across the gravel road near the pond, and when I peeked out my window there were two cop cars parked over there and the cops had their guns drawn and were running into the field following what looked like a silvery slime trail. My heart sunk; either Glenn was about to suffer a slow, painful death, or he was going to turn on the cops and leave two human skeletons standing out there and this was all my fault. I was probably going to go to the big house and eat bread and water and wear striped pajamas all day and night - and all because I wanted a monkey of some kind.

My brother Carlos had insulted Glenn the Sea-Monkey® one too many times, and suddenly I realized Carlos hadn't been home all day. I wondered where he was, but truthfully was too afraid to ask. I imagine being at one of the tunnels fishing and looking out into

the field and seeing my brother's skeleton standing there right
where Glenn had spit him out. The second day when my brother
was nowhere to be seen and hadn't come home the night before,
I started to worry a lot!

   I was about to ask my mom about my brother when my
walkie-talkie went off. It was my friend Andy telling me that
he and some of the other guys had spotted Glenn slipping into
the lake down the hill. We all bolted out of our front doors, climbed
on our Stingray bikes and cruised down to the lake with slingshots,
bee-bee guns, pellet guns, wrist rockets and some other cool ammo.

Glenn was at the bottom of the lake scooping up trout and catfish like they were guppies. An entire raccoon family was in his gut. You could see through him because he was still clear, and suddenly four raccoon skeletons shot through the lake water and spewed way up into the air, landing right at our feet on the raft, where we were hiding waiting for our moment to attack. We screamed all at once, and suddenly Glenn started to swim up to the surface, licking his giant Sea-Monkey® gums and rolling his eyes around hungrily.

My friends and I in the Secret Detective Club had laid a trap for Glenn, but we weren't sure how it was going to work. All at once we started firing our weapons down at him as he was surging up. He bellowed and screamed in a huge monstery voice like I had never heard before. Out of nowhere my friend Murph, the army nut, hurls this giant bomb made up of M-80s, Black Cat firecrackers and pop-bottle rockets all bungeed to a football down into Glenn's huge mouth. You could see the wick all wound up together and getting closer to igniting through Glenn's clear skin. When the fire hit the joined fuses, the football and all of the fireworks ignited at once, blowing a hole in Glenn the size of a horse. Slimy, scaled clear flesh blew in plasmatic patches all over us, drenching us with Glenn. Glenn looked at me as his innards were blown sky high with the saddest Sea-Monkey® regret, and I felt bad, but it was the only thing we could do. Then I started to cry. My friends all looked at me like I was crazy, because they were all celebrating like wild Indians.

When I explained that Glenn had eaten my brother, my friend Tony started to laugh really hard. Then he explained that my brother and one of his brothers had gone on a two-day overnight field trip with their class to Mesa Verde, and Glenn had nothing to do with his mysterious disappearance. For a moment I was totally relieved, then mad, then sad, and then I started to laugh like a maniac, wondering what secret mission Glenn was actually going to go on before he got snatched and ended up in my dumb comic book.

## THE END

I am not very happy about this. After Carlos made so
much fun of me about the Sea-Monkeys® being a bogus
rip-off, I asked Dad, and he and I looked in the dictionary
and encyclopedia under Artemiasalina and Artemia salina
and here is what we found: – brine shrimp. brine shrimp,
common name for a primitive crustacean that seldom reaches
more than 1/2 in. (1.3 cm) in length and is commonly used
for fish food in aquariums. Brine shrimp, which are not closely
related to true shrimp, can be found almost everywhere in the
world in inland saltwaters, although they are completely absent
from oceans. They can live in water having several times the
salinity of seawater, but they can also tolerate water having only
one-tenth the marine salt concentration. Brine shrimp usually
occur in huge numbers and can be seen in vast windblown lines
in the Great Salt Lake. Their absence from the sea has been
explained by their vulnerability to attack by predators and the
absence of the latter in their inland saline habitat. Although
brine shrimp are considered to be members of a single genus,
Artemis, and possibly a single species, there are several varieties.
Generally, they have stalked, compound eyes and tapered bodies
with a trunk that bears 11 pairs of leaf-like legs.

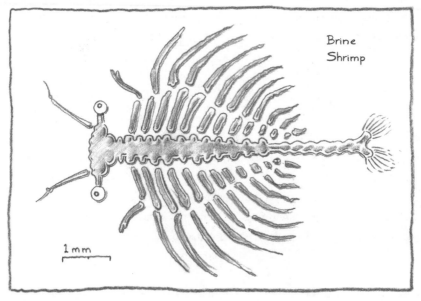

Brine
Shrimp

1 mm

Females have a brood pouch from which active young are liberated under favorable conditions. Otherwise eggs are laid parthenogenetically or fertilized and can either hatch immediately or be dried and remain viable for many years. These eggs are remarkably resistant to adverse environmental conditions, which is why they can be hatched so easily in saltwater and used for fish food; adult brine shrimp are also used as food in aquariums and are generally sold frozen. Brine shrimp are classified in the phylum Arthropoda, subphylum Crustacea, class Branchiopoda, order Anostraca.

Okay, I get that the three Sea-Monkeys© that came with Glenn were brine shrimp and I am not happy that the comic book people took advantage of a kid. But whatever Glenn The Sea-Monkey© is or was is not what the Science company meant to send. I think they are working on a secret weapon, and Glenn was one of them who got away. As a matter of fact, I think, like I said at the beginning of this paper, that the comic books ad for Sea-Monkeys© might actually be a communication device for our military to let them know where they can get these secret-weapon, actual true-to-life, magnificent monstrous Sea-Monkeys© like Glenn.

Now that it is all over, I found something really cool. You know how this all started? By me being a normal kid, wanting a monkey. Well, a Sea-Monkey© isn't really the same thing at all, but this might be pretty cool... check it out for only $18.95

DARLING PET MONKEY
$18.95

# CHAPTER TWENTY-NINE

# SPRINGTIME MEANS SUMMERTIME IS SOON...

Most of the past months kept me busy with school, scout meetings, drawing my comic books, hanging out with my buddies inside at each other's houses and the skating rink and lots and lots of homework, homework, homework.

As it was getting warmer again, I was planning on going down to Lawn and Leisure in the morning to get a red cream soda and to ride one of the new Indian motorcycles if mom would sign the permission note. Mom was kind of hoping for some calm, so maybe I would wait for a little while to talk to her about it. I was working in the garage when I heard Andy knocking on the front door

He was holding *the* book under his arm, *the* book being the holy grail of all books that is. He told me his dad took him down to the newsstand to pick up the book today. He is so lucky. He got the only copy they had left. But since Andy is my best friend, and he would let me borrow his anytime until I got my own.

It's hard to believe a year has gone by since I had the new one. Now my Guinness book has bent pages and looks like it's been through a war, and in some ways I guess it has.

Andy's book had come all the way from Dublin, Ireland where the Guinness family is a big deal and comes out with a book every year updated about all the coolest stuff people do all over the world.

Andy moved from the front door to stand under my window. He was calling me and throwing pebbles at my window.

"G-Gabe, g-g-guess what I g-got?" he said loudly.

"Andy, I'm down here!" I pushed the garage door up and stood under it, holding the garage door with my arms spread out like a superhero, like I was lifting a giant boulder or something. I had been banging caps with Dad's hammer in the garage, which was making my ears ring. I couldn't believe Andy didn't figure out that all that racket was coming from the garage, and that it was me.

I yelled to him, "Hang on, I'll be right back!" Then I ran up to my room and grabbed a notebook, a pencil and my last year's Guinness book. I ran to the refrigerator and grabbed two of mom's soda pops called TAB. It was all we had, besides a box of Space Food Sticks and the box of Count Chocula cereal.

Andy and I walked across the gravel road and took the book up into the tree house and compared our favorite records to the ones in last year's book. We sat up there for hours, munching and slurping and pointing and reading to each other, noticing that no one had the record for the world's biggest spit pool.

When it was time to go in, we walked across the road, making plans for the game of hide-and-seek that we were going to play all night long, since it was spring break and the tents were coming out to sleep in. We had a little trick up our sleeves for Murph and Butch, now that they were kind of best friends. They still argued all the time, but now it was kind of funny because we weren't all worried about whether they were going to fist-fight or not. Tonight we were going to prank the two of them in a big way.

@

I sat up in my room in the lower bunk, thinking about how a whole year had passed since we were trying to get into the Guinness book, and how another edition that we weren't in was already out. I put the photos of the spit pool taken from the tree house and from the ground, and stuffed them into an envelope with the official application for entry into the book. Dad was going to drop it by the post office, where they could add the postage we needed to get it all the way to Ireland.

*The Partridge Family* was playing loudly on my new eight-track stereo: *"I woke up in love this morning... Went to sleep with you on my miiiind..."*

I had won the stereo by selling garden seeds door to door. The speakers kind of crackled, and Dad said it wasn't the best quality, "But not bad for winning it, you future millionaire!" My phonograph, the one I got from Mr. Povich a few years back for mowing his lawn, was better. Maybe I would go get the newest Partridge Family album for my phonograph. I thought David Cassidy, or "Keith" on the show, was pretty cool, and Mom was letting me grow my hair out like his.

Carl's hair was getting long too, and Dad said, "Oh well, it's just a sign of the times. My boys are hippies, but that's okay. Some of my favorite students are hippies."

I explained, "I don't want to be a hippie, Dad. But Carl says the girls like bellbottoms and long hair."

"Oh, so now you *like* the girls?" Dad said, laughing a little.

"Well, yeah, kind of," I muttered, just a bit embarrassed.

"Well, that makes sense. After all, son, you are growing up! Some day you might even looove a girl..."

"Gross, Dad," I snarled, but I knew he just might be right.

"Well, I didn't always like girls Gabe." Dad smiled really big. "But when one is special..."

"Well, there's this one girl at school...her name is Haley and she has long, bl..." Suddenly I realized Carl might be within earshot and decided not to talk about her. "Forget it. Let's talk about that stuff some other time, okay?"

Dad gave me a hug and ruffled my hair. "Anytime buddy."

Dad walked out of my room. My mind was on other things. This upcoming summer could be different for The Secret Brotherhood of Boys. If we put our heads together and could come up with something totally original, we just might make it in to the Guinness book.

I was thinking about how we started our club and called it the detective part, but didn't really do any kind of detective work. It was time to change that. Trying to set the records was fun, but there were so many mysterious things going on in our neighborhood that I figured we could probably spend a lot of our time solving crimes, mysteries and other things

There were certainly many more mysterious things out there to solve. So much more to know about the crazy old lady up on the hill, the haunted schoolhouse, and the legends of the dead dog, the Indian in the lake and Killer's owner. Mr. Patchett seemed to be keeping some secrets too. That gave me a good idea. How many mysteries — real mysteries — could six or seven boys solve in one summer? There had to be a Guinness record in there somewhere! If only school would hurry up and be over!

My music was so loud I barely heard it when the doorbell rang. I heard Dad calling up the stairs, "Gabe, Carl, time for dinner! PIZZA NIGHT! WHOOOOIEEEE!"

I had just dialed up Andy on the phone. I turned the stereo down.

"H-H-Hello?"

"Hey buddy, you need to start The Secret Brotherhood of Boys phone chain, NOW!"

We needed to meet, but this was going to be a totally different meeting. Spring was just starting, but the weather was unseasonably warm and felt more like summer. I had just come up with a big idea.

Andy asked, "Wh-Why? What's up?"

"I want everyone to meet at my house, in the backyard, in my tent before we play hide-n-seek. It's really important!"

"C-Come on, t-tell me wh-what's up, Gabe?"

"I can't explain it right now, buddy. Tonight is pizza night, and Dad doesn't like it when I'm late!"

"Okay, we'll b-b-be there wh-when the streetlights c-c-come on!" Andy said.

From the bottom of the stairs I heard Dad's voice bellow, "PAGING GABRIEL PETERS! PAGING GABRIEL PETERS! ITS TIME FOR DINNER! THIS IS YOUR THIRD AND FINAL CALL!"

Dad's shout again sounded like the people who page you when you are at the airport, but a little bit angrier, more like my brother's as it boomed up the stairs, down the hall and flooded under the door to my bedroom. It was even louder than the Partridges coming from my stereo.

"Seriously Andy, I really gotta go. Write down ten mysteries you think we could solve..."

"Wh-Wha..."

"Kay, see ya, buddy."

I hung up, looked out my bedroom window because the sky looked like it was all on fire on account of the sunset and noticed a light burning bright up the hill at Grizelda's house, and thought I could see her standing in the window looking straight at my bedroom window. I shuddered and headed out my door, down the hall to where Carl was stuffing 'pizzaz' in his mouth.

"SURPRISE!" Mom and Dad said, and pointed out into the backyard to a brand-new trampoline, set up right next to my tent.

# CHAPTER THIRTY
# THE ANSWER

We had been waiting for about six months for a return letter from the Guinness people when Dad finally handed me a letter one morning.

Dear Master Peters,

Thank you for your submission to the Guinness Book of World Records. Though your pictures were clear and gave the committee a true look at your attempt, we all came to the same conclusion that it wasn't quite right for the Guinness book.

We respectfully decline your application and wish you great success in any future endeavors to enter our book.

Might I suggest the Ripley's Believe it or Not people for your "spit pool". It is truly hard to believe how many hours were spent hanging from one's ankle while suspended within a tree to fill a child's wading pool with saliva.

Might I also suggest that any future attempts do not include the aid of such saliva-inducing products such as chewing gum, candy or any other foreign objects, in that it is no longer clear what is actual spittle and what is simply the sugary confection of the aiding product.

Your obvious fondness for our literature is very much appreciated, and we hope you will have many more hours of enjoyment from our record books in the future.

Sincerely,

Baines Wattleton

Baines Wattleton
Esquire, The Guinness Book of World Records.

I never told a soul this, but I knew my dad had written the letter and sent it back east to one of my uncles to forward back to our house. I knew that because I had overheard him on the telephone one morning when he thought I was across the road in my tree house. I also found a couple torn-up drafts of the letter in his wastepaper basket.

Dad also must have forgotten that he told me a story once about a funny boy in his class when he was a boy named Baines Wattleton; it's not a name you forget easily. I seriously doubted Baines Wattleton had found a job in Ireland working for Guinness. Besides, every adult we ever told about the spit pool idea had crinkled up their noses, and I had figured there weren't any kids on the Guinness deciding team. So I knew our attempt probably wouldn't get considered.

I thought it was really nice of Dad to take the time to try to make me feel better. The funny thing is by the time my Dad got around to doing it, my friends and me were on to new ideas and kind of forgot about the whole thing.

So, I guess the truth is the Guinness people never even responded to all of our efforts. That is kind of lame, don't you think?

# EPILOGUE

I'm an adult now, and my family and I had moved into a new house a short drive from my old neighborhood. My parents still live in the house I grew up in.

I drove down to the airport to pick up Eddie and Andy, and looked forward to getting back to town to meet up with the other guys who had already arrived and called to check in with me. We had a plan that had nothing to do with the reason we were all in town—our high school reunion. Everyone was going to be in town for a three-day event.

There would be another kind of a reunion for those of us who grew up out in the small country neighborhood. We planned to gather once again across the gravel road from my childhood home, and perhaps shinny up onto the remnants of our tree house and have an official Secret Detective Brotherhood meeting.

I hadn't seen Eddie or Andy for some time, and was quite excited to see them again. Andy and I had been best friends as boys and held onto that special bond all these years, even fishing in Alaska and Cabo San Lucas together. We kept in contact mostly by email, and we talked on the phone about once a month, but it was hard living so far apart.

As the three of us drove from the airport to our old hometown, we talked about our own families and what had happened since we were all together last.

"Did anyone call Tyler?" Andy asked.

I still had a hard time adjusting to the fact that Andy rarely, if ever, stuttered anymore. When we were boys it was just something everyone was used to, especially when he got really excited about something.

"Shoot... I forgot." Eddie whined.

Tyler was a year ahead of us in school, and had gone to his own reunion last year.

"Forgot Tyler?" I asked.

"Remember that time when...."

One story led to another, and before we knew it we had driven the sixty miles and headed for the restaurant everyone was planning to meet at.

The night was full of reverie and stories and memories. It was unbelievable how fast we all just went back in time and in many ways acted just like the boys and girls we were once.

After it got pretty late I dropped the guys off at their hotel and headed toward home. As I drove down the highway that went by the old neighborhood, memories just flooded into my head. So much time had gone by. I was the lucky one in that I lived close enough to the old homestead that I was able to take my own kids fishing in the old favorite spots and climb the fossil creek cliffs with them. I showed my kids the old cave hideouts, and told them the legends from a time long ago.

I called Dad and told him our plan about coming out to the old neighborhood. He asked me to make sure the guys could come around dinnertime to the house. We agreed on a good time to meet up there for a backyard feast.

The next afternoon, the boys from the old Secret Detective Brotherhood were all sitting up on the platform of the old tree house that had initials from another time etched in it. A car came driving up the now-paved road at a faster than usual neighborhood pace. We all saw the car as it crested the hill, and watched it curiously as it pulled over next to the curb and parked.

A man I didn't recognize at first jumped out of the car and sprinted across the road. He walked up the little embankment below us and looked up with a squint on his face.

"So, who was going to let old T-Bone in on the meeting?"

"T, oh my gosh!" I sputtered, "How, where..."

"I ran into some of the guys that are in town, and they told me about overhearing you guys making a plan at the restaurant last night."

"Well, come on up."

"Uh, I think I am safer down here. You guys are bowing those boards pretty good."

Soon we all started to climb, shinny and fall down the tree.

Before you knew it, we were all walking down the railroad tracks, past our favorite fishing lake and the tunnels. We headed up toward the old abandoned schoolhouse. The whole time we were walking and talking, we agreed that next summer we were going to bring our sons and daughters out to the old neighborhood to show them how their dads lived as boys.

Then we headed back to the old neighborhood and walked up and down the planetary-named streets. We headed up the embankment next to the ditch, and everyone looked over at Mean Mrs. Rickles' old backyard. No one said a word. All the time we were by the ditch, dogs in backyards barked at us and chocolate-milk colored water flowed lazily, making each of us hungry to strip our shoes and socks off and crawl up the ditch looking for crawdad holes.

We kept walking until we ended up at my old house where my parents still lived. Boy, the house looked a lot smaller than I remembered it as a boy.

As we walked into the backyard I noticed the old picnic table had a fresh coat of stain and was set for six people. Dad came bounding out the back door of the house, and the scent of steaks on the grill hit our noses with full force.

"Boys! My boys are home!" Dad cried out, and soon was engulfed in a bear hug by five full-grown men. Soon Mom came bustling out the back door and one by one hugged my friends.

As we sat at the picnic table talking to Mom and Dad and catching up on old times and what had been happening during the last ten years, I looked around the yard at where the trampoline had been and where we always pitched the tent at the beginning of every summer. That's where we always got the best night-crawlers for fishing, and I could almost see ourselves running through the garden, barefoot, tan and loving every moment of our summer freedom.

I glanced up at my old window that looked out over the yard and the ditch, and remembered the mornings I would watch the sun rising to bring a new day. I remembered the nights I would watch the moon coming large over the horizon, while I was usually waiting for the boys to come bounding up the ditch to settle into my tent to plan our next adventures. It was home. Home sweet home.

## BOOKS BY MATOTT

### FOR READERS OF ALL AGES
**Chapter books**

*Go Ask Mom!*
Stories From the Upper Bunk (Book 1)

*The World According To Gabe*
Stories From the Lower Bunk (Book 2)

*The Tails of Mr. Murphy*

*The Sky Is Falling*

**Poetry**

*Nitwittles*

*Chocolate Covered Frog Legs*

*There's A Fly On My Toast!*

**Picture books**

*Aliens - All Mixed Up*

*When I Was A Girl… I Dreamed*

*When I Was A Boy… I Dreamed*

*When Did I Meet You Grandma?*

*When Did I Meet You Grandpa?*

*Drinking Fountain Joe*

*Ol' Lady Grizelda*

*Oliver Kringle*

*Benjamin Bailey Goes to the Zoo*

*Miss Spell*

### FOR GROWN-UPS

*My Garden Visits*

*A Harvest of Reflections*

*Independence Days - Still Just Boys*

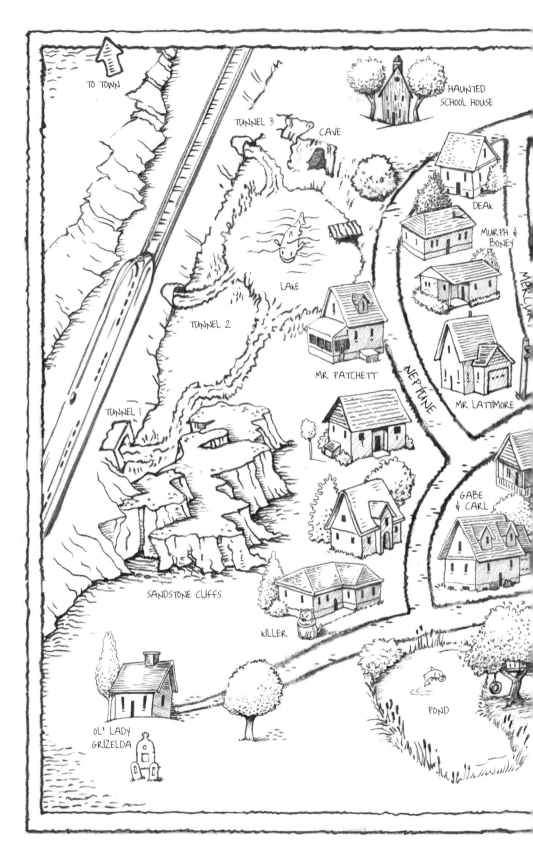